He was using her

Dammit all, nobody used Charlie Cossini.

"Listen, Ben, it's been fun, but I think it's time we stopped fooling ourselves that we have much in common besides fun."

"Fun? Is that what this has been for you, just fun?" Ben was aghast at her summation of their relationship.

"Charlie, how can you sit there—"

Ben abruptly heard himself, heard his own words, his aggrieved tone of voice and, in a painful moment of insight, knew he'd heard them in one form or another many times over the years. They were an echo of all the futile arguments women had used on him when he made a version of the speech Charlie had just concluded.

She'd switched roles on him. She was giving him the brush-off he'd perfected. And he, Benjamin Valentine Gilmour, was all but begging a woman—this damnable, infuriating woman, at that— not to leave him.

ABOUT THE AUTHOR

A native of British Columbia, Bobby Hutchinson is the mother of five grown children who lives in Vancouver with her husband, Alan, a retired member of the Canadian Mounted Police. Bobby says that she got the inspiration for this book when she and Alan went to a small surfer resort on the northern end of Oahu. She writes, "The first morning, and several thereafter, I awoke before dawn to the sound of a bugle playing reveille. Alan insisted it came from the military base over the mountains, but of course I knew that it was old Tom, standing on the beach and blowing his heart out."

Books by Bobby Hutchinson

HARLEQUIN AMERICAN ROMANCE
147—WHEREVER YOU GO

HARLEQUIN SUPERROMANCE
166—SHELTERING BRIDGES
229—MEETING PLACE

These books may be available at your local bookseller.

Don't miss any of our special offers. Write to us at the following address for information on our newest releases.

Harlequin Reader Service
901 Fuhrmann Blvd., P.O. Box 1397, Buffalo, NY 14240
Canadian address: P.O. Box 603,
Fort Erie, Ont. L2A 9Z9

Welcome the Morning
Bobby Hutchinson

Harlequin Books

TORONTO • NEW YORK • LONDON
AMSTERDAM • PARIS • SYDNEY • HAMBURG
STOCKHOLM • ATHENS • TOKYO • MILAN

Thank you, Dorothy Vriend, carpenter,
for sharing your knowledge and experience.

For all my children: Dan, Dave, Rob,
Marlan, Anne and Trudy.
Life must be understood backward
and lived forward.
So treasure the past and welcome the morning.

Published November 1986

First printing September1986

ISBN 0-373-16173-5

Printed in Canada

Chapter One

"How's it look, Charlie?"

Eliza's enthusiastic tones floated through the ocean-scented air, up to the roof where her boss's long, lithe form crawled gingerly along the shingles.

Cheerful Hawaiian sunbeams bathed the decrepit two-story building, and even at this early hour, heat from the curling green asphalt tiles burned through the knees of threadbare jeans. Grateful for the crumpled brown leather gloves she'd pulled on at the last minute, Charlie inched a careful path up the sharply angled roof.

No doubt about it, the whole miserable thing needed to be redone. Even the substructure was spongy beneath her careful probing.

Fifteen feet below, Eliza's piquant face with its cap of red-gold curls was turned up like a flower, hand shielding her eyes as she squinted into the increasing glare and waited for her boss's instructions.

"Get me that small ladder we saw propped against the wall, Eliza. Bring it up here and I'll have a look at the peak." Charlie shifted so that she sat well braced, her feet in their blue Adidas runners firmly positioned on what she hoped was a secure area. The ancient house was built with a sprawling collection of rooms added on to an original two-story structure, rather like a tall, imposing female whose hips have burgeoned hopelessly out of control.

Charlie was still on the lower level, and the second-story roof loomed high above her head. No doubt it was in just as bad shape as the projection she sat on, but it would be wise to go up and look, anyway.

She'd learned never to take anything for granted. Carpentry and renovation required meticulous attention to detail, and her fledgling company couldn't afford unwelcome surprises. Cossini Construction ran on a budget tighter than its owner's single pair of designer jeans, and this job was an incredible piece of good luck, tossed her way by Johnny Campenello, an old friend of her father's.

"We've done lots of work for these guys before, high rollers named Gilmour Developments," he'd told her father on the phone.

"Now they got some renovation in Hawaii they need done. Hell, all my guys are married; they don't want to uproot for who knows how long, even to go to Hawaii. Tell that girl of yours, that Charlie, that I'll put in a good word for her with the boss if she wants to bid on it. She's gotta pay her own way out there; then the company will reimburse her later. I looked at the specs, so tell her to make a bid in the neighborhood of—" He'd named a figure that sounded astronomically high. "That should get her the job and a nice bit of profit."

Johnny had been right. Shortly afterward, an anonymous male voice on the telephone had informed her that Cossini Construction had the job. They were expected to be on-site by August 15—two short weeks away, Charlie had calculated swiftly—and there would be someone there to supervise.

The three-woman Cossini Construction crew had celebrated wildly that night, wearing their best outfits and enjoying Gennero's homemade wine. A harried thirteen days later—yesterday—they'd taken the flight from Seattle to the Hawaiian Islands.

Charlie watched as Eliza's sturdy form hurried off for the ladder, winding among the desultory collection of huts and outbuildings that constituted the Reveille Reef Club. A half-dozen palm trees swayed high above the rooftop where she sat, while a million different birds chirped in what sounded like a strange language. Birds didn't make those particular exotic noises back home in Bellingham, Washington.

Charlie could hear the pulsing surge and retreat of the Pacific rolling lavishly over the reef in the sheltered bay and onto the empty stretches of beach fronting the dilapidated buildings Cossini Construction, Inc. had been hired to renovate.

The exact details of the resort's ownership were fuzzy, but Charlie knew the place had been used at one point by a church group as a retreat. Obviously nothing had been done for years in the way of maintenance, although some fresh paint had been applied here and there and everything was tidy, with no rubbish strewn around, as one might expect.

Renovating here would be a challenge and a delight. They'd get started right away, Charlie vowed. Today.

She'd be meeting the head honcho this morning, and she wanted to compile at least a rough estimate of the materials she would need and the time it would take before he got here.

The rattle of the extension ladder at the roof's edge signaled Eliza's arrival, and over the gutter appeared the top of the smaller aluminum ladder Charlie had requested, followed by Eliza's thatch of red curls and perspiring, cheerful face. Sliding nimbly down to grasp the top rung, Charlie relieved the other woman of the clumsy task of climbing one ladder while carrying another.

"Man, it's like an oven up here, and it's not even nine o'clock yet. Need me to hold this?"

Charlie glanced down at Eliza's skimpy blue shorts and shook her head, her own mass of golden brown curls held practically, if not glamorously, behind her head in a clumpy chunk and tied carelessly with a length of string.

"You'll wreck your knees. Anyway, I'm fine alone up here. Go see how Carol's making out in those huts." The third member of the crew was assessing what repairs were needed to be made to the interiors of the six primitive cabins that ringed the central building.

Propping the rubber grips of the small ladder securely against the second-story wall and muttering a fervent plea that its feet were on a section of the roof strong enough to bear her weight, Charlie tested it for stability and then slowly began the ascent. The ladder trembled and jerked but held fast. Luckily, heights had never bothered her. A half smile flashed across her face as she remembered the times her burly father had tied his stubborn small daughter to a chimney for safekeeping while he worked on his current roofing project. She'd become as adept as a mountain goat at scaling roofs.

A cursory inspection convinced her that the upper portion of the roof was in even worse shape than the rest. She hadn't really needed to inspect it to know. There was just something about housetops that intrigued her.

Conquering the last slippery yards, she straddled the peak as though it were a saddle and stretched her long, aching legs out on either side of the V, allowing herself to relax for a moment.

The view was spectacular, a postcardlike scene of ocean and reefs, palms and blue sky. The Reef Club was in an isolated location.

Yesterday, the taxi driver who brought them here had offered to give them a minitour of Honolulu first, and Carol and Eliza had enthusiastically agreed. Privately Charlie thought that it was a waste of time and money.

On the popular beaches he'd driven past she saw wall-to-wall people, and Charlie imagined that the whole of Oahu must reek of coconut tanning oil.

But here, little more than an hour away from the city, the shining sand was deserted. A half mile away, a picturesque Japanese temple squatted, half obscured by palms and thick ferns and an outcropping of lava rock.

In the other direction, the bay fronted a small park. Beyond that was the village, invisible from the rooftop, and then miles of sugarcane.

Far down the beach, she could pick out the skimming forms of surfers riding the breakers. She remembered reading that this particular stretch of beach was a surfers' heaven, and just a bit farther north was Sunset Beach, where international surfing competitions were held each November.

She wrinkled her nose at the thought. Swimming beyond a depth where her feet were able to touch terrified Charlie, and surfing was about the last thing she'd ever think of trying. Even if the inconceivable day should arrive when she had the leisure time and the money and the desire for such frivolity, she'd certainly put all to better use than that.

But the clean white sand on the beach directly below her was deserted, and the bird song and breakers and trees muffled any other sounds. She didn't notice the yellow Jeep nose its way into the driveway and come to an abrupt stop in the grass.

For an instant, perched alone high above the world, Charlie imagined herself omnipotent, queen of all she surveyed. A thrill of anticipation made goose bumps rise on her bare, tanned arms. For several long, warm months, she and her trusty crew would live here rent-free, actually paid to do what they liked best. The awful pressure of the past months, the constant fear that next week there wouldn't be any work for her crew, had disappeared with this lovely, long contract. Hard, hot work stretched ahead, but Charlie thrived on hard work.

She patted the roof tenderly.

"We'll give you the neatest face-lift, old girl," she promised the house, and then, giving in to impulse, she held both arms out toward the canopy of periwinkle sky, and tilting a determined chin up to the heavens, she roared at the top of her lungs, a wordless outpouring of triumph and joy.

BENJAMIN VALENTINE GILMOUR resented everything about the Reveille Reef Club. It took him away from what he considered his work, it involved dealing with his lovable but impossible opinionated Aunt Stella, and it necessitated making decisions—which he generally avoided, if possible—involving carpentry and renovations, about which he knew nothing and cared to know even less than he'd accidentally acquired by osmosis over the years.

Even worse, he had to take precious time this morning, when surfing conditions were at their rare best, to meet some brawny, brainless contractor hired by his brother as a favor to some friend of a friend.

Why hadn't Aunt Stella taken everyone's advice and allowed this termite-ridden disaster area to be torn down and a well-designed complex of high rises and cottages to be built? A development that would be a financial success. With some well-aimed publicity, this strip of beachfront could be a gold mine. He may not have his older brothers' acumen at business, but even Ben knew real estate potential when he saw it. Just the surfing competitions alone drew huge crowds.

Instead, Stella had insisted on keeping it basically the same as it had been since before the last war. That was going to cost considerably more than demolition and new construction would have. It was senseless. But Stella owned it, as well as substantial shares in the family business. About this project, she had the last word. Ben loved Stella dearly, but there was a limit.

He shook his head, mindful of the frustrating, maddening long-distance conversations he'd already endured this week alone with his intractable relative. She was one stubborn old woman. He grinned in recognition. It had been said that he was rather like his favorite aunt.

"I want it retained and restored to the way it used to be," she'd insisted.

Ben, primed by his brothers, had quoted figures, projections, rationality, income potential, land value per square foot. No amount of logic had worked. He'd remembered too late that logic seldom did on Aunt Stella.

Five million dollars' worth of real estate sacrificed to an old woman's romantic whims. That bothered Paul and Ralph and Mitchell a hell of a lot more than it did him. The part that got him hot was being shoved into supervising the disaster. It was like hanging an albatross around his neck, and even after all this face-lifting, the place still would operate at a loss, according to Mitchell.

"So what?" had been Ben's rejoinder to his brother's dejected assessment. The business could stand a few tax write-offs, couldn't it?

That earned Ben lecture number sixty-four.

"In case you've forgotten, little brother, you're now thirty-five years old. You have an expensive, frivolous degree in botany you've never used, and you're living like a beach bum at the moment." Mitchell's precise, dry tone had made Ben grimace with distaste.

"It's past time for you to justify your position on the company books as a consultant and start doing something to earn the salary that accompanies it," Mitchell lectured.

"Aren't you forgetting the wind-surfing company in Australia?" Ben asked sweetly. "And the motorcycle franchise in New Zealand?" Both had been his inspirations, and both were doing exceptionally well.

"Both temporary interests, Ben, and since then...?"

Ben shuddered in spite of the increasingly warm morning, slowing the Jeep and watching for the narrow, overgrown, rut-filled turnoff into the club.

Conversations with Mitchell made him appreciate the vagaries of a person like Stella. Eccentricity was wonderful compared with Mitchell's stultifying logic.

A faded wooden sign, half hidden in pink blossoms, announced his arrival at his destination. "Damned place should be called Stella's Folly," he muttered angrily, braking sharply and wheeling the Jeep through the overgrown foliage into the track that doubled as the driveway for the Reveille Reef Club.

The very first thing he saw was the trespasser on the roof, a blue-jeaned, pony-tailed youth, obviously acting on a dare, rapidly heading for the peak. Ben slammed his foot on the brake and jerked to a stop while adrenaline surged and anger gnawed at his stomach. Someone had let all the air out of his tires while he was here last week, and the Private—Keep off signs had been torn down again. That made three times he'd had to put up new ones. At least he'd caught this young criminal in the act.

Was Stella legally responsible if this imbecile fell and broke his neck? Visions of courtroom dramas with pathetic youths in wheelchairs and million-dollar settlements raced across the surface of his mind as he flung himself over the open side of the Jeep and raced for the ladder propped against the wall.

Careful, Gilmour, he warned himself as he clumsily mounted the shaky ladder. *You're no Edmund Hillary, and that stupid kid up there is probably hyped right out on drugs, anyway, and about to prove that he can fly despite any heroics on your part.*

Don't look down. Ben remembered clearly now why he'd always detested ladders. An aeon later, he attained the lower roof level, dropping cautiously to his bare knees and feeling the rasping bite of the rough asbestos. Why the hell did he always wear shorts?

"Son of a—" He swallowed the rest, reminding himself to be quiet, staunchly ignoring the abrasive roughness ripping his flesh to bloody shreds. Another foot and a half—his hands stung like fury, and his knees were bleeding—he grabbed at the second ladder, hauled himself shakily upright and swallowed convulsively as it shifted under his weight. One step up, another, one more—his lanky height allowed a view up to the second level, and he stared in disbelief at the apparition perched jauntily on the roof's crest.

It was a girl, a total nut case, talking to the roof and patting it as if it were a horse. A breathtakingly beautiful loony, a slender, long-limbed female tanned the color of Kona coffee with a dash of cream, her fine-boned face tilted up in drug-induced ecstasy toward the sky.

For just an instant, Ben forgot the rickety ladder that he clung to, forgot the daunting fact that he was hovering on a rooftop much too high above the earth.

There was a quality about her, an unholy, wild delight on her face as she grinned up at the heavens. An elemental force seemed to radiate from her, and the sunshine bathed her in a golden aura. Her uptilted perky breasts thrust against the thin blue T-shirt, braless, and her toffee-colored hair escaped in curling tendrils from its butcher-string tie.

She was absolutely, achingly lovely. Delicate, innocent, one of Stella's Dresden figurines sprung to outrageous life. Ben was about to call to her, softly, gently, so as not to startle her, when she abruptly opened her mouth and hollered at the top of her lungs, her strong, husky voice as shockingly loud and powerful as a rock singer's, throwing her arms above her head with careless abandon.

Ben's whole body jolted with shock, and as if in slow motion, the ladder he clung to tipped slowly but surely to the right. He instantly overcorrected to the left, and the ladder then reeled on one leg, slipped to the side and toppled over.

Ben's horrified roar brought Carol and Eliza racing out of the cabin just in time to see him crash like a drunken sky diver into the green shingled lower roof and to hear the truly impressive splintering and cursing as he exploded through the weakened structure. They gazed up in frozen, fascinated horror as his flailing body disappeared into the attic, his voice becoming muffled and far away, then fading abruptly. After a moment, the birds resumed their exotic melody, and the sound of the surf and the breeze filled the ominous silence.

As soon as she'd figured out what had happened, Charlie took charge.

"Eliza, get me down from here. There's a wooden ladder in the shed. Carol, go see if he's—"

The horrendous possibilities choked off the rest of Charlie's frantically shouted instructions. She'd glanced down toward the ladder just as it began its slide. A man with ash-brown curly hair and the thickest blond eyebrows she'd ever seen was gaping up at her, seemingly oblivious of the fact that the ladder he clung to like a limpet was starting to slip. She wanted to warn him, but it was already too late.

With an expression of utter amazement and outrage on his attractive bronzed features, he let out a bellow worthy of an enraged bull elephant and promptly crashed through the spongy lower roof.

The teamwork that followed was an example of the efficiency of Cossini Construction. Dust was still settling around a dazed Ben when Carol burst through the attic bedroom door, nearly taking it off its rusty hinges, and only seconds after that a ladder poked through the hole in the roof, and Eliza scuttled down, with Charlie close at her heels.

"He looks okay. Lucky thing he landed on that chair. His foot is twisted, though. Eliza, go see if we've got any ice. Just lie still, mister, till you get your breath back." Charlie had taken an advanced first-aid course, and she was mentally reviewing the page in her text headed "shock." *Loosen clothing around neck, chest and waist.* That was it.

Dust motes danced in peaceful filtered sunlight, and from where he lay sprawled, it seemed to Ben that the room was suddenly overrun with amazons, with the exception of one blue-eyed angel who'd floated down through a hole in the roof. He was either knocked silly and hallucinating or dead and gone to heaven. Either way, he was temporarily winded from his fall and it felt exceedingly pleasant simply to lie back and let things happen on their own.

Euphoria and placidity faded rapidly, however, as his willowy beauty from the rooftop made a decisive and shocking attempt to release the belt on his khaki shorts and pull the zipper down.

"What the hell—" He made a defensive grab at his midsection and struggled to sit up, then tried to heave himself to his feet, only to have the pain in his right ankle force out an expletive no gentleman should use to either amazons or angels. It didn't help the pain, either.

"Grab him, Carol," Charlie hollered as his huge frame began to buckle. Carol was closest, and she also was strong.

At six feet one and 183 pounds, Carol might just have a chance at keeping this hunk from landing on his butt on the floor and probably knocking a second hold in the structure. He was a one-man wrecking crew, judging by the hole he'd made in the ceiling.

Between the two of them, they just managed to get him back in the armchair. Puffing, they stood back warily while he cursed, and Eliza dashed in with a pitifully small bowl of ice cubes.

"The fridge isn't working; these were all that hadn't melted," she announced.

Despite his seeming ranginess, this was one big man, Charlie decided. He even towered over Carol. How tall was he, anyway? It definitely felt safer to have him sitting down again. He sort of loomed when upright. She discarded any idea of treating him for shock and voted for intimidation instead.

Charlie straightened to her own respectable five feet eight, put her fists on her slim blue-jeaned hips and glowered down at him while Eliza knelt to gently loosen the buckle on his Gulliver-sized brown leather sandal.

"Watch he doesn't kick you in the face, Liza," Charlie cautioned, mindful of the slap he'd delivered to her hand when she was treating him for shock. He shot her a really rotten look.

"What are you, a team of perverts?" he growled. But he gritted his teeth when Eliza removed the sandal, Charlie noticed.

"Shut up," she suggested forcefully. This guy was antsy about being handled, for sure. She bent over to peer at the pupils in his grass-green eyes, checking for unnatural dilation, and something in there suddenly made her feel almost queasy.

His lashes were short and thick and sun-bleached, as blond as his quirky eyebrows. He gazed back intently at her with a bemused expression parting the wide, hard-looking mouth. His steady, curious scrutiny made Charlie feel suddenly hot, prickly and uncomfortable. She was the one giving first aid here, for Pete's sake. What was this guy studying her for, anyway?

Thank goodness he didn't look fatally injured. Apart from a good many scratches, one gash on his left shoulder and badly scraped hands and knees, he seemed pretty fit. Well, maybe even fitter than average. She gulped a bit, glancing over his reclining body. There was so, well, so much of him. And it all seemed to be covered in soft golden fuzz, with an underlay of tanned biceps, triceps and pectorals.

Cripes. What was wrong with her? She couldn't even see his pectorals. This was ridiculous, imagining what was under his white shirt. His torn and dirty white shirt where his massive chest, moving up and down with each regular intake of breath, signaled that all was well within. You could almost smell good health radiating from him, Charlie concluded. Virile, masculine, husky good health, at that.

She tore her gaze away from him and drew in a deep breath of dusty air. Lucky he hadn't broken his fool neck. All brawn, no brains.

Perversely the good news of his survival made her suddenly furious. He was wasting her time, and time was money.

"What did you figure you were doing up on a roof with those leather-soled shoes on? Any ordinary fool knows you don't climb roofs in shoes like those," Charlie exploded, kicking the offending object halfway across the room in a fit of temper.

That got a response. His amazing brows beetled together, and he glowered angrily up at her.

"Me? Listen, little one, I'll have you know—ouch, oww, take it easy, for God's sake—" Eliza was applying her meager supply of ice to the rapidly increasing swelling on his ankle, and he shot her a reproving glare before turning again on Charlie. "Just what in supreme hell were you doing, you fruitcake, on the top of the house, baying at the sun? What the hell are any of you women doing on this property? Even ordinary idiots can read. Those signs say No Trespassing, and there's a law against breaking and entering. And removing those signs is a felony.''

Charlie's tan didn't hide her furious, slow flush of rage. Fruitcake, huh? She jerked a descriptive thumb up at the ceiling.

"Seems to me you're the one doing all the breaking and entering around here. You're the trespasser, wise guy, not us. We happen to have a contract to renovate this place, and I was checking out the roof. Now, just exactly what were you supposed to be doing up there, hotshot?"

A truly awful suspicion was forming in Ben's head. He looked at each woman in turn, the plump redhead kneeling solicitously at his feet, the quiet blond giant, and then his eyes returned to the fiery blue-eyed leader of the pack. It couldn't be, could it? His own brother wouldn't do this to him.

He directed his next question at her.

"Who are you, exactly?" His voice came out with less vigor than usual, and he waited, with a sinking feeling in his midsection, for her answer.

"My company is Cossini Construction, Incorporated. I'm Charlie Cossini. This is Eliza Blake." She indicated the redhead, who nodded and went on pressing ice to his throbbing ankle, "And this is Carol Thompson. We're carpenters."

The tall, muscular blonde held out a hand only slightly smaller than his own and gave him his first friendly smile of the day, along with a bone-crushing handshake. He responded with a sickly grin and a wince.

His Dresden figurine, with all the delicacy of a longshoreman, once again thrust her balled-up fists on each side of her slender waist and demanded in her husky voice, "Now, just who the heck are you?"

Before he could muster up the energy to answer, Eliza's soft voice interrupted from down at his feet. "Whoever he is, I think we'd better get him to the hospital, Charlie. His ankle's bending the wrong way, and it's swelling up like crazy."

THE MEDICAL CLINIC in Haleiwa was air-conditioned, but when two hours went by with no sign of Ben's reappearance, Charlie found she preferred to spend the time outside in the midmorning heat rather than inside surrounded by medicinal smells and starched efficiency. Hospital-like surroundings still reminded her too strongly—and painfully—of the months her mother had spent in extended-care units before death mercifully released her. The agonizing memories had begun to recede during the past year, fading with the healing passage of time, but odors seemed to call up painful visual clips of those events, like unpleasant news releases in her mind.

Today, however, it wasn't only the past that depressed her. She felt rotten about the dreadful way this first meeting with B. V. Gilmour had gone. And more than a little apprehensive about her contract.

She'd always been too fast with her mouth. Well, this time she'd outdone herself. Her sarcastic insults hadn't been enough. Worst of all, she'd allowed her temper to overcome her first-aid training, for she hadn't even had sense enough to examine that ankle of his right away and determine that it was broken. Then, when she finally had knelt and looked closely at the ugly purple swelling above the immense but well-shaped male foot, she'd become queasy and had to fight off nausea, closing her eyes and then opening them, looking up into his concerned face as if she were a candy striper with the vapors.

"You're not going to faint, are you?" he'd asked in that rough burr of a voice, reaching down to support her shoulder with his hand.

What had possessed her, letting herself get frazzled by a man's broken ankle, devastated by his green-eyed scrutiny? She'd seen plenty of broken bones. Construction sites were hazardous. And men had looked at her speculatively ever since she'd turned fourteen, which added up to twelve whole years of male speculation, and she'd never reacted this way before.

The truth was, this man made her feel fourteen. Prickly with newfound sexual awareness. And shy, of all things. Charlie Cossini, boss of her own construction crew. It was humiliating.

She stared down at the stained knees of her worn jeans and reviewed once again the colossal disaster the morning had become the moment he'd announced his identity in that deep, smooth voice of his.

Charlie really had come close to fainting then. She'd sat on her heels at his feet like a handmaiden turned to stone. The memory made her writhe with embarrassment. But how could she have guessed that the village idiot on the roof was none other than the one man in the world she couldn't afford to insult? B. V. Gilmour himself. She'd thought, of course, that he'd be older, wearing a suit, not so...whatever.

"I believe we have an appointment this morning, Charlie Cossini," he'd said with malicious enjoyment. "I'm Ben Gilmour, of Gilmour Developments."

Chapter Two

As though all the air had been let out of her balloon, Charlie had simply deflated and temporarily lost her ability to control the situation.

Not that it mattered. Quietly, but with an air of authority, he'd taken charge. Once they'd bundled him down the stairs, of course.

Charlie shuddered again despite the intense heat. That whole scene didn't bear thinking about.

Only the thin white line around his lips suggested that he was in considerable pain. And despite his injury, he'd been bossy, ordering Charlie to drive the Jeep and leaving Eliza and Carol concise instructions on whom to notify and which doctor to call at the clinic.

She had to admit he was tough, though. That had been an absolutely chaotic performance they'd gone through, getting him down the twisting stairs of the house. They'd done their best but still ended up bumping his injured limb several times because of the narrow staircase and his bulk. Charlie had been almost ill with reluctant empathy, knowing how much pain he must have endured in that torturous descent. But instead of cursing them out viciously, as she sheepishly felt they deserved, he'd just pressed his lips into an even thinner white-rimmed tight line and turned greenish pale under his tan.

Thank heavens he'd had the snappy yellow Jeep for transportation. It was a neat little unit, she thought covet-ously, glancing to where it sat by the curb. Without it, how would they have gotten him the three miles into town? On that rickety bicycle they'd found in the shed last night? Her mouth curved up weakly at the picture that presented.

Cossini Construction was going to have to spring for some sort of vehicle, given the distance from Waialua Bay into the village and the total absence of any taxi service at this end of the island. It would have to be cheap, because after the necessary cost of getting here, the business bank account was likely on overdraft.

Provided, of course, they still had the coveted renovation job after this morning's fiasco. Charlie rather doubted it somehow, remembering the expression on Gilmour's face when she'd blithely mouthed off at him. Damn, if she'd wrecked the chance of a lifetime just because of her tongue...

A smiling Japanese nurse opened the door behind Charlie, and a blast of artificially cooled air wafted over her perspiring back.

"Ms Cossini? Mr. Gilmour is ready to leave now."

A pale-faced Ben, supporting himself awkwardly on crutches, waited impatiently in the small waiting room. His right ankle was encased in a smooth, close-fitting cast, much more streamlined than the ordinary monstrous mound of plaster Charlie was familiar with. The lines around his mouth and eyes were deeper than they'd been earlier that morning, and Charlie felt a jolt of sympathy, making her voice come out jerky.

"The Jeep's just outside the door. There are steps. Can you make it down on those?" She gestured toward his crutches.

He flashed her an ironic half smile and nodded. "Just don't try to help me, okay? I have a feeling I can do better on my own this time."

Well, she deserved that. He was probably going to tell her off good, and she didn't blame him. He had every right to be mad. Her performance hadn't been wonderful back at the house.

She nodded silently, holding the door open for his slow exit, hovering helplessly as he navigated the stairs. He paused at the bottom, beads of sweat dampening the faint lines in his forehead. He felt drained after the long session of probing, X rays and the setting of the break. And now he had this batty woman staring at him expectantly.

"Getting hot out here," he remarked mildly, and she agreed it was.

He didn't sound angry. In fact, they'd actually almost had a conversation without one bad word passing between them. Maybe there was still hope.

Why not try Pop's favorite theory? "You catch more flies with honey than with vinegar," he'd constantly admonished his fiery daughter. Was it too late for honey?

Charlie hurried to the Jeep, holding the crutches while Ben leaned heavily on her shoulder and heaved himself into the vehicle.

His long fingers were strong enough to leave bruises. What did he do to stay so fit? His hands weren't marked by hard work, so it was probably some form of rich man's body-beautiful club. That figured.

No more of that, she reminded herself.

Charm, Charlie, charm.

For the rest of this trip, she vowed, racing around to the driver's side and hopping in, Ben Gilmour would be captivated and overcome by her delightful nature and impressed by her professionalism about her work. Even if she bit her tongue off restraining it. Her immediate future, and that of her loyal carpenters, depended on keeping this job.

She started the Jeep, skillfully casual, enjoying the motor's instant response, and then turned to her passenger with what she hoped was a bright smile.

"Where to?" Her empty stomach growled, and inspiration struck. Her charge card was in her wallet, in the back pocket of her jeans. It would be an investment in the business. "Could I maybe take you to lunch, Mr. Gilmour? There's a lot we need to discuss, and I know you're not feeling great, but maybe a beer and a sandwich would help?''

He stared at her, his thick brows raised in surprise at her diffident tone, and then the crinkles around his eyes deepened, and he chuckled.

''Planning to ply me with liquor, Ms Cossini? Or is it Mrs.?'' He sounded casual enough, but when she shook her head negatively, he let out the breath that had somehow gotten stuck in his diaphragm.

''Negative on the Mrs. It's just plain Charlie, Mr. Gilmour.'' Boy did it hurt to swallow humble pie on an empty stomach. She scowled, and he grinned.

''Well, plain Charlie, mine isn't Mr. Gilmour. But it isn't 'hotshot,' either.'' He couldn't resist triggering her, watching for the flash of suppressed temper in her tilted chin and narrowed blue eyes. Yup, there they both were, right on schedule. She was a firecracker, all right, despite the deceptive exterior.

''Call me Ben. Drive back to the highway and I'll show you where you can take me for lunch. Deal?'' After the performance at the clinic, he needed something cold and wet. Something to fortify him for the unpleasant scene ahead. Might as well get the whole thing over with this afternoon and see about hiring another crew. Women carpenters. What next? He squinted at her questioningly.

''Okay with you?''

She nodded once, decisively, and he admired the way she shot the vehicle into reverse, executed a U-turn and smoothly pulled into traffic. She was a better driver than he was, he admitted grudgingly. But then, machines had never been his thing. He preferred surfboards, any day, to cars. Obviously, this Charlie girl loved driving. How could such a feminine wrapping enclose such unlikely abilities?

In seconds they were at the intersection, and he glanced idly at her hands on the wheel, then gave them his full, horrified attention.

Her nails were cut neatly short and straight across, but several were cracked, and the backs of her long, narrow hands bore deep, old scars and new, raw-looking scratches. She wore no rings, no nail polish, and her skin was chapped and brown and rough. Calluses adorned the sides of several tapered fingers. He stared unthinkingly, unaware for an instant that she had stopped and was waiting patiently for instructions.

"Turn right," he directed absently, and then his anger caught him by surprise. Why the hell wasn't somebody taking better care of this delicious-looking girl, making sure her hands didn't have a chance to get in a state like that? He'd never seen a woman's hands damaged that way by hard work. Didn't she have a father, or brothers? He deliberately ended the list of possibilities there, uncertain as to why he was loath to add a lover to the list.

The parade of females Ben had more or less pursued, conquered and evaded during the adult portion of his thirty-five years had all had long, polished fingernails and smoothly pampered skin. Every single one. Velvety, well-cared-for, moisturized, perfumed skin. All over their bodies.

That brought intimate conjecture about other parts of Charlie's anatomy, and with it came a tightening surge in his own groin. The feminine shape beside him was disturbingly seductive, soft skin or not. The cooling effect of the Jeep's open sides and roof made the tips of her nipples evident within the snug blue T-shirt, and the clean, long planes of her thighs were outlined by the deplorably ragged, faded jeans that delineated a flat stomach and gaped a bit around the narrow waist.

She sensed his scrutiny and misunderstood the reason for it.

"Are you afraid the restaurant won't admit me in my work clothes?" she challenged.

"In Haleiwa?"

She noticed that he pronounced the word in two parts, Hallee-Eeva, soft and much more appealing than the way she'd been saying it. She moved her lips, silently memorizing the word, and when she looked over at him, he was smiling at her again.

"There are very few places in the village, or on the entire island of Oahu, that require dressing up. Certainly not here." He gestured toward a small storefront along the main street of the picturesque village, and she wheeled up to the curb and stopped.

"You do like hamburgers?" Ben asked, and now she had to grin. Her concept of B. V. Gilmour, poor little rich boy, hadn't exactly included a passion as avid as her own for hamburgers.

"They're my favorite," she assured him, and he quirked an eyebrow at her enthusiasm.

The proprietor of the narrow restaurant was anything but Hawaiian. He looked and sounded as if he'd just stepped out of Brooklyn. He kept up a running stream of sympathetic conversation with Ben, clucking over the cast and seating them at a table out of the heavy traffic area. Ben and he were obviously well acquainted.

"You and the lady want the usual?" he queried, and at Ben's nod he disappeared into the kitchen, which occupied the back half of the hallwaylike restaurant.

Within minutes, a smiling girl produced huge foaming mugs of cold beer, followed by giant-size burgers with all the trimmings. Charlie attacked the food with honest hunger before looking around at the decor.

Old snapshots of surfers and native villagers lined the walls, and lovely young brown girls in short white shorts and brilliantly printed shirts served and cleared tables. She might almost have been at a hamburger joint in Bellingham. Except, of course, for the man sitting quietly across from her. There was little that was familiar or relaxing about him. He looked tired, guarded and rather grim, and that wasn't a good sign. Charlie's appetite abruptly faded, and she sat up straighter in her chair.

Ben drank down half the golden brew in his mug in one long, thirsty draft. He ate his food without his usual voracious appetite and then slumped back in his chair with an audible sigh, stretching his cast out to the side and shutting his eyes.

For the first time in his life he wished fervently that Mitchell were here and that he, Ben, were safely back in the company's steel-and-chrome tower in Seattle, adding up boring numbers on a calculator. This woman-carpenter caper proved once and for all that Mitchell no longer knew the difference between boys and girls, a situation Ben had been predicting for years. Numbers, after all, had no gender.

"Is your ankle painful?" Charlie knew it was probably a ridiculous question. He kept his eyes shut and shook his head.

"It only hurt for a while there. Now it's just a bloody nuisance." Something told him it was going to be all of that and more before the next six weeks were up.

"That's a weird-looking cast," she commented sociably.

"This contraption's state of the art. It's fiberglass, which means I'll be able to swim now and then." No surfing, though. The doctor had been adamant about that. Ben glowered down at the sleek bulge on his ankle. Six miserable, lousy weeks, unable to run or surf, with this block of fiberglass hanging on his leg.

He opened his eyes and found her studying him with that characteristic frown wrinkling the golden skin above her dainty nose. He liked the way she refused to play coy, staring right back at him despite the slight rosy flush spreading over her cheekbones.

She didn't have any makeup on that he could see, and the lines of her face were both delicate and strong. Funny, he thought all women wore makeup of some sort. Belinda had worn light makeup even to bed for the whole eight months of their marriage. He'd hated the taste of it. For the first few months, anyway, while he still was tasting Belinda.

Charlie's generously curved lips were naked, even slightly chapped. Her bottom lip was short, which gave her mouth a slightly pouty expression. Kissable. *Can it, Ben. You're about to fire the lady.*

Damp tendrils of curly soft hair clung to her temples. She hadn't raced off to fix herself up, nor did she even carry a purse.

Impulsively, he raised his glass to her in a toast to nature, liking what he saw, loathing what he was about to say to her.

She lifted her own dripping glass, held it out in a challenging salute and took a healthy sip. Foam clung to her curved mouth, and irrationally, he wanted to lean over and lick it off before she could.

Man, what had they given him in that clinic, an aphrodisiac instead of a pain tablet? He was here to fire the woman, and all he could think of—

Get on with it, Gilmour.

"Charlie, I'm sure you're a fine carpenter," he began heartily.

"I am," she said calmly. "In fact, all three of us are. We've built four houses from the ground up, and for two years we've specialized in remodeling and finish carpentry." Far from sounding brassy, her tone was one of quiet confidence. "We have reference letters and photos of completed projects."

In spite of his resolve, Ben was impressed. She sounded as though she actually knew what she was doing.

Her voice became slightly more emphatic. "We also have a signed contract from Gilmour Developments instructing us to begin work at once on renovations at Reveille Reef Club."

She didn't add that the contract stipulated it was subject to approval by one B. J. Gilmour. Obviously, he knew that. And judging by the way he shifted uncomfortably in his chair and lowered his gaze from hers, he wasn't about to approve. Her fingers gripped the slippery glass and whitened with tension. And her resolve strengthened.

"Look, Charlie." The slightly apologetic tone made her stomach flop with premonition. "My brother Mitchell arranged this contract sight unseen for my Aunt Stella, who owns the property. Stella's seventy-four, and she hasn't visited Hawaii since after the war. Mitchell's the business end of the company. He sees everything in terms of dollars and cents, and I'm sure you must have submitted an attractive bid on the job."

She started to say something, but Ben went on firmly.

"Unfortunately, neither of them is aware of the actual situation at Reveille Reef Club. Nor do they know much about Hawaii in general, which makes my position difficult. I'm quite sure that as carpenters and renovators, your, um, workers are fine. The problem is, this particular job absolutely can't be done by women."

There, he'd done it that time. Her face was slowly turning magenta, and he could see the explosion coming. He held up both palms defensively.

"Now, don't read me the equal opportunities lecture or give me the chauvinism routine until I explain. I'm not questioning your ability."

Not entirely, he amended silently. But three women as carpenters? He was going to plan an appropriate, slow revenge for Mitchell over this one.

"Charlie, when did you and the others arrive in Hawaii?"

"Yesterday. We hired a cab to bring us from Honolulu Airport."

After the circuitous tour of Honolulu, it had been a good hour's drive on a highway, which wound past red-soiled pineapple fields, modern air force bases and ancient sugar plantations, to reach the rural village of Haleiwa, and another quarter of an hour on a narrow secondary road to get to Waialua Bay and the Reveille Reef Club.

The fare had been astronomical, and the taxi driver had shaken his dark head in confusion. "Don't know why you pretty ladies want to come way down here," he'd stated. "Better you stay in Honolulu. You saw yourself—lots of action there, plenty of clubs, shopping. Here, no taxis, no car rental, very primitive. Only surfers and artists stay here."

The three excited women had looked at each other and giggled. They were artists of a sort. Their first good look at

Reveille Reef Club had been something of a shock. The buildings were in pretty bad shape. But that fact only added to the challenge, and the three had explored first and then made themselves as comfortable as possible in bedrooms of the main house.

"Our contract stated that we were responsible for getting here and that we would be able to live at the club while we renovated it. We're prepared to keep our part of that bargain to the letter, Mr., er, Ben. You can't just—"

"How much do you know about Reveille Reef Club?" he persisted, determined to make her understand his reasoning.

Charlie held on to her rising temper with difficulty. He kept going off on tangents, deflecting what she tried to say. She shrugged impatiently at his question. "Not much. It was built as an army officers' club, and was used by the forces as a rest-and-rehab center during and after the war."

Ben nodded, adding, "It was then given to a church group, who used it for years as a boys' camp. Five years ago, they offered it for sale, and my aunt bought it, God knows why. As you know now, it's in bad shape. If Stella weren't so damn stubborn . . ."

He rubbed the back of his neck wearily, aware of the deep ache in his injured leg, and the thousand and one problems that had suddenly cropped up in his life. Uneasily, he studied the gleam of dogged determination in the blue eyes watching him steadily from across the small littered table.

"That's very interesting. Now, what exactly makes you think Cossini Construction isn't capable of renovating it? Why are you so unwilling to let us do the job we were hired to do?" she queried, icy challenge in her husky voice.

Ben sighed and with elaborate patience did his best to explain.

"Hawaii is in the midst of severe economic and labor problems. Growing pains, probably, but it's a time of confusion on the islands. Increased labor costs and competition in the marketplace have hurt the pineapple and sugar industries on which the economy here depends. Business is trying to remedy that by encouraging secondary industry, but the process is slow.''

He turned his glass in his fingers thoughtfully. ''Slow'' had to be the understatement of the year. He mentally reviewed the agricultural disasters he'd witnessed just during the months he'd been here, problems that interested him as a spectator. He'd even spent hours when the surf wasn't up dreaming up solutions to some of the more obvious problems—until he started puzzling over the trouble at Reveille Reef.

He recalled the incidents of vandalism at the Reef. His tires slashed. Senseless warnings scrawled on walls. The damned signs smashed to pieces every time he put them up. The new locks he'd had installed that were neatly sawn off. Dangerous or just mischief? There wasn't any way to know. That brought him back to his companion and reinforced the unpleasant business at hand.

''Ninety percent of the people on these islands are friendly, warm and welcoming. They understand that their future prosperity is linked to the islands' industrial growth, world trade and foreign and local investments. Unfortunately, there's a minority of radicals here, just as there are everywhere, who are young and unemployed and angry. They're tough rebels, and they can stir up bad trouble. They call people like you and me 'haoles,' and their advice to us is 'Go home.' ''

It was the explanation that the police had given Ben after the latest break-in at the Reef. He repeated it now, still not altogether certain, for some reason, that it was accurate.

Ben signaled to the waitress, and she cheerfully produced another beer for him and poured delicious local coffee for Charlie. He waited until she moved away, then continued. ''These attacks are just on property now, but they could get worse. You must have heard the news reports of attacks on tourists, including several murders. The local government and the police are doing everything they can. During the years the club wasn't used, it probably became a camping place for every type of vagrant. Those signs on the property are an effort to keep these people away, but all that happens is that the signs are broken or painted over with threats. Apparently they don't want the Reef changed. Most of the locals are scared and don't want to come near the place. That's why we decided to hire an off-island crew." How ironic that it had backfired. "Damn it all, Charlie, I feel awful about this whole misunderstanding. But I can't, I won't, be responsible for what could happen to three women, haoles at that, working in an isolated place like the Reef."

His voice grew louder, more adamant. "You're miles from anywhere, and you're women." He shook his head in disgust, and the next comment tumbled out before he could censor it. "Hell, when Mitchell told me he'd hired a crew headed by somebody called Charlie Cossini, I naturally envisioned a tough Italian who could take care of himself." Ben pursed his lips and blew out a frustrated breath, slumping back again in his chair.

Charlie forgot about honey and charm and acting reasonable. She slammed her cup down, sending hot coffee splashing over the wooden surface.

"Well, mister," she gritted through her clenched teeth, "that's exactly what you've got. A tough Italian who can take care of herself. Nobody's asking you to worry about our welfare. What do you figure, we need a bodyguard? Where've you been for the past ten years? Women like us aren't asking for any favors. All we want is an equal chance at jobs. We've been on hard jobs before, jobs with labor problems, jobs where men tried their best to make us look bad. Well, we managed then and we'll manage now—and also do excellent work. None of us are exactly shrinking violets, in case you hadn't noticed."

She stopped only because she was out of breath, and Ben sat watching her with infuriating composure.

The fact was, her tirade didn't surprise him at all. It did irritate him despite his seeming calm. This was one stubborn lady. He slowly assessed every feature of her face, ending his perusal with her full lips, now set in a hard, stubborn line.

"Oh, I noticed that, all right," he drawled maddeningly. "I just don't think any of you would be that effective in a fistfight."

He allowed his survey to extend insolently to her neck, down her shoulders and breasts, over her narrow rib cage, and then slowly to rise to meet snapping, angry eyes. His own anger was growing by the second, fueled by frustration. She had to realize what kind of people he was talking about.

"Nor do I think a fistfight is the type of attack you need to worry about," he added coldly.

He might well have saved his breath.

"If you're trying to scare us with threats of rape, we've all had training in self-defense," she spat out. "As to resentment of our being outsiders, I plan to subcontract to local trades—electricians, plumbers, carpet men. If you insist on brawn balancing our brains, then I'll also hire the biggest, toughest laborer I can find. But get one thing straight. I need this contract, and I don't scare easily. I'll fight you over this, because you have no legitimate grounds for giving us our walking papers."

Technically, he knew she was right. But technicalities had never bothered Ben. There'd be a way to ease Cossini Construction out, if that was what he wanted. What bothered him more than a little was that he wasn't sure he wanted them—or Charlie—gone. On the other hand, he was worried about her safety, damn it. Why didn't she realize that?

She sat ramrod-straight in the cushioned chair, her determined chin thrust belligerently toward him. He noticed her work-damaged hands clutching the coffee cup, and he was surprised it didn't shatter under the pressure she was exerting. The long tendons in the back of the scarred hands stood out rigidly, knuckles white. She was far more upset than her deliberate mask of defiance revealed, and his defenses crumbled.

"Truce, Charlie?" He couldn't stay mad at her, especially not while looking at those hands. "How about if we start over again and discuss this rationally?"

He hadn't changed his mind about the safety factor. But there might be a way around it.

"I was being rational," she insisted. "I effectively countered every single one of your legitimate concerns. That's rational, or didn't your fancy education extend to management mediation?"

He laughed; he couldn't help it. She was so pugnacious, so cocky, so foolhardy. And honest, maybe? Desperate, certainly. Why? He'd known a lot of powerful men who'd never dare challenge one of the Gilmours this openly, especially the ne'er-do-well youngest Gilmour brother. She stirred his curiosity, this Charlie Cossini, as well as more basic areas of his anatomy. He needed to know about her. He wanted to know.

"What made you decide to become a carpenter? Why is this job so important to you? Is your name really Charlie?" And would she answer?

She blinked, confused by his sudden barrage of questions. Would explaining do any good? Oh, what the hell. So far she'd struck out. Might as well start over.

"No, it's Charlotte. Charlotte Evangeline Mary Cossini. After my grandfather Charles and both grandmothers. I was supposed to be a boy; there were already two older sisters, and mother couldn't have any more children after me. So Dad made the best of it. He named me Charlie and treated me like a son." She recited the story matter-of-factly. Ben waited.

"Dad was a roofer, so I grew up around construction sites. He let me enter trade school at sixteen. For four weeks a year, for four years, I attended class. The rest of the time I apprenticed on the job. When I graduated, there was lots of construction going on, but gradually jobs became harder to get with the recession."

She'd done every dirty job in the book just to keep working. And she'd lost at least two jobs because the foreman wanted more than a good carpenter. But hard work paid off, and there were those good years when she'd met Carol and Eliza and formed the company. They were starting to do well, and then the bottom fell out of the construction business, Gennaro had the accident, the medical bills piled up, and her father grew thin and haunted. Charlie skipped over all that.

"Three years ago, I met Carol and Eliza and formed my own company. But times are tough, and the competition's fierce." She bit her bottom lip, then released it. The situation was much worse than she described, and she debated how much to reveal to him. What would an American prince named Gilmour know about hard times? She had more than her share of pride.

But pride was an expensive commodity. Should she tell him that if this job hadn't come along, Cossini Construction would have folded? That Carol would be back working as a nurse's aide, a job she detested, and Eliza would be waitressing? And she'd probably be in court for nonpayment of debts? She shuddered, a cold lump forming in her stomach. Had Ben ever had to worry about debts? She'd wager not. She didn't want his pity, just the chance to do the job and nothing more.

Ben watched her, noting the shiver and daring another question.

"How old are you, Charlie?"

"Twenty-six." The terse answer surprised him. If he'd had to guess, he might have said twenty. Although she talked a tough forty.

Enough was enough, she decided. "Do you want to know my mother's maiden name, too?" she asked, syrupy sweet, blue gaze wide and dangerously innocent.

Fortunately, the waitress intervened.

"Will that be all?" She scribbled out a bill, and Charlie produced her charge card, but Ben smoothly picked up the bill, handed it and money from his wallet to the smiling girl and slid the card silently back to Charlie.

"Look here," she bristled. Ben ignored her, struggling to his feet and retrieving his crutches.

"I said I'd buy lunch," she persisted stubbornly. He was already moving toward the door.

"How about buying me dinner instead? I'm in no shape to cook and you can discuss your suggestions for renovating the club." It was devious, but he had a feeling she'd refuse if he came straight out and asked her for a date. For some stupid reason like not mixing business with pleasure. If she agreed, it would give him another few hours to figure her out. He was clumsily trying to open the door and balance at the same time.

Charlie scooted in front of him, blocking the door with her back, impervious to everything except what she thought he'd said.

"Then you'll give us your approval? We've still got the job?" she asked breathlessly, watching as his bushy eyebrows beetled together in a mock frown.

"Well, I want to see your plans, of course. But yes, damn it, you've got the job. With strict conditions. Now, would you please open that door and get us out of here?"

"WHAT'S THE SCORE, Charlie? What happened with the hunk? Who'd have guessed he was Gilmour? How come you've got his Jeep?"

The barrage of questions poured like a flood from Eliza the moment Charlie braked the yellow vehicle to a halt in the rutted driveway at the Reef.

"I took him home. He couldn't drive this thing, so he loaned it to us," Charlie said wearily, adding, "Where's Carol?"

She felt exhausted all of a sudden, drained by the uncertainties of the morning, more than a little confused by the intensity of the emotions Ben stirred in her. Emotions such as anger, defiance, outrage. Attraction, desire? Ambivalence.

Sitting slumped behind the wheel, she decided there was no point in going over the whole thing twice, once with

Eliza, again with Carol. She didn't have the energy for it. Besides, the one question Eliza hadn't asked—did they have the job?—was the only one that mattered.

Eliza bustled off to find the third member of the group, and Charlie slid her body out of the Jeep and arched her arms over her head, tipping her head back and stretching the tension from her muscles, half closing her eyes against the brightness of the Hawaiian sun.

In response to Eliza's bellowing, Carol emerged, looking hot and sweaty and worried, from one of the buildings adjacent to the house. She wore her carpenter's apron over a pair of jeans nearly as ragged as Charlie's own, and her short sliver-blond hair shone in the sunlight.

There was a shy quality about Carol, Charlie mused, totally at odds with her size and her physical strength. Almost as if she expected to be hurt by life. Probably a hangover from the marriage and divorce she never talked about. As she walked slowly across the grassy yard toward Charlie, apprehension was evident on her Nordic features.

Unlike Eliza, though, she bravely went straight to the heart of the problem.

"We lost the job, didn't we?" she asked quietly, her hand clutching a tape measure like a talisman against misfortune.

A wave of relief washed over Charlie, and a feeling of fierce protectiveness for the big, vulnerable woman. It would have been horrible to have had to confirm Carol's worst fears. Instead, she shook her head and forced herself to smile widely at the other two, jabbing a triumphant thumb skyward in a gesture of victory.

"We're staying, carpenters. We're gonna do a number on this old place," she announced, and the women's whoops of delight echoed over the deserted collection of buildings. When the cheering quieted, Charlie repeated what she'd told Eliza.

"Ben, er, Gilmour, can't drive the Jeep. His ankle's broken, like we thought, so he loaned it to us for a couple of days. There's a catch, though." Charlie was beginning to suspect there'd be more than a few catches in any dealings with Ben.

"We have to help him move in here—today. The only way we got the job was if he and some surfer friend of his live here while we try to do our work."

"Why's that?"

"How come?"

Charlie did her best to explain the situation, repeating Ben's story of vandalism, the islands' economic problems and angry young men, not at all convinced of its validity. The whole thing still sounded pretty phony to her.

Typically, Eliza was delighted at the prospect of having the men live at the Reef while the women worked on it. Carol, however, was appalled, and Charlie knew exactly how she felt. Her own reaction to Ben's casual recital of his conditions had been negative. Extremely and loudly negative. Unfortunately, her objections had had absolutely no effect on Ben.

"Either we do it my way or no deal," he had stated smugly, knowing Charlie had to give in, however ungraciously. She didn't disappoint him.

"You'll be sorry. Living in a place while it's being renovated isn't at all like staying at some swanky resort, like you and this friend of yours are used to," she'd threatened. "Besides," she added petulantly, "you'll just be in our way. Don't you have a job you have to go to every day, at your office or something?"

He'd found that really funny. That's when he'd explained he was a professional surfer.

Chapter Three

Charlie couldn't believe what she was hearing. A professional surfer. She knew such playboys existed, but she'd never expected to meet one. An irrational tidal wave of disillusionment and anger swept over her.

Of all the frivolous, unproductive people she'd ever come across, Charlie decided in disgust, Ben Gilmour took the cake. An international playboy surfer, no less.

And this was the guy who had final say on Cossini Construction's ability to do their job? It was grossly unfair.

"How come they gave you the job of supervising the Reef, anyway?" she demanded, her contempt evident in her tone.

He'd watched her emotions play across her features. He should have expected her reaction, considering the work ethic she exuded like some unusual perfume. Still, he was surprised by its intensity, and amused, as well. This woman could even teach Mitchell a thing or two.

"A simple case of being in the right place at the wrong time," he said easily. "Now and then, in cases of expediency, the family reluctantly presses me into service. Fortunately it's not often." He'd quirked his thick right eyebrow at her, and it was all she could do not to snort in derision.

In suitably scathing tones, Charlie related the news now to Eliza and Carol.

"He doesn't even work? A real live playboy surfer, right here at Reveille Reef," Eliza enthused, emerald eyes sparkling wickedly. "Is he married? Is his friend rich, too?"

The questions annoyed Charlie unduly. "Who knows about people like that? He and his friends probably have an entire stable of ex-wives living off alimony their daddies pay for them," she said caustically. "We're not here to study the sex habits of the idle rich," she snapped, sounding irritable even to herself. "We've got a job to do, and it's going to be doubly difficult with him and his friends around. This afternoon we've got to come up with a detailed list of materials and estimated time. We'll also have to figure out where to put these guys in the house."

There were plenty of empty bedrooms. It wasn't a shortage of space that bothered Charlie. Somehow the idea of having Ben sleeping, eating, living, in close proximity to her was unduly upsetting and distracting.

"I already told B—Mr. Gilmour that they'll have to stay out of our way as much as possible. At six tonight we'll go and collect His Highness."

She didn't add that shortly after that she was neatly trapped into taking Ben Gilmour out to dinner. A short, explicit word spat from her lips, and her two carpenters glanced at her mutinous face and hustled discreetly off to begin the inventory.

Her bad temper was Ben's fault. She could see his face clearly in her mind, shrugging those eyebrows, looking as if he knew exactly what was making her uncomfortably aware of hidden parts of her body. Worse, and even more infuriating, he seemed to suggest without one spoken word just what was needed to remedy the situation.

The sun grew still warmer as the late afternoon progressed. Used to a more temperate climate, the three women were soon bedraggled and sweating profusely, physically drained by the effort of working intensively in such heat. But by five o'clock they had a complete and quite professional evaluation drawn up. It was Carol who finally lightened Charlie's lingering bad temper.

"I don't want a couple of strange men living in the same house I'm in," she burst out. It was obvious the matter had been on her mind all afternoon. "Mornings are hard enough without that. What do you say we fix up this cabin a little and put them both out here?" she asked Charlie.

The building she was referring to was hardly a cabin. One of the six outbuildings, it looked more like a windowless boxcar someone had dumped under the towering coconut palms.

The idea of putting Ben Gilmour in such an outrageous accommodation prompted a wicked grin to form on Charlie's lips. An adjoining lean-to held toilet facilities, showers and a kitchen of sorts.

Everything was old, rusty and much the worse for wear. It was perfect. With Eliza's help, they spent the next hour turning the water on, checking the plumbing, finding the right master switch for electricity and sawing a large window opening in the wall of the rectangular sleeping area, which was as hot as a griddle and stiflingly stuffy.

"We need another opening along the back wall," Eliza announced, plopping her rounded bottom on a sad-looking wooden chair and sprawling her bare legs on either side of the seat. "I'll do that tomorrow, and frame it in, and you can pick up some wire screen when you're in town, Charlie. Then there'll be a cross breeze, and it won't be half bad in here." She glanced critically at the gritty green linoleum floor, the cobwebs hanging from the exposed rafters and the sagging and dusty iron cots lining the unpainted walls. The new window let in more light, but it also exposed the dingy interior mercilessly. "When are we gonna have time to clean in here?" she wondered aloud, and then cowered dramatically under the outraged glares Charlie and Carol leveled on her.

"They want to live here? Then they clean, cook, wash their own clothes and completely take care of their own needs. No feeling sorry for them, either, Liza," Charlie cautioned sternly. Then she caught Carol's satisfied smirk and had to laugh. "This will be a learning experience for the dear boys,'' she said, and led the way in a mad dash to the main house to don bikinis for the quick, refreshing dip in the Pacific they'd been promising themselves.

Charlie stubbornly and uncharacteristically took her time, enjoying a shower after her swim, pulling on fresh khaki shorts and a plain brown cotton shirt, brushing the tangles from her hair and tying it back with a brown scarf but meticulously avoiding makeup or any suggestion that she'd done more than her usual minimum in the way of grooming. The weird part, she realized, was even noticing what she wasn't doing.

It was nearly six-thirty before she steered the yellow Jeep up the short driveway to his house, and it was obvious Ben was waiting for them.

He sprawled out on a wooden deck chair in the tiny front courtyard. Flowers of every exotic color and scent tumbled over cool red clay tiles, spilling from low planters scattered here and there around him. His crutches were propped against his chair, his cast stuck out in front of his reclining form.

Even with the crutches and the cast, he managed to give an impression of indolent grace, of lithe athletic power. Charlie swallowed hard, trying not to let her eyes dwell on the long, lean shape of him and the way his shorts clung to narrow hips and powerful thighs. His hair was soft, and it looked as if he'd showered not long ago. His expressive brows lifted in greeting, and his eyes, green as the foliage beside his chair, slipped past Eliza to settle squarely on Charlie, as if it were her, and her alone, he'd been waiting to see.

Everything inside her, from that moment and on through the next hours, accelerated, like an engine climbing a long, twisting hill. She met his eyes with a direct glance of her own, confused at the familiarity she felt for someone she didn't approve of or even know. Neither she nor Ben spoke, so it was lucky Eliza prattled on and on about the beauty of the beach house, the quietly luxurious furnishings. It filled the loud silence between Ben and Charlie.

"The company keeps this place for the use of its employees," Ben explained easily. He flashed a mischievous glance at Charlie, standing stiffly now, looking out at the view of the Pacific from the wide front window. "It's designed to encourage relaxation," he added wickedly, making Charlie conscious of her ramrod stance. Ben waited for a caustic response, but Charlie ignored his effort to bait her.

"This the stuff you want us to move for you?" She indifferently indicated a stock of boxes. Obviously he'd spent the afternoon trying to pack. It couldn't have been easy to do on crutches. His foot probably ached, too. Glancing covertly at him, Charlie could detect lines of fatigue etched around his eyes and mouth. She stifled a rush of sympathy and a fleeting remorse for the less than comfortable quarters he was being moved into.

Well, it was his own stubborn fault. He'd likely take one look and move back here, anyway. This comfort was what he was used to. She sniffed and picked up a box.

"Let's get it done today, Liza," she suggested.

Loading Ben's expensive luggage, his stereo and speakers, guitar, boxes of books and of all things his dozens of plants into the Jeep and transporting them and their owner from the small but luxurious beach cottage to the crude but larger cabin the women had prepared took much longer than Charlie expected.

Ben scowled when he learned they'd left Carol behind alone, and he lectured Charlie and Eliza sternly about it.

Exasperated, Charlie muttered, "For gosh sakes, she's a big girl, and we've been there two days already and never seen a living soul apart from you."

Ben ignored her. "After this," he reprimanded, "I don't want any of you alone at the Reef, day or night. We'll hurry back so Eliza can be there with Carol, and Pogey should arrive later tonight. Charlie, you and I are still going out for that dinner you promised me."

Charlie bristled. Eliza shot an archly teasing glance at her boss, assuming from Ben's words that Charlie had taken the initiative and actually asked him for a date. Charlie speared her with a challenging glare that kept Eliza from making any smart remarks, at least for the moment.

They rode back to the Reef, with Ben in the front beside a disgruntled Charlie. Why couldn't he ride in the back beside Eliza? Every single time she glanced to the side, he was watching her, smiling or some damn fool thing. It made her nervous. She was vastly relieved when they arrived at the rutted driveway and she could pull up with a flourish near the infamous cabin.

Ben disappointed all the women by not showing the slightest sign of surprise or shock at his questionable lodgings at the Reef. He took one quick look around, said not a word, and simply showed them where to put his things.

"Pogey, an Australian surfer friend of mine will be staying here with me and he'll be back soon. He's over on the big island visiting friends, but he knows where to come. I called him and told him we were moving. He'll pick up all the rest of the stuff tomorrow."

"Pogey?" Charlie muttered under her breath. He sounded like a real nerd as far as she was concerned, another fair-haired scion who'd probably never done a good day's work in his entire life. And probably never would either.

Her mind easily categorized exactly what sort of individuals Ben Gilmour and his friends were. Rootless, spoiled, selfish, frivolous. Living off money they had no ambition to earn. Her brain understood all of that perfectly. The disconcerting part was the way her body reacted the moment she was in Ben's presence.

Pure sexual magnetism brought every nerve ending into startling awareness, and no amount of logical reason controlled or subdued that instinctive response. It irritated her, confused her, angered her. But it didn't go away.

THE RESTAURANT Ben suggested for dinner was in Haleiwa. It had a pleasant, unpretentious dining room with a large outdoor eating area, roofed but without walls, making the heavy tropical evening an intimate part of the atmosphere.

As they entered, Charlie hoped fervently that it wouldn't be too expensive. She didn't intend to work herself half to death under that scorching sun just to pay for elaborate and unnecessary dinners.

At a word from Ben, the smiling host led them to a table in the open courtyard. There was room for Ben's crutches and space for him to stretch out his injured ankle. Ben sighed with relief as he carelessly shoved his crutches under the table.

A trio of cheerful Hawaiian musicians were playing soft background music, and candles encased in glass chimneys flickered as daylight faded.

Charlie had stubbornly refused to change into anything resembling dressy clothes. She still wore the khaki shorts and blouse she'd put on earlier, but a furtive glance around assured her that others were dressed just as casually. Not that she really cared, she told herself.

Ben wore a fresh, short-sleeved white shirt that made his tan deeper and the green of his eyes more emphatic. He, too, wore shorts—navy mid-thigh dress shorts.

"None of my pants will fit over this cast. I'll have to do something; maybe split the seams, do you think?"

Charlie was careful to shrug noncommittally. If he wanted seams split, he'd have to find a tailor. But her eyes, of their own accord, checked out the whole landscape the split seams would have to encompass, and a fresh wave of tension twisted through her. He was so—*virile*, she guessed the word was. A hunk, just as Eliza had said. Too bad he was an empty hunk.

Gradually, however, the sweet tropical smells blended with the odors of food and good cooking, lilting music filled the spaced around them, the excellent crab appetizer Ben ordered cast a spell over Charlie, and she relaxed. Nothing had been discussed about the job.

"First we eat, then we do business," Ben had declared when she'd tried to spread her papers out. "Everything looks better on a full stomach.'' So Charlie sipped the pine-apple-and-rum drink he'd ordered for her, studying her surroundings curiously.

The tiled courtyard had an aura of peace about it despite the muted sounds of laughter and clinking china. Beyond the sheltering beams of the roof, purple shadows crept across the neighboring old wooden buildings. Day had fallen into night without the intervention of the long twilight she was used to during the summer in her native Washington.

Everything was strange here, and for an instant a sense of being alien to this land filled her with homesickness. She'd traveled so little and never before to anyplace the least exotic. She'd never really had a vacation, yet all around her were young, vivacious people who probably vacationed all the time. How would it feel, for instance, to be the young woman at that nearby table, lovely in her sensual white dress, being wined and dined by the handsome man seated across from her? Although the man wasn't nearly as handsome as Ben, she mused dreamily, and then caught herself with a start.

Face reality, Charlie, she cautioned herself. *In your position you can't afford to dream. Dreams are a waste of time, and time is money. You're a businesswoman, remember?*

But the subtle seduction of the moment lingered longer than she intended, and Ben, closely watching the flitting expressions in her flashing eyes, sensed a wistfulness in her and saw how quickly she rejected it. The candlelight made golden patterns in her hair, and the beauty of her face made him long to trace its pattern with his fingertips.

The wistfulness in her deep blue eyes gave way to caution, then genuine alarm, when the waiter appeared for their order. Ben missed the way her eyes flicked to the prices on the wine list as he swiftly ordered a bottle of fine white German wine to accompany the specialty of the house—freshly caught whitefish, called *opakapaka*, in a special delicate sauce, with crisp, barely steamed vegetables—for two.

Charlie listened aghast as he blithely added several extra exotic dishes to the original, barely masking her reaction when the waiter left, and Ben's attention was again on her.

"Hungry?" he inquired, misinterpreting her wide-eyed gaze.

"What makes you think you're an expert on what I want to eat?"

He was completely unperturbed by her question. "I've been here before, and you haven't. I know what's good, and you don't." His smug confidence annoyed her further.

"I suppose you think carpenters are more familiar with hamburger than with fancy sauces and German wines," she snapped waspishly.

"Don't you like wine?" He deliberately ignored the rest of it.

Her voice softened slightly. "Of course. I grew up having sips of my father's homemade wine. But I don't expect you've ever tasted anything that didn't cost seventeen fifty a bottle."

He laughed at that, and she found herself loving the way his laugh sounded, the way his eyes sparkled.

"You'd be surprised, Charlie. I've downed more than a few bottles of real rotgut, mostly when I was younger and wilder."

"Seeing how the other half lived?" she pursued stubbornly just as the waiter proudly brought huge platters of colorfully arranged and delicious food, interrupting Ben's reply.

The next half hour was safely devoted to eating, and Charlie was famished. The food was extraordinary, and for short periods she actually forgot what it was going to cost in the sheer pleasure of savoring a fine meal.

Ben ordered them macadamia-nut torte smothered in cream for dessert, and Charlie loved it.

"Want the rest of mine?" Ben asked, and she nodded greedily. No point in wasting it. She hadn't noticed it on the menu, but it probably cost more than a sheet of top-grade plywood.

Ben loved her honest gluttony. Here, finally, was a woman not on a diet.

She scooped up the final morsel of creamy sweetness and sat comfortably back in her chair, stuffed with food. Ben ordered liqueur.

How far would they let her go over the limit on her charge card? She shivered at the thought of having the manager phone for verification and reject the card, staring at her with raised eyebrows as he refused to take a check. And wisely so, for it would bounce. She had no cash. Her newly filled stomach clenched as the scene grew worse in her imagination. As usual, her tongue betrayed her fears, although Ben didn't recognize it.

"You rich guys sure know how to live, all right," she purred, and then felt slightly ashamed of herself.

Ben decided it was past time to challenge her. Her remarks were starting to get to him. What did she have against money? Every other woman he'd ever met— But Charlie wasn't at all like every other woman, he reminded himself. Charlie was a law unto herself, and right now she was acting like a vixen.

"It would be nice if we could be friends," he said quietly. "I'd like to get to know you, Charlie." *Liar.* He wanted much more than her friendship. He wanted to be her lover. His intentions were absolutely lascivious. He wanted to kiss every inch of her, to explore those delicate, long curves and planes, to fit his body into her dark, secret spaces. That little fantasy caused a spontaneous reaction, which could prove embarrassing, and he forced himself back on track. *Hold it, Gilmour. Take it slow and steady.*

"You seem to have a real problem with prejudice. You don't appear to like me much. What have you got against silver spoons, Charlie?" He made his voice matter-of-fact rather than accusatory.

"Silver spoons?" She flushed warmly at his assessment of her opinion of him, abashed even though it was the truth, but now he'd lost her.

"Yeah, like the one I was born with," Ben said. "A person can't help what he's born with. I was the youngest of four boys, born nine years after my nearest brother, Ralph. Consequently, my brothers were already doing worthwhile, acceptable things by the time I grew up. They were running the business, making money hand over fist. I figured the family didn't need another banker or lawyer or economist. Anyway, I wasn't that good at adding or subtracting. I liked growing things, making plants produce food, but I didn't feel like being a wealthy gentleman farmer. There was no need. The impetus for what we do comes from need, and there's nothing I really need enough to make me want to do it." His steady, clear green eyes were unfathomable across the candlelit table, and Charlie wanted to shake him. Or comfort him. Or embrace him. Poor little rich boy.

"So you don't do anything at all? Don't you ever feel as if you ought to accomplish something?" she challenged.

For a brief second a flicker passed over his features, but his confident, charming grin was firmly in place again before she knew what it had been.

"My brothers are so good at accomplishment there's no reason for me to be, as well. Besides, every wealthy American family needs a remittance man to add much-needed color to their drab family tree. The English had them. Why shouldn't we?"

She knew he was teasing. Wasn't he?

"Haven't you ever had a job, done honest-to-goodness labor?" There was such wistful pleading in her voice. Why did she want him to be other than what he was?

He nodded his head, surprising her for an instant.

"Sure, lots of different jobs. I worked as a fire fighter once in Canada, and I crewed on a fishing boat in Sweden. I worked for a couple of months on a sheep station in Australia."

His recital simply confirmed what she already suspected. He'd never really worked. He'd played at work, like a curious dilettante.

"And now you're a surfer?"

He inclined his head in agreement, the ash brown of his short curls catching glints of gold from the candle, his eyebrows punctuating his level gaze.

"For as long as it interests me."

That about said it all, Charlie decided, wondering why his comment should make her feel so bad. Everything in Ben's life was strictly fun and strictly temporary. And everything in Charlie's was absolutely serious and very permanent. And that was that.

The table had been cleared as they talked, and cups of rich Hawaiian coffee steamed between them. She moved the cups to the side and retrieved her notebook from where she'd placed it under the table, opening it so the careful calculations faced Ben, forcing him to deal with their reality.

For the next hour, she insisted on completing the business for which the dinner had been arranged, arguing decisively over points she knew were necessary.

Ben asked questions, some incisive, about subcontracting and time management, some sadly ignorant concerning construction. To her astonishment, he silently penciled in a substantially higher figure under the wages column, leaving Charlie with a head filled with arguments she'd planned to use to accomplish that very concession and no need to use them. But after all, she cynically realized, it was easy to spend money you didn't have to earn.

When they were done, she excused herself, pretending to go to the washroom. She found the waiter and settled the bill using her charge card, crossing her fingers and praying silently they wouldn't phone for verification. They didn't. Trembling with gratitude, she added a satisfactory tip to the staggering total. Then she returned to the table and suggested briskly that since they had finished their business, it was time to leave.

"I paid the check," she said shortly when Ben started to signal the waiter. He stared up at her for a second, brows beetling together angrily. Then he scooped up his crutches and stumped toward the exit behind her. He paused outside the door, and she hesitated before descending the wooden stairs.

"Don't do that again, Charlie," he warned softly. "Not ever again. If I take a lady out for dinner, I pay. I'm a remittance man, not a gigolo." He was furious, she realized in amazement.

"It was a business arrangement," she stated primly, turning her back on him and hurrying down the stairs. "We agreed this afternoon that I'd buy dinner."

He caught up with her in the parking lot, heaved his crutches disgustedly into the passenger side of the Jeep and hoisted himself lithely into the seat. When she was seated haughtily beside him, about to turn on the ignition, he slid a powerful arm around her shoulders, immobilizing her, causing a shivery thrill to course down her body and an apprehensive warning to sound in her brain. She tried to jerk away, but his other arm passed smoothly just under her breasts, forming a cage, effectively trapping her against the seat. She was an unusually strong woman, but Ben was immeasurably stronger.

His face was inches from her own, the cool grass-green eyes behind their thick lashes boring down into her own.

"You bought me dinner. Now I owe you some loving. Isn't that how this scenario is supposed to go?" he purred, an undertone of danger evident in his low voice.

Without waiting for her answer, he lowered his lips to hers, moving a steadying hand to her jaw when she tried to turn her head.

"Be still, Charlie. For once in your life, stop fighting," he whispered, his wine-tinged breath mingling with her own.

In her throat, her pulse hammered as though it would leap from her body, and as if he'd hypnotized her, she sat immobile for the endless time it took his lips to finally cover hers. Then she could feel the hard strength of his mouth engulfing her, devouring her, and a hard knot of wanting sprang into life, making her breasts ache, her belly throb.

His tongue slipped into her mouth and caressed her inner lips, flickered across her teeth, darted deeper, in and out like the tidal rhythm pulsing through her body. Her hands moved, without her willing them, up his sides, memorizing the lean muscle they found there, tracing a path over smooth, heated male flesh until, beneath her palm, she felt his heart thundering like a tribal drumbeat, answering her own.

Her reaction was deep and urgent. Between one heartbeat and the next, she was kissing him back with a sort of frantic passion. She felt his hands slowly rise to her aching breasts, felt her hardened nipples leap, anticipating his touch. A ribbon of pure longing tied a satin bow in her abdomen, and he caught her upper lip gently between his teeth, nipping delicately. A moan slid from Charlie's throat, instantly echoed back by Ben.

But the throaty, sensual sound he made soon became a muffled curse. The Jeep's steering column, Ben's cumbersome ankle and the gearshift mechanism between them on the floor made closer contact impossible despite Ben's best intentions and Charlie's drugged cooperation. Reluctantly, they drew apart, their ragged breathing loud in the tropical darkness.

"Tomorrow," Ben joked shakily, "I'm trading this damn Jeep in for a car with an old-fashioned front seat."

His arm was still around her shoulders, but the cool, humid night air was restoring Charlie's sanity by slow degrees. She was trembling. What in blazes was she doing? If ever she'd met a man who was absolutely wrong for her, Ben Gilmour was the man. Her brain knew that. What the heck was the matter with her body, acting like this?

She brought the Jeep to life with a roar, reversed out of the lot and spun the wheel hard, making Ben grab for a handhold and shoot her a surprised look, but he was as moodily silent as she during the twenty minutes it took to reach Reveille Reef.

Steering slowly down the bumpy ruts of the driveway, Charlie saw light spilling from the windows of the house into the encompassing blackness of the deserted resort. She braked and turned off the motor.

Far away a car squealed, but here at Reveille Reef Club silence wrapped around them as soon as the sound of the motor faded. Ben reached over and ran a finger softly down her cheek, making her long to turn her face into his palm and give way to the hunger his lightest touch created.

Stubbornly, she jerked away from the tantalizing touch and swung her bare legs over the open side of the Jeep, feeling grass tickle her skin above her sandals.

"About that car with the big front seat—" she said flatly, staring at the lights in the windows of the house. Her voice sounded far too loud. "Don't bother on my account."

She started to walk away before he could reply, but her dramatic exit was ruined. Just then Carol, with Eliza close behind, exploded out of the front door and came rushing toward the Jeep. Eliza's voice was preceding them, high and thin and frightened.

"We were just sitting around talking when somebody threw a huge rock and broke that big window facing the ocean. It had a note tied to it. Pogey ran after them not more than five minutes ago, and he hasn't come back. We were just going to phone the police when you arrived. What should we do, Ben?"

Chapter Four

Two distinct reactions to Eliza's words raced through Charlie.

The first was anger, mixed with a lick of fear, and incredulity at the idea that anyone would do such a thing.

The second was absolute outrage at Eliza for transferring all authority to Ben when she, the head of Cossini Construction, was standing right there, up to her ankles in wet grass and plainly visible. What was the big idea asking Ben what they should do?

Her voice was sharp-edged when she ordered, "Carol, you and Eliza run to that little market and phone the police right now. Which way did this Pogey go? Did you see? I don't suppose he had sense enough to take a club or anything along?"

All she needed was for Ben's illustrious friend to get himself beaten to a pulp. He must have arrived after she and Ben left. The nerd was probably five feet one with delusions of heroism and shoulders the size of a twelve-inch ruler.

Ben's quietly authoritative voice countered, "Hold it. Nobody's going anywhere by herself, Charlie."

There was no phone at the Reef as yet. The women had been using the one at Chung's Market, three blocks away.

"The driveway's pitch-dark, and probably the market's closed by now. If I know Pogey, he'll turn up any minute. I'd rather we stayed together till he gets back."

It was said tactfully, but there was no question Ben expected to have his orders followed. Before Charlie could open her mouth to object, a quietly deep voice sounded out of the thick shadows to their left.

"I lost him along the beach somewhere, Ben. I think there was only one, but he seemed to fade into the night and just disappear. The tide's coming in, so that'll be the end of any footprints."

The owner of the voice stepped closer, and Charlie gulped. Even by the uncertain moonlight, he didn't look as if he'd need a club. Pogey was every bit as tall as Ben and built rather like the football player they called the Refrigerator—a rectangular block of seemingly impenetrable material. Heaven help the guy he got mad at. For an instant, she was ridiculously glad the intruder had escaped.

Pogey had already called the police from a pay phone near the park. They moved in a group toward the main house as he quickly told Ben the exact details of the attack, much as Eliza had described them. Trust a man to want to hear the story from another man, though.

But once they were inside, Charlie felt shaken by the view of shards of glass all over the floor and of the small boulder lying ominously against the dingy wall. What if it had hit someone? For all her show of bravado, she was secretly grateful now for the presence of the two men.

"Charlie, this is James Crawford, better known as Pogey," Ben said as an introduction, and her hand was swallowed by a wide paw. In the harsh light of the naked overhead bulb, she took better stock of Ben's friend, finding him strangely gentle and rather shy. He had blond hair, not as silvery blond as Carol's but sun-streaked, straight and rather long. His skin was tanned a deep bronze all over his amazingly muscular frame, and with his light blue eyes, the effect was devastatingly attractive.

He was not, however, as damnably, wickedly irresistible as Ben. It was too bad, Charlie concluded, because she'd just bet Pogey was lots easier to get along with.

She gave him a brilliant, sparkling smile, demurely saying how nice it was to meet him. Pogey held her hand a second too long, and she was rewarded by the sharp, speculative glance Ben shot her.

The police car had just pulled up in the driveway with a crunching of tires on gravel, and there was a sudden banging on the door.

If Charlie had considered Pogey to be a large, muscular man, she was forced to reassess her opinion when the policeman ducked his head under the doorjamb and entered the room.

"Chief Kimo Nakanani, of the Haleiwa Police." He identified himself simply, standing straight and tall, towering over everyone else, as if he were a legendary Hawaiian king. He was truly magnificent, seemingly larger than life, dark-skinned, with limbs like tree trunks and huge, soulful eyes. He had a dramatic mustache and a short, well-trimmed beard. His lavish black hair curled in a frenzy around his well-shaped head, and his teeth gleamed.

My gosh, Charlie thought, gaping up at him in awe, *if I had a dollar right now for every pound of handsome male flesh gathered in this room, I might be able to pay off all my bills.*

She glanced over at the other two women, and Eliza's bemused expression seemed to exactly mirror Charlie's own thoughts.

But Carol wasn't even glancing in the chief's direction. She had turned her back and was fussing with the coffeepot, adding water and putting it on to perk. There were times when Charlie worried about Carol. After all, it was perfectly natural to look, wasn't it?

Ben and the policeman obviously knew each other. They seemed on friendly terms as Ben introduced everyone. The Hawaiian had a natural dignity, combined with an easygoing manner.

"Call me Kimo," he suggested. "We're relaxed around here. Hawaii does that to you."

He paid close attention as first Eliza, then Pogey, went over the evening's disturbing events. He looked at the crumpled note that had been wrapped around the rock and smiled and shook his head.

"What does it say?" Charlie asked as she gingerly accepted the paper from Kimo. In black lettering, written in bold but uneven script, she read "No Trespassing."

"Our friend has a sense of humor," Kimo remarked. He examined the shattered window, and the three men all spent a long time outside, investigating.

"Well," Charlie demanded impatiently the moment they returned, "do you have any idea who might have done it?"

After Carol silently handed everyone a cup of freshly perked coffee, they carried the cups into the screened living room and took seats on the collection of old, mismatched chairs and couches.

To Charlie's chagrin, Ben waited until she was seated and then plunked down beside her, trapping her in a corner of a small settee only big enough for two people. His expression was absolutely innocent, but his thigh rested disturbingly close along the entire length of her leg. She squirmed, but unless she got up and pointedly moved elsewhere, there was no room for escape. She stayed where she was.

"No gearshift," he muttered so only she could hear, and she gave him a killing glance, which he chose to ignore.

"I could make like Sherlock Holmes and pretend to know what's going on here, but the truth is, I'm baffled," Kimo admitted. "Ben reported all the other acts of vandalism, and we've investigated each incident without any success. There isn't any obvious reason for somebody to do this. And that note doesn't tell us anything." He frowned, obviously annoyed at having to admit his investigation had been fruitless so far. "There's a gang of young toughs around who could be responsible. They're unemployed, fool around fixing up old cars and get in mischief. They used to hang out on this beach a lot. I'm not discounting them, but nobody heard a car tonight, and it's pretty unlikely they'd hike from town along the beach just to break a window. There are no footprints. The tide is coming in fast.''

His wide brow furrowed again in puzzled thought. ''There had to be a motive behind it. But it's sure got me guessing.'' He looked directly across at Carol, sitting apart from the others, her long denim-covered legs tucked up under her.

Charlie realized she hadn't said two words since Kimo arrived. Perhaps Kimo had noticed too, because he directed his next question at her.

''Miss Thompson—it is Miss, isn't it?''

Carol's cheeks turned an intriguing shade of rose. ''It's Mrs.,'' she supplied, her soft voice barely audible. Kimo's expression altered slightly until she added, on her forthright fashion, ''I'm divorced.'' His relieved half nod spoke volumes, and he directed his questions gently to Carol.

''Are you women living alone here at the Reef?''

Carol explained about the company and the renovation job, adding that Ben and Pogey were now living in one of the cabins.

''It's a good thing the men are around,'' Kimo said soberly.

Charlie didn't even grimace at the statement. She very honestly was glad of it herself.

''I'll be back tomorrow morning,'' Kimo added. ''I want to make sure there's nothing we missed in the dark.''

His eyes were centered on Carol when he said good-night, but she didn't look up. She appeared to be intently studying her fingernails.

When the sound of the policeman's car faded away, Pogey stood up and stretched, yawning hugely. Charlie caught the other women staring in awe at the relaxed giant. What did they feed kids in Australia to grow them that big?

''Time for bed for me,'' Pogey announced, innocently unaware of the attention he was attracting.

''Perhaps one of us should sleep in the house tonight,'' Ben suggested, his arm touching Charlie's with disconcerting intimacy. ''I'll go and get my shaving kit,'' he went on boldly.

"No, you won't," Charlie blurted out. How could she get any rest if he was snoring away nearby in pajamas? Nope, he wouldn't wear pajamas. He wasn't the type. "We're not afraid," she said stoutly. "Besides, we're excellent screamers, aren't we?"

Ben's wicked grin flashed wide. "Can I see references?" he asked, and Charlie narrowed her eyes at him.

"We don't need you here. Right, Carol, Eliza?" Charlie appealed to the other two women, and Carol agreed vigorously. Eliza showed considerably less enthusiasm, but silent pressure from the other two finally convinced her.

"We'll be okay, I guess," she finally granted reluctantly, and the men left reluctantly, too.

It took longer than strictly necessary for the women to gather the coffee cups and turn out the lights. Suddenly the darkness on the other side of the windows seemed thick and palpable, and the constant roaring of the surf became a perfect cover for mysterious noises.

Finally, there was no longer any excuse for lingering. Bidding each other falsely hearty good-nights, each of the women went to her second-floor room.

It wasn't anything she'd ever admit, but Charlie was reassured when she peeked out her window and saw the light of the men's cabin shining like a beacon across the grass.

Comforted and secure, she stripped quickly, pulled on her old striped cotton nightshirt and fell in exhaustion onto the lumpy mattress. The day's events marched through her brain.

"No Trespassing."

She tried in vain to imagine who might write such a message and be desperate or vicious enough to toss it through a window. Was the warning sinister—dangerous, perhaps?

Such conjectures kept her wide awake, and she determinedly turned her thoughts instead to the other, equally confusing events of the evening.

She stopped the mental video when she reached the part where Ben kissed her, holding the image as she whirled down into sleep.

THE DAWN WAS STILL a gray uncertainty when she awoke. The faded yellow chintz curtain on the window moved leisurely in the coolness of the early-morning breeze.

Charlie had been deeply asleep, curled up on her side in a relaxed kittenlike ball. She flopped groggily over onto her back, brushing away the tousled hair that tickled her face while she listened.

She was subconsciously waiting for the sound that had filtered through her rest, seducing her into dreamy wakefulness.

As she waited, floating back toward sleep, the sound of a bugle drifted again into her room, the final notes of a vaguely familiar tune, clear and poignant. It faded slowly, and she lay unmoving for several moments, bemused by the clear and haunting melody. Now the only sound outside the window was that of the exotic birds she'd heard the morning before.

She sat up, straining to hear more.

Reveille, that was the tune. What had her brother-in-law called it? "Wakey-wakey." Well, it certainly had worked this morning. But where was it coming from? She tumbled out of bed, splashed her face with cold water in the bathroom down the hall and pulled on faded jogging shorts and a jersey. Running a cursory brush through her mop of curls, she crept past the silent rooms where the other two slept, retrieving her battered running shoes by the back door.

Grayness was giving way to daylight on the beach, and the entire stretch of sand and sea was empty in both directions. No bugler there. She shrugged, looking once again in both directions. Nothing. Should she go for a jog along that isolated beach? Thoughts of last night made her hesitate, and finally, feeling like a coward, she ran back to an open, grassy area beside the main house and began her morning exercise routine.

Deep knee bends, stretches, sit-ups. Crunches, leg raises, push-ups.

BEN, EXASPERATED after a restless night spent trying to get used to rolling over in an unfamiliar bed with an immobilizing lump for a leg, finally gave up at first light of morning and headed grumpily for the shower in the lean-to outside. The doctor had advised using a plastic bag and a large elastic band as double insurance, despite the fiberglass, and Ben wrestled his foot and leg inside the black bag, swore copiously as he scrubbed under the lukewarm spray that trickled out of the ancient equipment, then toweled and pulled on a pair of tattered cutoffs.

He saw Charlie as soon as he came out the door. She was facing away from him, clad in shorts that bared a delicious amount of firm, rounded buttocks and a brief top that ended intriguingly just under her breasts. Delightfully braless breasts, he decided, leaning on his crutches with his eyes feasting on her every movement. The morning had begun to improve.

There was plenty of movement to see. She bent forward from the hips. Those shorts should be banned as lethal weapons, dangerous to a man's health. Her long, slender legs curved into firm, shapely thighs. Her hips were narrow, her waist ridiculously slim.

Seductively uptilted breasts moved freely under their sparse blue covering, and her arms were willowy as she raised and lowered them, agilely bouncing up and down and scissoring her legs alternately apart and together in a rhythm that made Ben swallow hard.

Her hair, carelessly tied back, bounced on her long neck in a ponytail, and Ben remembered vividly how her warm female body had felt in his arms last night, how she'd kissed him back with a response that had nearly driven him out of control, and would have, had they not been in that damn Jeep.

There was a wildness in her, a hint of passion, primitive and violent, if only he could tap it. He had an uneasy conviction that Charlie wouldn't make it simple for him.

It had been years since a woman had presented him with any sort of a challenge. Most women he'd met had been almost embarrassingly eager to satisfy his admittedly virile appetites. He was adroit at making the pleasure mutual. His relationships had been casual, short-lived and enjoyable. Clearly defined and easily ended.

Charlie wasn't one of those women. He couldn't exactly say why he knew it, or how, and watching her now, he didn't dwell on reasons. Instead, he fantasized how he'd swoop her into his arms, fling her prone on the first flat surface he could find and remove that scanty outfit.

Her graceful body would be bare beneath him. He'd kiss her until her lips were puffed and pouty with wanting more, until those blue eyes took on a smoky haze. He'd kiss her everywhere, until her hips surged uncontrollably beneath him and that husky, powerful voice entreated him softly—

"Ben Gilmour, what do you think you're doing, standing there and staring at me? Surely I have a right to a certain amount of privacy, for heaven's sake—"

Startled, he nearly dropped his crutches. She was stomping toward him, hands on her hips, fire in her eyes. And because of his stupid fantasy, he was in no shape for close inspection. He gritted his teeth, wondering if he should head quickly back into the bug-infested shower room and turn the water control deliberately to cold.

"Calm yourself," he managed to say, shifting into an awkward slouch on the crutches. "Don't be so conceited, woman. I was admiring the sunrise."

Sure enough, out beyond the palms and reef, the ocean was obligingly turning pale rose, and the gray sky was streaked with the promise of a crimson glory.

She shot him a suspicious glance and turned uncertainly to look over her shoulder at where he was pointing. When she turned back, Ben was quickly heading for the screened-in kitchen lean-to tacked on to his cabin.

"How about I make us some breakfast and we watch the sunrise together?" he suggested. "That is, if you can loan me some eggs and coffee. We haven't had a chance to shop yet," he added apologetically, riffling through the rough shelving that masqueraded as cupboards.

"Oh, and bread? We don't have any bread, either."

Charlie sighed, her Italian sense of hospitality warring with yesterday's intentions to let the men starve out here if necessary.

"All I ever eat for breakfast is bran flakes. If you want some of that, I'll go get it. And coffee."

"Bran flakes?" His disappointment was evident.

"Take it or leave it," she bristled.

"That's fine; that's great," he hastened to say. "Unless you'd drive us out for breakfast?" he tacked on hopefully. "Haleiwa has one place that opens early. The surfers eat there," he suggested enthusiastically.

She gave him a scathing look. "Whether you know it or not, today happens to be a working day. Ordinary people don't go out for breakfast on a workday. They can't afford either the time or the money."

"Bran flakes it is. I don't suppose you've got any cream and raw sugar?" he added mournfully, lifting his thick brows at her.

Rolling her eyes heavenward, she hurried off toward the main house, irritated because she'd missed the time slotted for her morning jog by wasting time with Ben and unwilling to admit that the sight of him in those faded denim cutoffs, with his bare chest and muscular limbs, had stirred errant pangs in her stomach that had little to do with bran flakes.

"Did you hear the bugle earlier this morning?" she remembered to ask, watching in fascination as he used a mixing bowl for his cereal and added most of a quart of milk to it along with sliced bananas.

He nodded, attacking the huge mixture with honest hunger.

"I've heard it before here at the Reef. There's a military base some miles away, and when the air currents are right, the sound carries over the mountains."

"But he sounded as if he were right here, on the beach," Charlie protested, loath to give up her romantic image of a bugler in the dawn.

"What's the difference where the music comes from? It's a nice addition to the morning. It's a recording, anyway," Ben commented idly, refilling his bowl and adding more milk. "This stuff doesn't really stick with you, does it?" he said, spooning up the other half of her week's supply of bran flakes.

By eight-thirty, Cossini Construction was on the job, hard at work demolishing all but the bare skeleton of the first of the cabins. Charlie had decided to leave the main lodge till last, thus keeping her crew's living quarters intact as long as possible.

By nine forty-five, Charlie was ready to drive Ben to some busy intersection and leave him there in the traffic without his crutches. He was driving her berserk.

Eating her whole box of bran flakes and drinking both quarts of milk at breakfast hadn't particularly bothered her. She had a brother-in-law, her sister Gisella's husband, Tony, who was like that. Gisella routinely doubled recipes that were supposed to feed six people. Usually, it made barely enough for her and Tony and their two little boys.

It wasn't his appetite. It was his interest.

As soon as she started work, Ben began following her around, asking questions, offering advice about things he obviously didn't have a clue about, whistling, singing, joking with her carpenters.

He was getting in the way and wasting their time, Charlie thought in disgust, watching from the corner of her eye as he made Eliza giggle with some nonsense or other, thereby slowing to half the time whatever she was supposed to be doing. Ripping out those blooming rafters—that's what Eliza should be doing. Not wrinkling her cute little nose and flirting outrageously that way.

"Ben," Charlie called with only a trace of acidity in her voice, "could you come over by this pile of old lumber and pull nails for me?"

Carol glanced at her curiously. Charlie had a thing about not using old nails, ever. Ben didn't know that, though. He borrowed her hammer and clumsily started yanking them out.

For half an hour everyone worked undisturbed.

She might have known it wouldn't last long.

"Don't you think it's time for a coffee break? You can get dehydrated fast, working so hard in this heat."

Seven minutes later, her quelling glare stopped working on him.

"Charlie, I know you showed me the specs on this, but could you explain again exactly what it is you've got planned for this cabin?"

Twenty minutes of impatiently explaining what she could have sworn he already knew and she was back at lifting rotten floorboards.

For barely four minutes, however.

"Charlie, I understand the reasons for this demolition, but don't you think—"

Finally exasperated beyond belief, she demanded, "Where's Pogey? Shouldn't you be doing something with him? We've got to get on with this work, and I hate to say this—" she didn't at all; it gave her great satisfaction "—but you, Ben Gilmour, are wasting our time. I know you're paying for it," she added sweetly, "but I do have an hourly estimate to meet."

He ignored most of that.

"Pogey? He's down at Sunset Beach. The surf's up." He looked longingly out at the Pacific. "He left before daybreak. We always go early; that's when the waves are at their best." He held out both palms. "But I give you my word that from now on I'll be invisible. Scout's honor."

She narrowed her eyes at his too-earnest expression.

Ten minutes later, he suggested, "Let's all drive into town for lunch. I didn't have much breakfast, and if you'll drive, Charlie, I'll buy."

It was hopeless. At this rate, she'd murder him within a week, or something worse. She untied her carpenter's apron in defeat and flung it into the cabin. Usually, her materials were handled with the care most women gave to expensive jewelry.

"All right, Ben, you win. But as soon as we get back, you take a nap."

His eyes twinkled roguishly. "About that nap. Is there any chance—"

"Don't push your luck," she warned, struggling to stay mad. It was difficult with that wicked grin aimed her way.

Besides, she decided maliciously, today he was buying. She wasn't about to argue over the bill. If he wanted to waste the Gilmour millions by buying starving carpenters lunch, well, he could write it off as a charity donation.

"Get in the Jeep, everyone."

She drove them all into town, and it was fortunate Kimo Nakanani wasn't running radar that morning, for Charlie cut at least three minutes from the existing land-speed record from the Reef to Haleiwa.

It was disappointing that Ben was totally unperturbed and refused to even hang on around corners. He slumped over onto her side instead.

Coincidentally, Kimo did arrive shortly after they'd parked. Ben had directed Charlie into a small shopping center and suggested they eat in a cheery café named Rosie's Cantina.

The patrol car drove in right behind them, and Kimo unfolded himself from behind the wheel.

"Why don't you join us for lunch?" Ben invited. Charlie had a hunch Kimo had planned exactly that all along.

Rosie's was half a restaurant. It served tacos and huge pitchers of beer and shared its floor space with Papa's Pizza, which, predictably, served pizzas, with huge pitchers of beer. Owned and operated separately, the two establishments, Ben said, existed in perfect harmony, dividing up their customers' palates with great good nature.

Charlie found herself seated cozily close to Ben. Kimo, imposingly official in his uniform, was sharing a narrow bench with Carol. Eliza, obviously unattached, was getting star billing from a gorgeous blond waiter. This was turning into a regular *Mix and Match the Couples* game show, Charlie decided.

Without consulting anyone, Ben ordered what sounded like half the menu, plus several pitchers of draft beer.

"You must be thirsty," Charlie said primly. "We can't drink, of course. We have to work this afternoon."

Carol and Eliza immediately feigned deafness and drank down their first amber glassfuls nonstop. Charlie gave up and drank her own, ignoring Ben's amused expression. It was so darned hot out in that sun.

After the second glass, Carol stopped trying to balance on the four inches of bench to avoid touching Kimo, and she even smiled once at him.

Charlie had no choice. Her bench ended in wall, and Ben casually made certain his entire calf, thigh, hip, arm and shoulder were touching her.

Why should touching Ben make her so aware of plain old ordinary skin? She gave up trying to figure it out and experimented with eating left-handed. That way, the touching wasn't interrupted.

Eliza had majored in conversation as well as carpentry.

"Did you grow up in Hawaii, Kimo?"

"Sure did," the amiable giant confirmed. "I'm native Hawaiian. When I was little, my great-grandfather was still alive, and he used to tell me stories about his ancestors sailing here in canoes from Polynesia."

Carol, usually quiet, unexpectedly spoke up. Her soft voice was filled with honest enthusiasm, and everyone paid attention.

"I read that the Polynesians who sailed here and settled in the Hawaiian Islands crossed about five thousand ocean miles in those canoes. They did it seven centuries before Captain Cook, using only the stars for navigation."

Charlie felt a proprietary pride in Carol for knowing something like that, and she beamed a smile at her friend.

Kimo had turned toward Carol to listen, and his features, made rather fierce by the dark beard and mustache, changed as he watched the blond woman, becoming almost tender.

Charlie noted how striking Kimo's dark skin was beside Carol's Nordic fairness. Kimo was immense, dwarfing the bench they sat on, creating the impression that Carol was much smaller than she really was.

"Not many people who come to the islands bother to read our history," Kimo said softly. "I've got some books you might enjoy, Carol."

"How about you, Charlie?" Ben's voice was a murmur close to her ear. "What sort of books do you read?"

Charlie opened her mouth to tell her she had no time to read, but before she could, Eliza answered for her.

"You should just see what she reads," the pretty redhead blithely revealed. "Technical books on architecture and things about how they built the Leaning Tower of Pisa." She rolled her eyes in horror. "Weird."

Charlie had no idea why this bit of trivia about her reading habits should make her feel uncomfortable. Ben didn't comment; he just gave her a long, serious look.

When lunch was over, it was much later than Charlie expected it to be, and she herded her carpenters hastily into the Jeep.

"Why not ride along with me this afternoon?" Kimo suggested to Ben. "I have to check on some campers."

"I really ought to stay at the Reef. These women need my supervision," Ben said regretfully, and when Charlie seemed ready to explode with exasperation, he laughed and accepted Kimo's invitation.

"First," Kimo declared firmly, "we'll drive to the Reef and make sure Pogey's there."

Obviously, Kimo, too, had now assumed guard duty for the Cossini Construction crew. Much as she appreciated the high-powered police protection, Charlie suspected Kimo just might have an ulterior motive. Carol's rich color when he was around wasn't entirely due to the Hawaiian sunshine.

Chapter Five

"Thanks, Charlie, but I couldn't hold one more bite. We dropped in on Kimo's sister Lona and her husband, Jim, and they insisted we eat with them."

Ben had arrived back at the Reef late from his excursion with Kimo, and he quickly decided it was a good thing he'd eaten with Kimo's relatives. The remnants of dinner that Charlie was offering on a chipped plate looked, well, revolting. Gray and sort of dejected.

Carol gave him an amused conspiratorial look. Charlie shrugged indifferently and dumped the mess into the bag of garbage propped against the table leg. A hasty glance into the bag suggested to Ben that more than just his plateful had recently landed there. He deposited the bags of groceries he'd brought on the battleship-gray linoleum that covered the counter.

"These are breakfast supplies, in return for what I ate up this morning." He unloaded cereal boxes, bread, milk cartons and pounds of bacon, and Carol efficiently stowed it all away. The other bag was much more interesting.

"Kimo's sister insisted on giving us stuff," he explained, pulling out orange-and-black-speckled mangoes, a gigantic bunch of thumb-size ripe bananas and several huge, emerald-green avocados. "I took another bag like this one over to our cabin. Pogey and I sure can't eat this much before it goes bad."

Carol took one hungry look at the fruit, and within minutes she'd put together a fruit salad large enough to serve everyone.

"Pogey, take the Jeep and run down to Chung's Market and get some ice cream to go with this," Ben suggested.

No doubt about it, Gisella's husband, Tony would be right at home with these two surfers, Charlie decided when Pogey returned with six pints of ice cream for five people. But maybe he'd known Kimo was going to drive in just then. At least that made it six for six.

After one spoonful of the concoction, everyone agreed it was ambrosia. It was the women's first taste of the tangy mango, and they agreed that the dwarfed, unimpressive-looking Hawaiian bananas were sweeter and more flavorful than any of their larger relatives on the mainland.

"The mangoes are from an old tree beside Lona's house," Kimo explained. "She'll keep us supplied for the whole season." Kimo wasn't in uniform tonight. He wore comfortable old khaki shorts and a brightly patterned cotton shirt, with thong sandals on his gigantic feet. When the group moved out to the screened porch to sit, he chose a spot close to Carol. But he directed his questions to Eliza.

"Where are you all from?" he queried. "At lunch we explored my roots. Now it's time for you to tell me yours. How'd you get to be carpenters, anyhow?"

"Ever hear of a city called Bellingham, in northern Washington State?" Eliza supplied chattily. "It's near the U.S.-Canadian border. Well, we all grew up there, but at different times. First Carol; she's thirty-six. Aren't you Carol? Then Charlie, she's twenty-six. And then me; I'm twenty-three."

Carol and Charlie exchanged a look of exasperation and rolled their eyes.

"Liza, watch it," Charlie warned. Given an opportunity, Eliza would next recite their weight and their measurements, recent love affairs and whether or not any of them slept in the nude. But Eliza was not to be easily quelled once she had the floor. She ignored Charlie, blithely going on with her recital.

"We met because we were the only women carpenters around. Charlie went to trade school before Carol and I enrolled—she was a pioneer, the first woman to attend."

"Charlie, you don't look old enough to be a pioneer," Kimo said.

"Started at sixteen, finished at twenty." Charlie was brusque, very aware of Ben's intense interest in Eliza's comments.

"Didn't you mention wanting to hire a laborer to work with you?" Ben commented now, remembering a previous conversation. "I've found an applicant for the job." Charlie looked over at him suspiciously, and he shook his head, mockingly rueful. "Sorry, no, not yours truly. But Pogey thinks he'd like to give it a try."

The group turned to Pogey curiously, and he flushed. "I've got to find a job, so when Ben mentioned you might need a laborer—" He flexed his muscles in a comic show of strength. "Think I'd do?" he asked Charlie.

"Why do you need a job?" she asked bluntly.

To her considerable surprise, he replied. "Money. What else?"

"But I thought..." she stammered. "Aren't you, don't you, I mean, Ben—"

"You figured Pogey was a remittance man, too?" Ben was obviously enjoying her discomfiture. "Pogey's working his way around the world."

Charlie swiftly reshuffled her opinion of the burly Australian.

"It's hard work," she warned him.

"That's great," Pogey said. "Keep me in shape for surfing."

"Charlie's a slave driver; don't say we didn't warn you," Eliza put in with a dimpled grin, and everyone laughed.

"You're hired," Charlie confirmed. "We start at eight thirty; don't be late."

That first week established a pattern at the Reef.

When the sun shone, Pogey disappeared before dawn to surf, appearing punctually on the dot of eight-thirty to do the heavy work of three men before each day ended. Hiring Pogey was the best bargain she'd ever had, Charlie told herself gleefully. The renovations on the first cabin were already shaping up beautifully.

Ben wasn't quite as convinced that things were going well.

Every morning he made a point of breakfasting with Charlie. Bran flakes. He was considering buying a case of the damn stuff.

He started swimming in the protected waters of Waialua Bay, mostly so he could watch Charlie each morning jog far down the beach and back again. He loved watching her move, the long coltish legs gracefully covering the distance, her head thrown back and her arms pumping.

Swimming was anything but easy with the cast. It overbalanced him, and he had to learn to counter the effect. But with no one else in sight, there was a serene quality about the mornings, just he swimming and Charlie running and the sound of the reef out beyond the bay, taming the monstrous breakers before it allowed them into the cove.

But that was as far as it went between him and Charlie.

"Care to come for a burger in town?" he'd ask.

"Sorry, I don't go out during the week."

"Care to come for a drive down the coast?"

"Sorry, we've got to finish the forms for the patio."

Sorry, Ben, I have no time for you. It was a great blow to his ego.

THERE WERE NO repeat incidents of mischief at the Reef, but maybe that was because one of the men—Ben, Pogey or Kimo—was always present. She'd never admit it, but Charlie found having them around reassuring, as long as they didn't interfere with her work. Ben certainly did. But there didn't seem to be a thing she could do about it.

The demolition of the outbuildings went ahead strictly on Charlie's rigid schedule despite Ben's "supervision."

The first short workweek passed like a speedboat, she was so busy. By Tuesday of the next week, however, she realized that there were two priorities Cossini Construction could no longer live without. One was a telephone at the Reef. Ordering lumber, talking with suppliers, trying to locate materials, couldn't be done efficiently by running to Chung's all the time, despite the chubby proprietor's good nature.

The second priority was a vehicle of some kind. She had to have her own transportation despite Ben's insistence that she use his Jeep whenever she wanted it and Pogey's casual urging that they use his Land Rover whenever they liked.

Reluctantly, Charlie borrowed the Jeep for what she hoped was the last time and drove to Haleiwa that Tuesday afternoon.

On Thursday a happy-go-lucky young Hawaiian workman came to install the telephone. His cheerful whistling sounded through the open doors and windows of the main house.

After he'd been working for over an hour, Charlie headed inside to get a pitcher of ice water for her crew. She hurried into the kitchen in time to see the man begin to undo his belt buckle and loosen his pants.

Telephone wires were hanging, and tools were carelessly strewn all over the kitchen. The telephone sat on the floor, still unattached.

"What, exactly, do you figure you're doing?" she demanded, ready to beat a hasty retreat if the striptease continued.

He gave her an offhand glance. "Going for a swim, of course."

"A swim? Now? Aren't you working?"

The wiry young man—he looked barely out of his teens—continued peeling down to skimpy purple swim trunks, which he seemed to wear instead of underwear. At least it was a swimsuit. Not much of one, though.

Charlie gulped and kept her eyes firmly above his neck. Her temper began to rise at his casual attitude. She was counting on having phone service today, and it was already late afternoon.

"This is a construction site. I'm the foreman, and we need that phone right away." She put every ounce of authority into her tone, but to no avail.

"Hey, the sun's out, the water's cool, it's ninety degrees out there," he explained as if she were a bit slow. "Besides, my friends and I have used this beach for years. It's practically public property."

Then he took a closer look at her sweaty face, the T-shirt stuck to her body. His eyes lingered slightly longer than necessary on her midsection, and his tone became wheedling.

"This is Hawaii; you oughta try converting to Hawaiian time, lady," he suggested. "Whatever you have to do today will keep fine till tomorrow. It's a lot more fun that way. Why not come along for a swim?"

Charlie was appalled, and about to say so, when Ben stumped in just in time to catch the appreciative gleam in the man's eye and his purple bikini trunks.

Charlie saw Ben's green eyes flash dangerously, the muscles tense in his biceps, and she explained in a rush what was going on. Ben actually looked as if he were about to take a swing at the guy.

After her hasty recital, Ben became coldly authoritative. "I represent Gilmour Developments, and I'm expecting a call from my head office in exactly forty-five minutes," he said in a lethal tone. "So I'd suggest you put your pants back on, friend, and have this telephone service working by then. Oh, and this beach area is now private property. If you choose to swim here, I suggest you ask permission first."

Charlie watched him, mesmerized. He exuded power, both physical and somehow monetary, and the young telephone man recognized it and reacted.

It wasn't what Ben said. It was how he said it. It certainly wasn't his clothing. Nevertheless, the result was astonishing. In cutoffs and a cotton shirt, wearing a running shoe on one foot and a cast on the other, Ben suddenly became Mr. Gilmour. Sir.

The phone was working within thirty minutes, and the installer had prudently decided to swim elsewhere. Ben watched him drive away and coldly noted the number on the truck. Then he hurriedly swung himself over to the new phone and snatched up the receiver.

He'd tell Kimo about the encounter, just on the off chance the guy might have had something to do with the problems at Reveille Reef. He seemed to think he damn near owned the beach, Ben mused, dialing the police station.

Was the man lazy and harmless? Or was there a more sinister meaning behind his words and actions? Either way, he was lucky Ben hadn't used his crutch as a battering ram on his head, leering at Charlie that way and standing there half dressed.

"Kimo? Ben here. Listen—" He told Kimo the facts, and when he hung up, he stood for a moment, balanced on his crutches. Kimo had promised to investigate the guy, but Ben could tell that Kimo thought his concern was unwarranted.

"If this kid came across like you said, sort of laid back and not ambitious but not really a criminal type, he's probably just your ordinary workman. His attitude is fairly typical here on the islands; you know that," Kimo had gently reminded him.

It was, too. Ben himself ran on Hawaii time. So why had he gotten bent out of shape over it all?

He rubbed a hand over his face in chagrin. It was hard to admit, but he'd been jealous. He'd been instantly, blackly jealous of that guy in his swim trunks, with Charlie standing there in a wet T-shirt, and the open admiration on the man's face.

Ben shook his head in disbelief, shoving the screen door open with the tip of his crutch and heading over to his cabin, half ashamed of himself. As far as he could remember, he'd never been jealous like this before. He finally concluded that the problem was simply libido.

He wasn't getting the usual amount of exercise with this lousy cast on. That bit of a swim in the mornings was nothing, and his sex drive was skyrocketing.

Besides, he'd developed a fixation over that troublesome woman. With all the lovely, willing, half-naked women on every beach in Hawaii, he had to want a carpenter with calluses on every finger and a time clock built into her brain, which was starting to affect even him.

He swung into the doorway of the cluttered cabin, threw the crutches down with a crash and slumped onto his bed. Well, a good, hot affair would soon cure him. He'd learned that close association with a woman shortly led to boredom. The excitement he felt around Charlie was the challenge of pursuit and the hope of the triumph of eventual capture. After that, it would all go downhill.

He half closed his eyes in speculation. He needed Charlie in his bed; the sooner the better. Now how was he going to go about seducing her? The boss of Cossini Construction worked hard from daylight till nearly dark every day, and he'd bet his best surfboard she didn't have energy left for lovemaking at night. He'd asked her out each evening, for dinner, for a ride, for anything she could want, but she simply shook her head wearily each time.

"Can't," she kept repeating. "I have to figure out the order on the shingles." Or do the time sheets. Or—Ben shuddered—make dinner. "Haven't got time during the week," she insisted, and after watching her closely for these few days, he reluctantly had to agree with her.

The first weekend had been filled with chores, such as grocery shopping, laundry, cleaning house—all the mundane necessities of everyday life. Even he and Pogey had things that had to be done, and the rather primitive conditions made it all the more time-consuming.

So when was he going to be able to seduce her? A guy had to put some time into it, lead up to it gradually, at least get her alone once in a while. It was a challenge.

He hadn't quite figured out a game plan by the time Pogey finished work for the day.

The blond Australian ducked his head to clear the door-jamb as he stepped into the cabin.

"How's the ankle?"

Ben was getting heartily sick of that question.

"How's the surfing?" he countered, and for twenty minutes Pogey filled him in on winds, boards, a new kind of wax, a group that had just arrived from the Eastern Seaboard and, inevitably, injuries. Surfers took for granted cuts, bruises, scrapes and the occasional more serious accident. Ben knew without asking what his surfing companions would think of breaking an ankle by falling off a roof. It was humiliating, not even getting injured in the line of duty.

"That foxy Debbie Lou you took out a couple times was on the beach looking for you, the guys told me this morning," Pogey announced. "Man," he said admiringly, "has she got a body."

Vaguely, Ben remembered the general topography of Debbie Lou's attributes. He waited hopefully, but absolutely nothing stirred at the memory, and in disgust he let the foggy visual image drift away. Charlie's was the image he could clearly visualize.

Pogey's voice continued. "Hey, want me to tell her where you're holed up? She'd probably be happy to keep you company." He glanced around the musty cabin. "Better go to her place, though. This joint's hardly fit to live in, never mind using it to romance a lady like Debbie Lou." He thought his remark over and hastily added, "Don't get me wrong, mate. I couldn't care less where we bunk. You and I've lived in worse places than this." He grabbed a towel and headed for the shower.

It was true. Ben and Pogey had shared some questionable quarters, all right, generally some bunkhouse or other with transients like themselves.

But they'd also stayed in several unpretentiously luxurious places, depending on Pogey's bank balance and whether or not he was able to get a good-paying job wherever they were.

Like Ben, Pogey had little real regard for money. Unlike Ben, he worked for whatever he had, although that difference in their life-styles had not yet come between them. Life was an adventure. Money was incidental. They lived in an easygoing ambience, and if Pogey felt he couldn't afford luxury, they simply lived somewhere reasonable.

Here in Hawaii, Ben had to admit he preferred the Gilmour beach house to this place. It had little to do with luxury, however, and everything to do with the simple fact that the beach house had a cleaning woman who appeared every second day, unobtrusively keeping the men in order.

Once things were tidy, they managed quite well to keep them that way. The problem was that Pogey and Ben had no idea where to start on their own.

Here they'd put their clothing into the drawers of the rickety wardrobe, hung the rest in the closets, set up the stereo and filed everything else in one corner under miscellaneous. Ben's plants flourished outside on the narrow porch, but inside sand gritted underfoot, cobwebs hung in corners, and it seemed there was always a stack of laundry to do.

Ben slowly turned his head, assessing their dismal surroundings. "This is no palace, that's for sure," he muttered to himself, "but the main house isn't all that much better. Those women work so damned hard all day, they hardly even cook for themselves at night. Carol's the only one who had a clue about food preparation. Charlie's a disaster as a cook. Wouldn't you think an Italian female would at least know how to make spaghetti? What the whole lot of us need is—" Ben slowed and stopped. "A housemother," he added thoughtfully. "Pogey, drive us into Haleiwa and I'll treat you to a steak. I just had one hell of a good idea."

The next morning was eventful. The crew had barely begun working when a truck lumbered into the driveway. Charlie took one look at it and gave an excited squeal.

"That's it; that's our truck. I bought it for the company." She untied her leather apron and raced toward the incredible vehicle chugging into the yard like a time-warped mastodon.

"Hi! Hey, park her over here," Charlie hollered at the grinning man behind the wheel, and he wrestled with the steering wheel until he finally had his recalcitrant steed parked where Charlie indicated. He opened a rusted door and stepped down, and the three women mobbed the truck.

The delivery driver thrust a handful of papers at Charlie and jogged back to the road where an old Volkswagen was beeping its horn, waiting for him.

"What kind is it, and how big?" Eliza demanded. She climbed up into the cab to examine the torn brown leather seats and poke at the switches on the dashboard. "No radio, but maybe we could get one installed," she said hopefully.

Carol was a bit more hesitant. She walked around the outside, scanning the peeling khaki paint, the places where rust had chewed holes into the metal, and noting the missing window on the driver's side.

"She needs some TLC," Carol decided.

Pogey had been spraying the new concrete deck they'd poured that morning, keeping it moist so it would harden properly. He turned off the hose and strolled over.

"How do you like Cossini's new truck?"

Eliza grinned engagingly at him from the high cab. For the first time since they'd met him, the women saw Pogey actually become agitated.

"You didn't buy this, mates. Tell me you didn't buy this," he begged, striding around the truck and shaking his head. "This is an antique from the Second World War. We had some of these on sheep farms in Australia, but the last of them hit the junk heaps ten years back." He stood beside Charlie. "They paid you to get this off some lot, right?" he asked hopefully. "They gave it to you right?"

Charlie glared at him. "This truck is indestructible. It's a three-quarter-ton-four-wheel-drive Fargo. I looked it over, and the motor's in good shape. The body's a little rusted, but the guy at the garage in Haleiwa said every vehicle here on the islands rusts after a couple years, anyway, from all the salt in the air." She tilted her head up and narrowed her eyes at Pogey, daring him to malign her choice.

"I like it," she said, drawing each word out and leaving no room for argument. "I bought it for the company, and I like it."

Pogey groaned. He made one last attempt at reason. "See there?" He pointed at a line of rust along the window above the cab. "First good blow we have, that roof will part company with the rest of this baby. You'll be going down the highway, and bingo, the whole hood will be gone. Instant convertible. It's rusted through, and I tell you, it'll blow away."

Charlie had pondered a bit about that very problem. "We're going to tie it on," she said offhandedly. "With rope, through the missing window. Then it can't go anywhere."

Pogey silently looked down at her for several minutes.

"I give up," he said hopelessly. "God knows I tried." He retreated to the cabin and his cement.

"Start her up, Charlie. Can we go for a ride?" Eliza was bouncing on the seat, testing for springs.

Charlie was sorely tempted. But there were only so many working hours in a day.

"When we quit, later this afternoon," she declared, turning reluctantly back to the job. The first cabin was now gutted, ready for rebuilding, with strong new cement foundations to replace the rotting timbers.

Eliza and Charlie were stripping out the old iron plumbing and worn electrical wires, preparing for the local electrician and plumber to replace the services before the walls went up. Carol was working on the openings for wide doors to the new deck, putting in supports for the sliding doors and also the floor-to-ceiling windows that would stretch along one wall.

Charlie had ordered lumber and plywood that should come this afternoon. Maybe it was here now. She could hear a car turning into the drive.

It wasn't the plywood delivery. It was Kimo. Earlier that morning he'd arrived in a great hurry, picked up Ben and driven away.

Now he steered carefully around the hulk of the truck. Charlie could see Ben in the back seat and a passenger in the front. The car drew to a halt near the women, and they watched curiously as Kimo stepped out and courteously held the car door open. A Rubenesque woman wriggled her way across the front seat and got out, and Ben, hampered by his cast, bumped his way out of the back, unfolding his long length and shooting a devilish grin at Charlie.

How did he always know when she was watching him? By the self-satisfied look on his face, he was up to something, all right. Charlie ignored him and hammered at a nail much harder than necessary.

"Everybody, come over here," he called. "I want to introduce you to someone."

"Fine, boss," Charlie shot back sarcastically. She saluted smartly. "We'll be right there." She made a show of taking her apron off again. "Our master's voice," she muttered to Carol as the three women walked toward the group standing by the car. "I'm now charging him overtime for every single interruption."

But she couldn't help just glancing once at his wonderfully mischievous green eyes and those curiously tufted expressive eyebrows. It always seemed as if he were having so much fun. She had to struggle not to smile back at him. He was obviously enjoying himself, whatever he was up to, she concluded.

Then her attention was fully drawn to the woman whom Ben was introducing.

"Carol, Eliza, Charlie, this is Auntie Lani."

She nodded to them regally, like a queen acknowledging her subjects. She wasn't tall, maybe five feet one or two, Charlie assessed. But she had a certain presence. She was round. Round body, great round breasts, round, dimpled face with snapping, black Oriental eyes. Her hair was cropped short, with a bit of fullness on top, and she wore large diamond studs in her pierced ears. Her body was covered from shoulder to toes in a flowing magenta muumuu, with thongs on her feet.

"How do you do; pleased to meet you," everyone murmured.

Charlie extended her hand in greeting. "Happy to meet you, Mrs., ah—"

"Just Lani, Auntie Lani. Half the island calls me that; you might as well, too," her lilting low voice commanded as she grasped Charlie's hand in a powerful grip. She had a wonderful voice, Charlie noticed, rich and full and deep.

Auntie Lani's eyes met Charlie's with a direct gaze. The woman might have been anywhere from fifty-five to seventy years old. She could be any number of racial mixtures. Age and nationality aside, there was that indefinable something in her manner that commanded respect.

Her eyes measured Charlie, making her wonder uneasily if her face was clean and if she'd flossed her teeth that morning. It was a familiar maternal look.

Charlie decided Lani probably had raised at least a dozen kids. Charlie's great-aunt Rosa had had a dozen kids, and one look from Rosa was enough to quell a tornado. Auntie Lani had the "look," all right.

Charlie was about to tell Lani she reminded her of her great-aunt when Ben dropped his bombshell.

"Auntie Lani has agreed to live here and keep Pogey and me in order."

However, Ben had the strangest feeling that it was Lani who'd hired him. Kimo had introduced them, and certainly she'd done all the interviewing, questioning him closely about the people who lived at the Reef and what they were like. He'd been scrupulously honest about the possible dangers, too, telling Lani all about the recent vandalism.

"I've heard about it" was all she said. "News travels fast on the island. I think it's a lot of fuss over nothing."

He'd offered her a generous salary, and she'd eyed him shrewdly.

"Can you afford that much?" she inquired. "If so, I'm happy to take it."

She gave him the impression that money wasn't the issue here, at all.

Charlie was giving him an inscrutable look.

"Lani has her own house trailer, and a crew is coming today to fix up a sewer and an electrical hookup. As long as that's okay with you, of course. Charlie?" he asked respectfully.

This time he'd caught her completely off guard. He'd gone out and hired someone to make his life comfortable. She kept forgetting he was rich, that he didn't have to struggle with everyday problems the way the rest of the world did.

She kept forgetting that she, too, was working for him, that she was his employee, just as Auntie Lani was. Although he didn't have to ask anyone's permission for what he chose to do, he was being so polite that she felt like kicking him.

Even if it wasn't all right, what could she say? The resort, after all, belonged to his family—the rich, pampered Gilmours.

She liked Lani fine, but she was tempted to ask him nastily when his butler and valet were arriving. She wanted to say that if he kept adding more people to the staff, they'd have to apply for zoning laws.

Lani was to be a housemother. She'd cook and wash and clean and make sure his pants fit over his cast. Charlie was suddenly uncomfortably reminded of what she'd originally told Carol and Eliza about the men staying here.

"They clean, cook and completely take care of themselves." That particular joke had certainly backfired on her. She had a sudden mental picture of the stacks of laundry languishing in the main house, the need to scrub out the cupboard where she'd spilled the sugar, the milk dripping in the refrigerator, the sticky places on the linoleum.

Whose turn was it to cook today?

She glanced at Auntie Lani, who was watching her closely, and she forced a smile at Ben.

"That's a great idea," she said weakly.

It was a great idea if you were a rich playboy. She had a feeling Ben had just outsmarted her again.

She felt a bit better, though when he squinted over at the truck.

"Who does that thing belong to? It's blocking the driveway."

"Cossini Construction," she replied proudly. "It's our new truck."

"New truck?" Irritation drew his brows together in a frown. "Charlie, I told you over and over to just use the Jeep. It sits there half the time; I can't drive it. You didn't have to go and buy a piece of junk like that. Why are you so stubborn, woman?"

"You watch what you're calling a piece of junk, Ben Gilmour. I happen to believe in independence. That's a perfectly good piece of machinery, and more to the point, it's mine." She added sweetly, "If you ever want to borrow it, I'd be more than happy to—" Suddenly she caught sight of Auntie Lani. A delighted smile split Lani's round face as she watched Ben and Charlie, squared off as usual, glaring ferociously at each other.

Now why should that be amusing? Before she had time to puzzle over it, the materials she'd been waiting for finally arrived, and with the confusion of unloading and stacking the lumber, covering it against the rain that consistently fell during the night and blew away by morning, Charlie forgot about everything except the job at hand.

Lani's trailer arrived that afternoon, a rather battered twenty-five-foot long yellow-and-silver box that fit right in with the boxy cabins and the generally bedraggled atmosphere of the rest of the buildings at Reveille Reef.

Pogey supervised the placing of the trailer under a huge coconut palm close to the men's cabin, and soon afterward, the electricity and sewer connections were complete. A set of wide wooden stairs was attached to the entrance, and the sound of a radio playing fifties' rock-and-roll music floated out of the screened doorway.

Auntie Lani was firmly in residence. By the time the women quit for the day and wearily headed to the beach for their predinner swim, ravishing odors of cooking food were floating over the area, and Charlie could see Lani bustling around the men's kitchen. The wonderful smells had intensified when they returned from their swim.

It was Charlie's night to cook. She eyed the greasy stove, the dishes still draining from breakfast. She opened the fridge, remembered the dripping milk carton and slammed it shut again.

"Let's go try out the truck and have a burger in town," she suggested. Eliza cheered, and Carol looked relieved.

Ben watched the women leave, the truck wobbling uncertainly down the drive as Charlie got used to the steering.

"You can't run away from me every night," he warned her silently. "With Auntie Lani on my side, Charlie Cossini, I'm gonna win."

Winning was also on Charlie's mind just then, but the battle wasn't with Ben. It was with the truck.

Perched on the seat beside her, Eliza watched the struggle quietly, then commented after a mile or so, "You have to sort of herd her along, don't you, Charlie?"

The remark was apt. Their recalcitrant beast ambled along cheerfully enough, but it definitely had a tendency to wander at will from one side of the road to the other. The motor sounded surprisingly healthy, however, and the brakes were good, although the truck had obviously been built before the advent of springs. Every pothole in the rough road bounced the women up alarmingly close to the roof and banged them down again. After one particularly bone-jarring encounter, Charlie muttered, "This could land our kneecaps inside our shoes."

All in all, Charlie figured that the loose steering and the flakes of rust that sifted down on them from the roof, even the missing springs, were all bearable in a vehicle that had cost only a hundred and fifty dollars, and the missing window was no problem in a climate such as Hawaii's. For the four months she estimated the job at the Reef would take, the truck was great.

It certainly had character. They'd have to tie that roof on, though. Every gust of wind made it flap alarmingly, sending even more rust filtering over the three of them.

"Big Mama has dandruff," Eliza complained, vigorously brushing the rusty flakes out of her cropped red hair when they finally parked on the street in Haleiwa.

Carol and Charlie laughingly agreed, and with that the truck was christened. Big Mama was a part of the family, flaws, dandruff and all.

The next morning Charlie awoke once again to the sound of a bugle playing the now familiar reveille, sweet and hauntingly sad in the early dawn. She let the notes wash over her, let them draw her reluctantly out of sleep to face the new day, half resenting the bugler for awakening her.

Her body ached, as it often did the morning after a particularly grueling job, and as the clear notes faded, she got out of bed with less energy than usual. It would be easy, this morning, to flop back into the warm bed and sleep longer, to ease the muscular soreness with rest.

What was getting into her? Up and at it, she encouraged herself, and within minutes she was in her shorts, doing warm-ups out on the lawn. There was no sign of Ben yet, and she felt a small stab of disappointment. Sharing breakfast with him had already become a habit she looked forward to. He was disturbing, but he was also fun to be around and easy to talk with.

She started off to the beach for her run. He'd probably be up when she returned.

"Good morning, Charlie."

The musical voice belonged to Auntie Lani. She was already coming back from a walk. Her turquoise muumuu had scarlet roses climbing up its front, and she carried her thongs in her hand, enjoying the damp sand, washed cool and clean by the tide, squishing up between her toes. She moved with a graceful, rolling gait.

"Morning, Auntie Lani. Say, did you hear the bugle this morning?" Charlie immediately demanded. She was beginning to feel as if she were the only person at the Reef who paid any attention to the dawn serenade.

Ben was maddeningly offhand about it, dismissing it as an ordinary military custom. He still insisted the sound came from a military base, a recording that echoed all the way to the Reef if the air currents were right.

It annoyed and puzzled Charlie that the refrain held such fascination for her. And several times the bugler had missed a note here and there.

Lani reacted strangely to the question. She looked straight into Charlie's eyes for an instant, and then she let her glance slip beyond Charlie, out toward the ocean where the sunrise was painting on the water.

"Yes, I heard it. A fine way to welcome the morning, don't you agree? Ancient Hawaiian priests used to stand on these shores and blow conch shells to lure the sun back from the night. This bugle does the same, I believe."

Auntie Lani's fanciful words distracted Charlie momentarily. She found herself glancing along the shoreline, almost as if— She brought her attention sharply back to the practical matter that puzzled her.

"But where do you think it comes from, the sound of this bugle?"

Lani's face was inscrutable. "From everywhere. From nowhere." She looked past Charlie, and now a smile lit her face. "Here comes your man," she said placidly. Ben was loping toward them on his crutches, clad only in a brief pair of yellow trunks.

"He's not my—" Charlie began to protest vehemently, but then Ben was directly in front of her, and she stopped. He'd want to know what had been said, and she suspected that with Ben and Lani both in on such a discussion, things could go from bad to worse. She'd have to set Lani straight another time.

He must have overheard, however. He balanced in the soft sand and gave her a quizzical, slow look. Then he said gruffly, "Don't be too sure of that, Charlie." He shifted, planting one crutch on either side of her bare legs, neatly trapping her, and before she could guess his intent, he bent and planted a quick, hard kiss directly on her lips, using the tip of his tongue to flick a provocative caress rapidly in and out before he released her.

It was over between the breaking of one wave and the next. It was a blatant, passionate challenge, and it aroused all the emotions Charlie was doing her best to ignore. It reminded her, quite simply, how much she wanted Ben Gilmour. She pulled back, putting distance between them, needing a moment to recover. Her body felt as if she'd gotten sunburned.

"He's a bad boy, that one," Auntie Lani chortled, wagging a finger at Ben. She'd watched the incident with obvious delight, Charlie realized.

"You two go and play," Lani ordered archly, and now Charlie blushed in earnest at the obvious innuendo. "Have fun; in half an hour breakfast will be ready." She padded off, still smiling.

Charlie turned on Ben, hands jammed on her hips.

"You dope, what'd you do that for? Now she thinks—"

Ben was still balancing where she'd left him. He met Charlie's furious glare unashamedly.

"She thinks we're lovers, Charlie. I don't find that such a bad idea." His glance wandered over her, and the thin jersey top and shorts she wore suddenly felt invisible beneath his hot gaze. "Do you?"

She didn't find it such a bad idea, either, but she certainly wasn't about to tell him that. Without answering, she turned and ran, her feet digging into the wet sand, the tide playing cat and mouse with her legs as the breakers rolled and ebbed along the shore. Her long, lean legs pumped like pistons, and she drove into the rhythm with her elbows, farther and farther down the empty stretches of Reveille Reef.

Ben confused her. He frightened her. He thrilled her. Like the mysterious morning bugler, he awakened emotions she hadn't felt before, awakened her when she half wanted to go on sleeping.

She ran as hard as she could, as far as she could away from him. But eventually she had to turn back, and in the first warmth of the tropic morning she could see Ben waiting for her, his ash-brown hair wet from the ocean, his magnificent, tanned body glistening in the sun as she drew near. Seeing him from a distance, a sculpture etched against the brightness of the sky, she understood that her appreciation for fine architecture was also part of her attraction to Ben. He was beautifully made, strong, sinewy, lean. The muscles in his shoulders rippled as he moved forward on his crutches to meet her.

But this was no art form. This man was perfectly male, he was nearly naked, he was Ben—and all Charlie could think of was how it would be to have him make love to her, here on the beach in the seductive Hawaiian morning.

Chapter Six

"Three eggs?" Charlie stared at the table when they returned from the beach. "Lani, I can't possibly eat three eggs. All I ever eat for breakfast is—"

"Bran flakes," Ben finished for her, his tone indicative of his opinion of that cereal.

They'd found Lani setting two breakfasts out on a large, round wooden table she'd dragged outside from somewhere.

"Anyway, I have to shower. You go ahead—"

"Shower. Hurry up. Then you get back here and you eat." Lani was scowling at Charlie, and her voice left no room for argument. "Look at you, skin and bone, working all day without a decent breakfast. From now on, three eggs. Two pieces of toast. Fruit. Go, go. Ten minutes, you be back here." Lani's tone was a command.

Charlie was back in seven, and she meekly ate every scrap. She was savoring the second cup of Lani's coffee when Eliza stuck her fiery, tousled head out the door of the main house and yelled, "Charlie, telephone. It's your father."

Charlie sprinted across the grass, and Lani called to Eliza in the same threatening voice she'd used on Charlie, "You and Carol get out here. Your breakfasts are ready, and I get mean if people don't eat when I cook for them."

But Eliza wasn't about to argue as Charlie had.

"No problem," Eliza hollered delightedly, and hauling Carol behind her, she hurried to the table before Lani could change her mind.

Inside, Charlie pounced on the receiver. "Papa, is that you? Yes, yes, I'm fine. We're all fine." She shook her head and smiled tenderly. "It's ten to nine here, Papa. Yes, in the morning. Yeah, I know it's earlier there. Uh-huh, it's sunny and hot. You've got snow already?"

She listened as her father gave her reports on the whole family.

"Tony's thinking of going back to school? That'll be hard on Gisella, working all day, the kids at night. But if they guarantee him a job when he's done, it's wortn it."

She listened again, shaking her head from side to side. "Papa, I told you and I told Rosa, too, don't worry about the money. I'm sure to make enough here to pay off the whole damn loan." she grimaced at the tirade of rebuke that poured into her ear and grinned ruefully. Her father still bawled her out if he thought she needed it, twenty-six or not.

"Sorry, Papa, no more swearing, promise," she apologized. She listened and imagined the high-ceilinged kitchen where Papa was standing, in the house she'd grown up in, the house that seemed to have relaxed and become more like a home when her mother left it. Charlie had stayed on there with her father, thinking of getting herself an apartment and never doing it. Papa would have been so alone in that huge place by himself.

"This job's a winner, Papa. Tell Johnny Campanello thanks again when you see him. And tell Rosa I'm happy for her about the new baby. When's it coming?" She closed her eyes, picturing her father's fringe of white curly hair, the drooping mustache, the eyes so like her own . . . A wave of homesickness made her voice gruff.

"Papa, for cripes' sake, would you forget the damn bank loan? I'm making enough to pay it off, I tell you." Her voice had risen, and she bit her lip, forcing lightness into her tone.

"Yeah, otherwise we'll need another loan to pay the phone bill. Bye, Papa. I will, for sure. Bye. Love to everybody."

She hung up slowly, and her face crumpled. Tears rolled freely down her cheeks, and she swiped them away angrily with her fingers. Damn, she hated crying. It was just hearing Papa's voice, all the details of the family troubles, and realizing that in two short weeks everything back home was changing. She'd never been away from her family before. It was scary, most of all because she suspected that maybe she was changing, too....

"You all right, honey?"

She jumped, startled at Ben's soft words, and then ducked her head to hide the shameful tears. His tender endearment made her cry harder, of all things. She swiped at her face impatiently, trying to stop but not succeeding.

He'd come in quietly, heard most of her conversation, and now he tipped her chin with his fist, forcing her to look up at him. She scowled, humiliated that he'd caught her crying. He shook his head at her, a tender, warming light in his eyes.

"Tough guy, huh? Haven't you heard that even carpenters get the blues?"

He looked around for tissues to wipe her streaming eyes, found none and finally unbuttoned his pale blue cotton shirt, casually using the bottom to wipe her face, scrubbing at the tears.

"Ben, not on your clean shirt." Her voice was husky with tears. She suspected that in another moment he'd order her to blow.

"Bad news from home?" he queried, smoothing back her shower-damp, tangled hair, letting his fingers linger on her neck.

She sniffed hard. "No more than usual. Gisella's husband's still out of work; Rosa's pregnant again. It snowed last night."

He propped himself against the counter and took advantage of her distraction to draw her tenderly into the cradle of his arms. His thick brows lifted quizzically, his eyes filled with gentle amusement as he rubbed a hand up and down her back. It felt good, and she stayed, aware in a moment or two of the masculine outlines that poked out where hers went in.

"So why are you crying, then? Unemployment, okay, I understand that, but a baby and a snowstorm?"

"Rosa has two preschoolers already, and her husband doesn't make that much money. Because of the snow, Papa can't get out to go for therapy. He hurt his back; he was a roofer. Now he runs a little store, and he hates it." She shrugged in a weak attempt at nonchalance. "Middle-class America. This is how the other half lives, Ben."

"The bank loan, Charlie. You mentioned a bank loan."

"For my mother's hospital expenses. She was in a private hospital." It suddenly dawned on her that he'd listened to her conversation. Her eyes narrowed, and she drew in a deep breath, preparing to accuse him of snooping. Before she could, he tightened his grip on her so she couldn't move away, and he nodded, looking her straight in the eye.

"Yes, I overheard part of it. No, it wasn't deliberate. I came to see if you were all right. Phone calls sometimes aren't good news." Determinedly, he persisted. "What bank loan, Charlie?"

Would it do any harm to tell him? He'd just hire the CIA to do a dossier on her entire family if she refused.

"My mother was a miserable woman, Ben. She probably never should have married, but in a strict, Old World Italian family, I guess she had no choice. I don't really know. Anyway, she felt life had somehow passed her by, saddling her with us kids and a house. She wasn't a loving woman or wife or mother. Oh, she kept everything fanatically clean, cooked and all that, but she made us all feel guilty for her having to do it, especially Papa." Charlie's eyes brimmed again, and she fought the tears back.

"Anyway, as she got older, she retreated into a childish state that wasn't mental illness but certainly wasn't normality, and she absolutely refused to do anything, not even take care of herself. My sisters and I, and Papa, did the best we could, but finally Papa decided to put her in a private hospital. She didn't qualify for any insurance program—it was sort of a voluntary rebellion." Charlie gave a small, sad laugh, but her eyes were bitter, remembering. "She went on strike, I guess. And then she did get sick, really sick instead of just pretending. And she begged Papa not to make her move; she was used to all the luxuries and the pampering by then. So his insurance got eaten up at a wild rate. She died, finally. It was a relief." Charlie wasn't watching Ben, and she missed his reaction to her matter-of-fact statement, the sympathy on his strong features.

"Then Papa fell and cracked a vertabra and needed care himself. I was doing well, so I took out a loan to pay the medical bills until he was on his feet again, which never happened." She shot Ben a challenging glance. "And that's the sad tale of the Cossinis. Tragic, huh?"

"Every family has problems, Charlie. They're nothing to be ashamed of."

"Even filthy-rich families?" The words were out before she thought, and she was suddenly ashamed of being spiteful when he'd just been nice to her.

But for once the remark didn't make him at all defensive. He just gave her a lopsided, quizzical grin and ran a playful hand over her hair.

"Even so," he agreed. "Look," he began tentatively, "money's absolutely no big deal with me. I don't even spend what I'm paid each month. Why not let me make you a loan or—"

She tore away from him as if he'd suggested an act of perversion.

"Absolutely, positively not. And don't even mention it to me again." For a long, warning moment, her furious eyes and tilted chin challenged him.

He shrugged and held his hands out in a supplicating gesture, and right then she caught a glimpse of the clock on the wall. The anger in her expression gave way to astonishment, and her eyes grew shocked and round. "Is that the time? Damn it to hell. We're going to be late starting work."

Ben watched her fly out the door, and he shook his head. "Crazy, impossible, proud woman. What would your father say if he heard you swearing like that?" He tilted his head to the side and stared thoughtfully after her for long moments after she was gone. What was there about Charlie that made him want to protect her? She touched some inner place he hadn't even known was there.

Every morning after that Lani made breakfast, and the women ate it gratefully. On her next trip to town, Charlie bought a lavish supply of bacon, bread, eggs and fruit and plunked it down in the men's kitchen.

"Our share," she stated. Lani judiciously checked the grocery bill in the bag and shook her head in horror at the prices.

"This is robbery. If you really want to share expenses, I will buy our supplies from local farmers, and you and the men can split the cost. What do you say?"

Of course, Charlie said yes. The scheme appealed to her sense of frugality, and by now she couldn't have reverted back to bran flakes, anyhow.

But she'd eat them till she choked rather than let Ben know that.

The next inevitable step was sharing the cost of all three meals.

Charlie gave easily on lunch. After all, what was a sandwich here and there or a glass of juice? Well, there was often fruit salad and Lani's macadamia-nut cookies. Nobody could possibly resist those. But dinner was a matter of principle. As long as they went on making their own dinner, they remained satisfactorily independent.

Thus, Charlie held out against the first few dinner invitations Lani extended. The first time, Carol was cooking, and Charlie knew their own dinner would be edible, if not fancy.

The next night, however, Eliza served lukewarm canned vegetable soup, raw carrots and yogurt while the delectable odor of roasting beef filtered over from what they now called the cookshack.

Listlessly, Carol spread Cheez Whiz on a chunk of cardboard bread.

"Lani invited us to dinner again today." She took a bite of the bread, grimaced and laid it down again.

"I don't know about you, Charlie, but the smell of that roast is driving me nuts." She glanced at Eliza for support and announced, "I vote that we hand over all our food money to Lani and eat with the men. If we're gonna work like men, we should get to eat like them, and I can't stand yogurt."

Eliza jumped up from the table and pounded her chest dramatically, if not hard. "Meat, I need meat," she groaned. "And tomorrow's Charlie's turn to cook again. I can't stand that, either. I second the motion to join the men. You're outvoted, Charlie. C'mon."

The parade to the cookshack was almost a stampede. Over generous helpings of rare barbecued beef and sweet potatoes, Charlie watched carefully for smugness or gloating from Ben. He hid both reactions with all the deadpan finesse that brother Mitchell used in heavy financial transactions, but inside he reveled at what he felt was a major victory.

He got around to examining his motives the next morning when he stood bent in an S-curve, trying to shave and still balance on one leg while not smashing himself silly on the low roof of the shower house.

What was it that made him care for Charlie? Why should it be urgently important to him that she get better nutrition and more leisure time? Why did those hands of hers cause a peculiar tenderness in him?

He finally shrugged, lost his balance for one precarious instant, cursed satisfactorily and rationalized the whole thing by telling himself he was deliberately plotting to increase her sex drive so he would benefit. He tried a sinister leer on the mirror. He wasn't much good at leering, he decided. But he sure as hell would be good at relieving Charlie's incipient sexual urges.

God knew his own libido didn't need any help, what with her flitting up ladders wearing those damned army-issue leg shorts. She had the best sort of legs, long and curved and sort of coltish. His libido reacted to Charlie's legs in a predictably healthy manner, and he groaned.

THE FIRST WEEK she was at the Reef, Auntie Lani got the women to build a makeshift extension of the roof on the cookshack and then enclose the whole thing in screen, forming a large outdoor seating area protected from insects. They furnished it with a haphazard selection of lounge chairs as well as the huge picnic table, and it became a kind of social center where they lingered after supper to sip the addictively delicious coffee brewed from Hawaiian beans and listen to Lani pick out rock tunes on her ukulele. Ben brought out his battered old guitar and joined her, delighting everyone by doing a fair imitation of Elvis.

In the background, the ever-present booming of the surf sounded as counterpoint to the unlikely melodies in the softness of the early tropical night. There was usually a moon later, giving the entire scene the exotic flavor of a *South Pacific* movie set.

"This outdoor living room makes me wish I had a porch on my trailer," Lani commented one evening. "It'd have to be portable, though, and I guess that just isn't possible."

Charlie spent the next afternoon hunched over a sheet of graph paper, and when she showed Lani the sketch she'd made of a charming extension for the trailer, which folded handily on hinges for moving, Lani was enthralled.

"You carpenters build it for me and I'll housekeep for you." The bargain was made, and gradually cleanliness and order reigned at the Reef, although Lani administered tongue-lashings if she felt men or women were being unnecessarily messy.

The group felt like a family, Charlie concluded, a large, unlikely, happy family.

More often than not, Kimo would drive in sometime during the evening and quietly take a seat as close to Carol as he could get. He would talk, and usually she would ignore him or nod or answer in monosyllables.

Charlie decided after watching this scenario several nights running that Carol was making it unreasonably hard for the affable policeman.

Eliza must have thought so, too, because during a break the next afternoon, she abruptly demanded, "How come you're giving that poor guy such a hard time, Carol? He's a hunk. You're just lucky I don't decide to give you a run for your money with him."

Lani appeared just then with a pitcher filled with cool green juice tinkling with ice cubes.

"You will drink this," she ordered ominously. "It's full of vitamin C and minerals. You all look dehydrated. Your breasts will shrink unless you keep up your liquid intake; don't you know that?"

They all giggled at her outrageous threats, and she poured them each a glass, and one for herself, then slowly lowered herself to the grass beside them, spreading the wide hem on her muumuu like a sail around her.

The breeze was cool under the coconut palms. It was a relief to get out of the blazing noonday sun, however briefly, and they all slumped like rag dolls.

Eliza gulped her first glass down without taking a breath and then gasped, "Lime. That's heaven. Thanks, Lani. Don't you agree with me about these two?" she demanded of the older woman.

Lani poured her another glass. "What about them?"

"Here we are in a tropical paradise, with a corner on the market for available bachelors, and these two are acting like vestal virgins, for gosh sakes."

"Virgins were useful in ancient times for tossing into erupting volcanoes," Lani replied placidly. "I'm afraid virginity was never prized here in Hawaii. Far too perishable a commodity." With that startling bit of trivia, she turned and regarded Carol with a great deal of interest, her large, round head tipped to one side.

"Now, honestly, tell me. Why is Kimo not acceptable to you? Don't you find him pleasing? He is an honest, virile man. You are a woman of great beauty, more beautiful than most because you're big and strong. Together, you and Kimo would have wonderful babies."

Carol's face, already tanned, now looked as if it might be sunburned all over again. She had a mouthful of juice, and she swallowed with difficulty.

Auntie Lani obviously expected an answer. She was watching Carol and waiting with the patience of one prepared to wait all afternoon if necessary.

"It's not Kimo. I mean, I, well, the problem is—" Carol stopped, then started again. "It has nothing to do with Kimo. It's me. I was married, and it didn't work out, and I'd rather not try it again." Her soft brown eyes seemed to look inward, and she dropped her head, avoiding Lani's continued regard.

Lani reached out a plump brown hand, nails short and lacquered scarlet, and laid it compassionately on Carol's arm.

"This haole you were married to obviously wasn't man enough for you, that's all. Kimo, now he would cherish you. I see the way he looks at you. Besides, one marriage isn't enough to judge by. I myself have had three husbands. One died, one left me for another woman, one I left—he was a crazy Englishman. But I'm not against another if he happens along." She lowered one eyelid slowly and opened it again in a huge wink. "However, he will have to be very rich and very good at loving. It's difficult to find both virtues in one man, but I keep hoping. But you, Carol, to let yourself be defeated after only one attempt. That is madness."

She heaved herself up and gathered up the empty pitcher and glasses. "As for you—" she said sternly, fixing her attention now on a squirming Charlie and giving her the "look." "You, stop running so fast. You have to give him a chance, at least, to catch you. And try to curb that tongue of yours."

No one asked who "he" was. Charlie nodded weakly up at Lani and then watched with profound relief as she made her way back to the cookshack.

The women shared astonished glances with each other. Auntie Lani was something else, all right.

Charlie was about to order everyone back to work when Eliza asked curiously, "How long were you married, Carol?"

"Six years." Carol's short silvery-blond hair gleamed in the sun as she dipped her head again. "I should have left him long before that, but I was a real dishrag in those days." She shrugged and picked idly at the grass beside her bare leg.

"It had to do with being big. I was already six foot one when I was fourteen, and I outweighed every boy in my class, never mind the girls. They called me Tiny, and I laughed along with them, but I never had a date." The uncharacteristic flood of words faltered, but she cleared her throat and went on. "You see, inside I felt exactly like all the other girls, but with one difference. I'd have given my left leg to be tiny."

"C'mon, Carol, it's great to be tall. Why, lots of times I wish I was taller. Clothes look so good on tall women," Eliza protested, but Carol shook her head.

"Not when you're a teenager and nothing fits. Or you're dying to have a boy kiss you and he can't reach your lips even if he stands on a stool. You've never really thought about it, Liza. You're cute and small and sexy. But the whole social thing, when you're growing up, is geared to size in a way. Cheerleaders, in school. Ever see a cheerleader six foot one? Girls didn't play football in those days. At a dance, who wants to cuddle an amazon? I wasn't interested in sports. Of all things, I wanted to act. Now, in little theater how do you cast a girl the size I was? Not as the female lead, that's for sure. I gave that pipedream up in a hurry." Caught up in her story, she forgot to be reticent.

"Jackson came along when I was seventeen. I still can't figure out why he wanted to marry me, but he did. I thought it was my one chance at being like every other girl in Bellingham, at having kids and a husband.'' Her eyes were sad more than bitter, and she met Charlie's look squarely.

"I trained to be a nursing aide, and he quit his job. I earned our living, and he drank more and more.'' Carol's blue eyes were shadowed with grim memories, and she drew her shoulders into a rounded shield, folding her arms over her breasts.

"He started making fun of me, joking about my size in front of other people. He'd always pretended he didn't care that he was a couple of inches shorter than I was, that he was smaller than me. The thing I didn't realize was that his soul was small. He was a mean little man. Finally, I got the nerve to leave him. And I learned to live with my size. I've accepted myself, I guess. But I don't want to be married again, ever,'' she added vehemently. "It hurt too much.'' She scrambled to her feet, dusting off the bottom of her shorts. "Shouldn't we be getting back to work? I see Pogey coming back from his swim.''

Charlie got up, too. She threw an arm around Carol's waist.

"Look, if Lani says you're gorgeous, then believe it. She's not someone you argue with. Besides, it's true.'' She knew the reassurance was clumsy, but Carol honestly didn't seem to realize how attractive she was.

"It's something you either feel about yourself or you don't,'' Carol said in a low voice. "I don't.''

She walked over to the work site and tied on her leather apron.

"Are you two just going to lie around all afternoon and watch me work?'' she called in a deliberately breezy voice.

The discussion was over, but Charlie thought about it off and on during the days that followed. What would it take to convince Carol? How did anyone ever trust anyone else with his heart?

She also thought about Lani's warning to her. Was she ready to stop running and let Ben catch her? What would it take to make her yield to the ever-increasing desire she felt for him?

She banged a row of nails in with twice the force they required.

Another Friday came around. The women had now been in Hawaii a full month, Charlie realized. Time enough to fall in love with the long, eternal summer of the days, the rain-cooled nights, the eternal whisper of the ocean.

At breakfast that morning, Lani said, "I've decided today is my day off. I want to visit my cousins; they're fishermen down the coast. I'll come back tomorrow, and on Sunday night we will have luau, a Hawaiian feast."

She shot Charlie a reproachful look and added portentously, "Too much work and not enough play around here, I think."

"If Lani's not cooking, let's all go out for Mexican food tonight," Eliza suggested.

But Ben calmly stated, "The rest of you go ahead. Charlie's coming out with me for dinner tonight." He held his breath, waiting for her to refuse, but to his delight she glanced a bit guiltily at Lani and then nodded her agreement.

Lani gave Charlie an approving nod and poured them all more coffee. "My other cousins raise pigs, and I'm going to cook fresh pork and fresh fish, traditional Hawaiian style, in an underground oven. You two men can dig the *imu* pit today, over there." She indicated a spot near the beach. "Kimo will come by and help you; he knows what to do."

She gestured to where Big Mama hunkered under a tree by the cabins.

"Can you stand taking enough time off this morning to drive me to Weed Junction, Charlie? I catch the bus there to go up island."

Lani had developed an affection for the truck, just as the other women had. She'd even helped paint the monster several evenings before.

Big Mama was now resplendently pink and blue and yellow; the vibrant colors had been sworled onto her rusted frame in an unlikely approximation of the army's attempts at camouflage. Eliza had bought spray bombs, and they'd had a wonderful time one evening, ignoring the horrified comments made by Ben and Kimo and Pogey.

Big Mama was an individual, and she deserved to dress like one, Eliza grandly informed them.

Charlie started the truck, a matter of cunning, muttering oaths that would have seared her father's ears right off and technique, and soon she and Lani were bouncing happily along the narrow highway toward Haleiwa. Over the roar of the motor, Auntie Lani pointed out a tidy little house on a small plot of land, one of many similar houses that bordered the rutted road. "Stop here a moment," she ordered, and Charlie obligingly pulled to the side, idling the motor.

"That's where I grew up," Lani announced, and Charlie gave her a surprised look.

"The Martins lived over there." Lani pointed to the next neat little house, and an expression of deep sadness passed over her round face. "Their son was my friend."

For some reason, Charlie had never imagined Lani growing up and living all her life here on this island. Lani seemed timeless, cosmopolitan, a trifle exotic.

Lani was still looking at the houses as they pulled back onto the road. "My mother was Japanese, my father Hawaiian," she explained. "They're both dead now, but they were lovers all their lives. I think they wanted many children, but they had only me. So I was wonderfully spoiled, wonderfully loved. The Hawaiian people adore children, as do the Japanese."

"Was it hard for you, having parents from different cultures?" Charlie remembered uneasily that kids back home who were "different" in any way usually had a rough time of it. Carol, for instance. Charlie, too.

But Lani laughed her big, rolling laugh, the sound blending comfortably with Big Mama's engine noise.

"Hawaii is a melting pot," she explained. "People on the islands are a happy mixture of Caucasian, Japanese, Filipino, Chinese and of course Hawaiian."

They were approaching the bus stop at Weed Junction, and she gathered up her immense straw bag embroidered with garish flowers. Then she added thoughtfully, "During the war, being part Japanese was difficult, though. Not so much for me, because I was a girl. But for others, yes, it caused heartbreak." For a moment her face was sad again. Charlie thought she was going to say more, but just then she happened to glance past the gas station to the junction.

"Ayee, that's my bus. Step on it, Charlie."

Charlie did as she was told, drawing up with a groaning objection from Big Mama's capricious brakes. Lani bailed out of the truck, waved and hurried across the street, holding up an imperious hand to halt oncoming traffic. A truck filled with marines stopped for her, and she climbed onto the bus like a queen, head high and buttocks rolling majestically beneath her scarlet muumuu.

Charlie drove home thoughtfully. She'd never have met a person like Auntie Lani unless she'd come to Hawaii. Or Ben, either, probably. Her mouth quirked ironically. Bellingham was not exactly a playboy's retreat. No, for sure she would never have met Ben in Bellingham.

Being in Hawaii was changing her, affecting the way she thought about things and even the way she acted. Here it was, ten in the morning on a workday, and she was ambling along slowly, smiling at these beautiful brown children riding bikes along the side of the road.

She waved to them and impulsively saluted by honking the horn. It sounded like the first discordant notes on a bagpipe, and the kids waved delightedly and shouted greetings to her.

She wanted children to raise. She wanted babies to hold, toddlers to chase, kids like the ones on the road. She'd ride bikes with them. She'd teach them to build things with nails and wood. Yeah, she wanted children. She just didn't plan on getting married to get them.

"HOW CAN YOU SIT THERE and say you want kids and then in the next breath tell me you don't plan on getting married?" Ben sounded as exasperated as he felt. "It's not fair to a kid to deliberately deprive him of a father," he objected.

Every time he was around her, she came up with some new confounded idea that raised his hackles. She was the most exasperating woman he'd ever met, and she was beautiful tonight.

They sat at an intimately small, round table in the sunken, glassed-in dining room of the Turtle Bay Hilton, an elegant resort hotel ten miles up the coast road from Haleiwa and light-years removed in luxury accommodations from the Spartan conditions at Reveille Reef.

"Oh, I'm not planning on producing them myself." She speared another of the small deep-fried balls of shrimp and crab on the lavish hors d'oeuvre tray that the waiter had placed between them, dipping it into the spicy sauce and munching on it.

"I'm not planning on either pregnancy or marriage for myself. See, I'm going to adopt kids nobody else wants, little kids like you see in the paper every so often. Single-parent adoption is quite common now, you know."

"Wouldn't it be easier and more fun to find a man who wanted the same thing? Any kid has to benefit from having both a mother and a father. I sure did."

Before she could stop herself, Charlie said softly, "Yeah, well, I didn't."

Ben felt the pain behind her words. His eyes softened, and he reached out to capture her hand, but the waiter appeared with the wine that Ben had ordered, staging the elaborate tasting ritual. Ben sipped, nodded, the man poured the wine, and the tender moment was gone.

"Do you care for the buffet, or would you like to see menus?" the cheery waiter inquired, and Ben raised an eyebrow at Charlie.

"The buffet, please. Oh, unless it would be easier for you if we ordered." Although Ben was now using only one crutch, it still would be hard for him to balance himself and a plateful of food safely.

"I'll be your bearer, sir, if you want the buffet," the affable waiter offered. "Sports injury?" he inquired, nodding toward Ben's foot.

"Skydiving."

"Dangerous, isn't it?"

"Yes, but the thrill is worth it," Ben assured him earnestly, and Charlie rolled her eyes.

The succulent display of food was irresistible, and at the end of the table a broadly smiling cook presided over the largest beef roast Charlie had ever seen. Waiting for a massive slice of the delectable meat, Charlie couldn't help grinning as she remembered Eliza pounding her chest. "Meat, I need meat." She must tell Carol and Eliza about this meal.

Soon their plates were heaped, and Charlie hadn't even made it halfway around the buffet tables.

"I've got a brother-in-law who'd die from gluttony in here," she murmured to Ben as they made their way back to their table, the willing waiter carrying Ben's enormous serving for him.

"I'd like to meet him. I'd like to meet your whole family someday, Charlie." The truth of it surprised him.

Giving him a surprised look when she realized he meant it, she said, "I doubt we travel in the same circles. My family's pretty ordinary. Except for Papa."

She felt very removed from her family in these surroundings.

The short tropical twilight was fading rapidly, and Charlie took a last look beyond the glass wall, which was all that separated them from the rocky shoreline and the wildly pounding surf. The juxtaposition of the opulence of her surroundings with the majestic and wild force of the ocean nearby was stirring to her senses.

Upstairs there were undoubtedly sumptuous rooms that overlooked this same scene. How would it be to stay in one of those suites, to look out on this magnificence, to have an obliging waiter bring morning coffee on a silver tray? To lie in a moonlit room between silken sheets and listen to that pounding rhythm—in Ben's arms?

"Chilly? I can put my jacket around your shoulders," Ben offered, and she quickly shook her head. It wasn't his jacket she wanted enfolding her.

Silken sheets weren't necessary, either; Ben's arms would be just as effective in a tent, she suspected, noticing his clean-scrubbed, well-tailored looks. He wore casual slacks and an open-necked lemon-colored shirt with his tweedy jacket. Ben wasn't the suit type, and she liked that. She liked the way his grass-green eyes crinkled at the corners when he smiled at her, making goose bumps rise again along her bare, tanned arms.

"Do people actually own those cabins along the shore-line?" Anything to get her mind off its stubborn fantasy. She gestured far down the beach, where several cedar-sided buildings clung to the edge of the cliff.

"Some. Others are rented out by the hotel. My parents brought my brothers and me to Hawaii several times when I was growing up, and we stayed in cabins like those. Not always on this island, though. We'd travel around—a week here, a week there. Dad would get restless after more than four days in one place."

"What's your dad like?" Charlie realized she'd never asked Ben much about his family. Had she always been too busy resenting his money to find out about the people in his life? Or was she afraid to fill in the gaps of his character, afraid to find herself liking him even more than she already did? A twinge of guilt flickered, and she tried to ignore it.

Ben finished chewing his beef, swallowed and thought for a moment.

"He's got more energy than anybody I've ever known. I read somewhere that energy like that is a common factor among high achievers. Of course, Mom got him to retire five years ago, and now they spend most of their time traveling. They might turn up here, sometime after Christmas, and you'll get to meet them." He smiled fondly across at her. "Dad will love you, Charlie. You've got that same urgent need to keep the world hopping." She decided not to mention that it was highly unlikely she'd ever meet the senior Mr. Gilmour. The job would be over in December.

"I take after my mother," Ben was saying. "She's a dreamer, and she's about the happiest person I know. I guess she's a little eccentric. She studies parapsychology and practices yoga."

Charlie's fork paused halfway to her mouth, and Ben laughed. "For instance, I was born on Christmas Day, but she named me Valentine. Benjamin Valentine Gilmour. She said anybody could be named Noel, that Valentine was much more romantic and wouldn't stereotype me."

What intrigued Charlie was Ben's total lock of self-consciousness about the name. Any other guy would never reveal it. Here was a man secure in his masculinity.

"You're sure it wasn't just because she was counting on a girl after three boys?"

Her tone was light, but Charlie had her own memories of her mother bemoaning the fact that Charlie was female. Growing up had cured that particular hurt, at least. She loved being a woman, most of the time. Well, all of the time she was around Ben, for sure. He made her aware of her femininity.

"Sorry I wasn't a girl? Not my mother. She always said that boys naturally married girls, and how fortunate it was she'd get her daughters by that method, and already toilet-trained. She hated toilet training, she claims. Anyway, she insisted my father train us whenever he was around, sending us into the bathroom with him to watch how it was done. After four of us, he said it took him years to get used to going in alone."

Whatever she'd imagined about Ben's family, it wasn't this. Private schools, exotic holidays, fast cars—those, certainly. But toilet training?

"Are your brothers married?"

"All but Mitchell. Mom despairs of Mitchell. She says he has no Zorba in his soul. Remember Zorba the Greek?"

Charlie shook her head.

"Well, he was a man with what he termed fire in his blood. It takes fire to get married."

"How would you know?" The comment was offhand, and she expected a teasing reply.

Instead, he met her eyes with a direct gaze and said seriously, "Because I was married once. For all of eight months."

Her mouthful of food was suddenly hard to swallow. She forced it down and tried her best to make her tone nonchalant. Some demon made her quote a statement he'd once made about work.

"Was that as long as she interested you, Ben?" He'd said that he worked at different jobs—as long as they interested him.

His green eyes darkened, and his whole face became still and wary. She was sorry as soon as the words left her mouth, because she could see that she'd hurt him.

Before she could find the difficult words to apologize, he said evenly, "That's how long it took her to find out she couldn't make me into what she thought I should be. She divorced me and married an oil tycoon who knew how to live up to his position in life." He poured more wine into their glasses, splashing a few drops on the table.

"I'm sorry, Ben."

One thick eyebrow quirked, and he said, "I swear, I think that's the very first apology I've ever wrung out of you, and it's for the wrong reasons. Belinda simply taught me what I didn't want out of life. It's been years since my broken heart mended." His ready grin brought an answering one from her, but inside she pondered this new information about him.

Had Belinda, who Charlie now despised sight unseen, made Ben into the footloose wanderer that he'd become? He must have loved her deeply. He'd never remarried, and he was so attractive plenty of women must have tried by now.

Well, that made two of them who were off marriage. Too bad the decision not to marry didn't automatically turn the libido to an off position, as well.

They wandered through the palatial lobby after dinner. On its periphery was a collection of specialty shops. The stores didn't interest Charlie at all, but the gigantic ceiling-high bird cage in the lobby's exact center fascinated her. It was easily ten feet around, and inside was the largest pea-green parrot she'd ever encountered.

He was rocking back and forth on a swing large enough for a small child, uttering noises that sounded as if they should be words, and he was surrounded by an entourage of smaller, brilliantly colored birds whom he appeared to bully in fine style. Charlie grinned at his audacity.

Ferns and flowers grew on the cage bottom, and vines trailed down the sides and from the roof. There was even a tiny stream threading its way across rocks and gravel. A bird cage done by a decorator, all right.

She stood still for several minutes, entranced by the sight and sounds, and she was hardly aware that Ben wasn't at her side until he reappeared, an embossed shopping satchel in his hand from one of the boutiques.

"Ready to go, or would you like to wander around some more? I'd love to take you dancing if I could."

"Well, you sky divers have to suffer for your bravery." She gave him a wide smile, an open, teasing Charlie-type smile that made his insides go all soft.

He studied her openly, standing as she was silhouetted against the background of the cage and birds. She was slender enough to be a model, and the classically simple white dress she wore skimmed and hinted at curves and hollows. It's neckline was deep V, and its sleeves were short and flared, letting the long, strong lines of her tanned arms show. When she'd leaned forward at the table and he'd seen the gentle swelling of her firm breasts and a wisp of frothy lace bra, he'd had to count slowly to ten and concentrate on cold surf.

"I've never seen your legs in a dress before," he commented, giving them what he hoped was a lewd once-over, just to see her flush prettily and scowl at him. "They're really very nice."

They were spectacular. She had elongated, beautifully shaped legs, as he'd noticed again and again during the past weeks with her flitting around in shorts or a bikini. But there was an aura of feminine mystery tonight about those same legs, encased in sheer panty hose, ending in dainty, strappy high-heeled sandals.

"The rest of you is very nice, as well," he went on judiciously, letting his eyes wander slowly up and down her. "In fact, the rest of you is absolutely gorgeous," he added, his voice husky and intimate as he watched the reactions to his words play across the delicate features of her face.

Charlie had a natural, personal elegance he was certain she wasn't aware of at all. Her deeply blue eyes were wide, watching him to gauge if he was serious or joking. His eyes centered on her short bottom lip, which made her mouth always seem as if it needed to be kissed. Her lips were moist and glistening, with just a hint of rose added to their natural color. Tonight, she'd gathered her curly hair up and pinned it back, baring her long, slender neck and dainty ears. If they didn't get out of here in five seconds, he'd attack her in full view of the parrot.

They were passing Sunset Beach, dark and deserted at this late hour, when Ben decided. Calmly he said, "Charlie, I want you very much. I want to make love to you. I've wanted to since the first day we met."

Cool move, Gilmour. Guaranteed to get you kicked out of this Jeep in the middle of nowhere. He held his breath.

She gulped, and her foot on the gas pedal made the Jeep surge ahead unexpectedly, the way her heart had at his words. But her voice was quite steady when she spoke, although her answer made no sense to Ben at first.

"I want you, too, Ben. Where can we be alone?"

He'd expected something so totally different that it took time for her words to penetrate.

"I have the keys to the beach cottage. It's still empty," he said hoarsely.

She made the turn off the highway with a confidence she was far from feeling. When they arrived, she turned off the motor and the headlights and said inanely, "Well, here we are."

It was where she'd chosen to be. She hated playing games, and the forthright way he'd asked her had been perfect.

She was twenty-six years old, and mature women did this every day. She'd had Eliza and Lani lecturing her before she left tonight on the finer points of male seduction. She wanted Ben exactly the way he said he wanted her. They understood each other, didn't they?

So why should she feel so frightened?

Chapter Seven

The pounding breakers surged in only inches from Charlie's bare toes, and she could see Ben's cast sinking into the sand close beside her. The wind was up. Charlie's hair had come loose and was blowing in the damp night breeze.

"Well, that sure as hell didn't work, did it?" Ben remarked in disgust.

Charlie silently agreed. It sure as hell hadn't. There was something about coldly planning a mutual seduction that had left both of them incapable of carrying out the mechanics of the exercise.

Oh, they'd done all the right things at the appropriate times. Ben had turned a small radio to a station that played romantic ballads. They'd stood, Ben's arms around her, admiring the breathtaking view of moon and ocean and deserted beach. He'd slowly slid his arms around her and kissed her deliciously. She'd kissed him back. They'd tried hard.

But before they even reached the unbuttoning stage, Charlie gave up and started to giggle helplessly.

"What's so funny?" Ben stroked up and down her arms and her back in a way that should have been arousing but instead was only ticklish.

"I keep thinking we should stop and turn to page forty-five of the manual," she managed to say. He was nuzzling her neck, and he nipped gently with his teeth. That simply made her laugh harder, and he felt an angry rush of frustrated impatience with her inappropriate response to what was, after all, a technique perfected by practice.

Had it been too long since he'd made love to a woman? Was his approach hopelessly rusted into antiquity in only a few weeks?

At that point, he nearly picked her up and resorted to caveman tactics. But he had a horrible suspicion that it would only make her laugh harder. Why, oh why, couldn't Charlie Cossini react normally?

Then he saw the humor of the situation, as well. Playboy lures beauty to secluded cabin. Object: carnal knowledge. Result: carnal amusement. He struggled against the image and finally succumbed, laughing a bit sheepishly. Laughing with her.

"I'm sorry, Ben. It's just that Eliza, and especially Lani, treated this project like a military maneuver. This is Liza's dress, and she did my hair. Three times. And Lani sprayed me with some exotic local perfume that made me choke. And they gave me instructions on how to, um, how to...act. Eliza had some insane article from a magazine."

She hadn't meant to reveal how detailed the project had become, but the rest slipped out, anyway.

"On how to seduce you." She giggled again.

"Me? You? Seduce me?" It was an idea he'd never considered, especially not from Charlie. "Seduce me?" he repeated incredulously, and with that his virile, healthy reactions, alive and well until that very instant, began to fade. To wither. With them went his tolerant amusement. "You mean magazines actually give women tips on how to—" Morbid curiosity overcame his pique, and he probed for details. "What did it tell you to do?"

Charlie's eyes were sparkling, and her cheeks were pink with mischief. "Well, first, Lani told me to keep my mouth shut and try smiling more."

"That's all? That's not such a bad idea."

She gave his arm a playful punch. "Of course that's not all. This whole lecture took maybe two hours when Lani got involved. With diagrams even. But I'm not going to spill the whole secret plan to the enemy, am I?''

Ben studied her, annoyed and intrigued at the same time, just as usual with Charlie. He'd planned to have her under him in the bedroom right now.

Hell and damnation. Nothing he ever did with this woman worked out the way he expected. Passion had fled.

''Okay, Laughing Eyes, what should we do now? I think there's an old Scrabble board over there in the cupboard.''

His attempt at sarcasm went unnoticed. Charlie was perched on a chair, and his eyes unwillingly traced the long curves of her leg as she drew up her knees and unfastened her strappy sandals one by one. Then he had an intriguing glimpse of silky thighs, and in the next moment she was stripping her panty hose off. She stretched both legs out and wriggled her bare toes with gleeful relief.

''They felt just like Saran Wrap,'' she announced. ''I hate panty hose. No wonder men don't wear them.'' She stood up, walked to the wide window and looked out at the beach. ''How about a walk?'' she suggested.

That had been an hour and a half ago. They'd wandered far along the sandy shore, confiding to one another silly tales from childhood days.

Ben told of hiding from his older brothers in his father's massive greenhouse when it was time for them to tutor him in math, and how the gardener, a dour Scot named Alan Stewart, became his friend and taught him about seeds and tree grafts and the magic of growing things.

''I was the kind of grubby kid who kept worms under my bed and ant farms in my closet.''

Charlie told about the clock tower.

''Sister Mary Francis used to lecture me all the time about what was proper behavior for girls. She knew Papa took me with him on jobs, and she said it was disgraceful. Even when I was little, my hands would have tar on them. According to both her and my mother, roofs were definitely not proper for little girls to climb, and they really got on my case. At one point they had me believing that there was something seriously wrong with me."

Ben noticed her voice changed when Charlie spoke of her mother.

"Papa found me bawling about it. I asked him if it was shameful and vulgar—scary words for a kid of eight—to like climbing roofs. He didn't say anything, but he borrowed or stole, I don't know which, the key to the clock tower in the local park. He took me over there and led the way up what must have been hundreds of circular steps, right to the top. Even I was exhausted when we finally got up there. It was a little room, full of bird droppings and smelly. But I looked out, and there was what I figured must be the whole world, spread out far below us. To a kid who loved roofs, this was the ultimate thrill." She laughed softly. How lucky she'd been to have Papa for a father.

"He let me look and look as long as I liked. Then he said simply—" she imitated a lilting Italian accent "—'Don't let anyone tell you not to climb. Some people never try; they're the ones who tell others what's right to do. You be your own boss. Don't let anybody tell you how high you can climb.' And we went down."

They walked along, not talking now, not touching, aware of each other but separate, as if they each needed room and time to absorb the things they'd learned about the other. They were nearly at the beach house again when Ben reached out impulsively and captured her hand in his own. The feel of her long-fingered, shockingly rough paw in his reminded him of the bag he'd brought from the hotel. He'd tossed it on the seat of the Jeep and forgotten it.

"Stay here," he instructed her, taking the path around the house in long, swinging strides on his crutches. He was back momentarily, the embossed bag swinging from his arm.

Charlie watched, mystified, as he propped himself against a tree trunk, letting his crutches fall to the sand.

"Come over here and hold your hands out," he ordered.

"Do I have to close my eyes?" she asked as she obeyed a little nervously, wondering what he was up to. Yet his tone of voice had been playful. She held out her hands, palms down. He gently turned them over, reached into his bag, and selected a bottle at random.

Unscrewing the cap, he poured mounds of pink, creamy, delicious-smelling liquid into each of her palms; then, with his own hands, he began to massage the liquid firmly into her skin.

"What's this? What're you doing?" She made an attempt to draw her hands away, but he held her firmly and went on massaging.

"These hands of yours are a disgrace, Charlie. They're all cut and sore and chapped. They make me wince just to look at them. Now, I've got eight different kinds of lotions that the woman in the store recommended for serious cases of neglect. Every evening I'm going to massage one kind into your hands, because you'll never remember to do it."

She felt annoyed, reprimanded and insulted. Her feminine pride was injured at his forthright words. Then honesty forced her to admit that he was absolutely right. Her hands were a disgrace, and she never did get around to doing anything about them. And, yes, they were sore.

His strong fingers rubbed back and front, over and under, between her fingers, along the fine bones in her wrists, rubbed a circle into her palms, skimmed down her fingers again. He frowned, concentrating on his task with clumsy intentness. A sweet, flowery perfume floated up from the lotion.

"This one's called—" He checked the label of the bottle in the moonlight. "It's called Plumeria."

Charlie stood motionless, mesmerized by the erotic stroking, the gentle concentration on Ben's face, the amazement she felt at his doing this for her. Then a disturbing thought made her ball her hands into fists. He looked questioningly at her.

"Does it embarrass you to take me out with hands like this? Is that why—" She pulled back so suddenly she tripped in the soft sand.

He reached out and caught her, and this time they over-balanced the other way, banging hard into the rough tree trunk.

They landed in a heap, Charlie half sitting on him. Ben was completely exasperated.

"Damn it all, Charlie, I'm fed up with you always thinking the worst of me. I don't give a hoot what anybody else thinks of your hands. I care because they look so sore. They're beautifully shaped, and you're so careless you make me mad enough to want to strangle you, so help me." He grabbed her shoulders in frustration and gave her a shake, then slid his arms around her helplessly, trapping her in his embrace.

Her head was tucked into his neck, and her breath was warm and fragrant against the skin on his throat. Tipped slightly back, leaning as they were against the tree, her body was off balance, pressed against his.

The exotic fragrance of plumeria lotion rose between them, and desire caught him unaware, although he was still fuming at her unfair accusation.

She felt so fragile, her ribs and narrow back dainty under his hands. He wondered fleetingly how she could be as strong as he knew her to be.

Then heat swelled furiously within him, and his arms tightened around her. He bent his head, searching for her lips in urgent, blind need. He trailed kisses across her cheek, the corner of her eye, the tip of her nose, before he trapped her full, petulant mouth with his own. The growing need of his body caused an urgent aching that sparked a hungry movement of his tongue across her lips, as if asking her a question.

She hesitated, but only for an instant. Then her mouth shyly opened beneath his, and he shuddered with the job of exploration, the sweetness and softness opening for him.

Charlie felt an answering shudder run the length of her body. Ben's arms were locking her into his embrace, the strong muscles tense and iron-hard. Liquid heat pulsed through her veins, and inside, her body clenched spasmodically in response to his evident need.

"Touch me, please, Charlie. I want your hands on my skin."

The drumming of her heart became an echo of his, and she slid her hands under his shirt, shy, yet wanting to caress the hair-roughened chest with its tight blond curls swirling around flat male nipples.

She found one with a forefinger, and it grew pebble-hard at her touch. He groaned and pressed his hips against her in helpless loving rhythm, his deep kiss and thrusting tongue telling her wordlessly what he wanted.

She was aware of the soft air and the night, which seemed to close them inside an intimate cocoon. His eyes reflected the moonlight, absorbing and kindling it into a spark that she felt warming her, irresistibly drawing her with him into discovery.

She breathed sounds into his mouth, meaningless, short exclamations of surprise and pleasure and wanting. His hands were large, powerful and slightly abrasive against her skin. She shivered, although the warmth growing from every part of her body was shooting dainty stars of heat to the very roots of her hair. Even her face felt flushed.

A tight knot somewhere in her belly loosened, turned liquid and spread just like the perfumed lotion he'd put on her hands such a short time before.

This time, there was no need for planning. What was happening was inevitable, spontaneous, and she moaned aloud as his mouth slid, hot and open, across her neck and down to where her breasts had become hard buds of desire. They strained impatiently toward his mouth, and for long burning moments he lingered there, wetting the silk that covered them, until, in a frenzy of impatience, he found the zipper and drew her dress up over her head, tossing it onto the sand.

Slowly, he adored her with his eyes, covered as she now was in only scraps of glowing lace. His legs were stretched out, and he lifted her body, encouraging her to cradle, legs apart, on his lap.

"Like that," he whispered, and his breath became roughly uneven as her softness and his heat touched through the clothing, which now was an intrusion between them.

Her legs straddled him. Long, brown thighs glowed in the moonlight, and her knees nestled into the damp sand on either side of his thighs.

He cupped her chin in his fist, fighting down the pulsing desire that threatened to carry him out of control. The lovely, intimate perfume of her inner self rose to his nostrils, engulfing him, madly erotic, musky and sweet.

"Charlie?"

It was question and demand, born of wild urgency, his husky voice part of the wind and the endless breaking of waves just below them, where the lonely beach became ocean. With urgent fingers, he loosened her bra and stripped it away from the proudly firm breasts with their prominent nipples. He ducked his head and tugged gently at them with lips and teeth.

"Charlie?"

She didn't immediately answer with words. She didn't need to. The rhythmic, instinctive movement of her lower body was answer enough, and her fingers fumbled with the buttons of his shirt until it joined the discarded dress on the sand. Then her arms locked around his trunk in an embrace as fierce and almost as strong as his own.

Her passion ignited, burned and fed on itself until it was a living thing, and she was almost angry with his holding back. She'd wanted him for so long. Why hesitate now, when everything was right?

Then she understood. He was waiting for her spoken, full acceptance of his lovemaking. She gave it freely, gladly, urgently.

"Love me, Ben. I want you to love me, now," she begged, and in a frenzy of haste he slipped off her silken panties, loosened his belt and slid his trousers and briefs down his thighs.

There was just time to strip his own clothing completely from his burning body, over the intrusive lump of the cast on his leg, before she ran her rough hands feverishly down him, needing to feel the evidence of his desire for her.

He lifted her above him, his hands cradling her, and when she slid slowly down, a long, gasping cry escaped her. His turgid flesh throbbed inside her slippery smoothness, and then she no longer could tell Ben's need from her own.

A guttural cry rose in his throat. He held her firmly still until he could control the ecstasy she was thrusting him toward too rapidly.

She was marvelously, unbelievably beautiful, and he told her so. He held her immobile, staring into her face in wonderment. Her heat seared him, her inner quickening was so delightful he could hardly bear it.

"Kiss me," he whispered. He watched the way her lashes fluttered as if she were lost in a dream. Then her swollen lips came closer and closer to his own, and all her moist and tender parts were one with him.

Like a pagan goddess tossed up by the sea, she echoed with him the tropical ocean's surge and ebb. Toward the last, she became formless and without control, incapable of movement of her own. She rode immobile on the flood about to break in her soul.

He wrapped her tighter in his embrace, took her rhythm and completed it for her.

A tidal wave of sensation clenched and drowned and aeons later, in some silent place, released her.

An instant later, Ben's climax exploded, and now it was she who held securely as the cry of joy broke from his lips.

The inner tides retreated, and Charlie was unwilling to let them disappear, but slowly she became aware of the damp sand and the cool night air. She shivered. The cataclysm of their loving was frightening. They'd each, separately, thought to light a small flame and instead found themselves in the grasp of a raging inferno. Neither dared confront the other with words to acknowledge the power of what had happened between them.

For Charlie, it would mean an admission of love she wasn't nearly ready to admit.

For Ben, being honest would mean changing the pattern of his life.

They both strove to diminish the truth to themselves and to each other. Still, there was no changing what they'd shared.

"I've wrecked Liza's best dress," Charlie moaned. She stood unself-consciously in the doorway to the small bathroom, clad only in her bra and bikini panties, her long, slender limbs and delicate curves appealingly feminine and rosy from her shower. The black scowl on her face was typically Charlie, however, as she brushed ineffectually at the smudges staining the white crepe.

Ben had longed to shower with her, cursing the cast that made every simple task difficult and cozy showering in a stall this size impossible.

Instead, they took turns. He'd hurried in and out, and Charlie had watched with unabashed interest while he dressed as he snapped shut the trouser leg Lani had cleverly altered for him. The closures were invisible in the seam, but they made it simple to get the narrow pant leg on and off over his cast.

She could see the smooth muscles and hard planes of his body she'd traced with her hands such a short time before. It astonished her to find herself wanting to touch him again, but more leisurely this time. She swallowed and turned away abruptly.

Something similar must have been going through Ben's mind, too. His green gaze deepened and turned liquid as he slowly took in every inch of her. He grasped his crutches and came over to her, balanced for a moment and then dropped the crutches with a resounding crash as he took her in his arms, gently tossing the dress over a chair.

"Forget the dress," he ordered hoarsely. "I'll buy Eliza a dozen dresses if you want." He buried his hands in her hair and rained tiny, nibbling kisses on her face.

"You, my worrywart, are nothing short of gorgeous standing here like this." His voice softened to a whisper. "Charlie, let's stay here tonight. There's no real need to go back to the Reef." His teeth grazed her neck in an erotic love bite. "I want to make love to you in a bed this time. I want to wake up beside you in the morning. We could swim naked in the surf. I'll phone the Reef and tell Pogey we'll be back late tomorrow."

The soft appeal in his voice charmed her, made her want to please him, and herself, by agreeing.

His touch was intoxicating, his body as ready for loving as it had been on the beach. She almost succumbed to the idea.

If she did, could she stop the love for him that had crystallized in the past hours? She heard herself making excuses and knew that they weren't the real reason.

"I've got to get back. There are time sheets to catch up on, a million things that have to be done in the morning." She dropped her gaze so he couldn't see the truth. She was plain scared by what had happened—the force and profundity of their joining, its impact on her emotions.

"There's too much work to do at the Reef. Besides, I'd feel strange, having everyone know I was staying overnight with you." She tried to lighten her refusal. "I guess I'm still a convent girl at heart. You know, the nuns taught us that even kissing was a mortal sin. Think what spending the night with you would be."

He wanted more than just one night. He wanted time to prove to himself that what had happened to him out there on the beach hadn't really happened, and here she was prattling about convents and kissing.

Unexpectedly, an agony of jealousy for what her past might have held forced the next question out of him.

"Haven't you ever lived with anybody, Charlie?"

She was struggling into her dress, tucking the panty hose she hated into Ben's pocket.

"Sure, with Papa," she joked.

"No serious relationships?" He was pushing, but he had to know.

She looked down at herself. Maybe the stains didn't show too badly from this direction. She let the silence stretch, debating whether to answer. "Once," she said shortly. "For a couple of years, when I was a lot younger."

Ben waited, unmoving.

She'd have to tell him more than that, but she hated revealing how naive and vulnerable she'd been.

"He was a lawyer," she finally burst out, "a local guy from a family much like mine who'd decided to get an education, to be something more than a laborer like his father." Her voice had become sarcastic and hard. She ran a brush through her hair, pulling viciously at the tangles.

"That was the problem. In the beginning, he was grateful for my job. I picked up the tabs while he was studying. We could go out for dinner; I loaned him money. Then he joined a law firm in Seattle, and I wasn't quite good enough for him anymore. He wanted me to talk different, dress better, be something I wasn't." She tossed the brush down and shook her tingling head. "Then I started the company. Having the boss of a construction crew for a wife wasn't the image he wanted. It took me a while, but I finally figured out being his wife wasn't what I wanted, either. So we agreed to disagree, and we split up."

She sounded pretty nonchalant, but Ben wasn't fooled for a second.

"Another Belinda, huh?" He was sitting on a chair, resting his arms across his chest. There was a world of understanding in his voice, and she relaxed. "It hurts, doesn't it, Charlie? Not anymore, but at the time."

She nodded hesitantly.

"They were alike, weren't they?"

Remembering what he'd told her, Charlie suddenly saw the similarities in the two people they'd dared to love. The defensiveness faded from her voice, and she said thoughtfully, "Wayne taught me a lot about myself without meaning to. I had to think about what I really wanted, and it wasn't marriage, home and family.'' She moved to stand in front of the dark window, seeing only the room's reflection instead of the view.

"I started thinking about what marriage did to my mother, and even worse, what she did to my father. She made him feel guilty all the time, because she wasn't happy. Us kids, too. She didn't really want kids at all, I guess." She gave a half laugh, a strained, small sound.

"Poor Papa. He's a good-natured, fun-loving guy, but she wore him down. Nothing any of us did ever pleased her. I wonder sometimes what she wanted out of life. Whatever it was, we sure as heck weren't it."

Ben saw the tension in her body, the clenching of her fists. "Why didn't they just divorce?"

"She was afraid, I finally figured out. Scared to try it on her own. When she made herself sick, that was a form of divorce, but she knew she'd be taken care of. Papa has a soft heart; he'd never have walked out on her and us kids."

The tragedy underlying her matter-of-fact words made him swallow a lump in his throat.

"You shouldn't let bad memories put you off marriage, Charlie. Your sisters married; they're happy, aren't they?"

She shrugged. "I guess they are. At least they act like it. But I always figured they married young to get away from Mother, and now they make the best of it. They were around her more than I was, growing up. I spent a lot of time with Papa, getting dirty and giving her lots to nag about."

She was restless, uneasy with all this talk about marriage and domesticity.

"C'mon, Ben, let's go." She fastened the straps on her shoes, wriggling her toes into place.

"Think you'll ever get married again?" She tossed the question behind her as she led the way out to the Jeep.

"God, no," he exclaimed, more fervently than he'd planned. "I don't think it's a bad thing. My mom and dad, for instance, are as happy together as anybody could be. But I enjoy my freedom too much. I've never needed another person, never met anybody I couldn't live without."

Why should his words sting her like insect bites? Why did they bring a picture of being in his lap on the sand, silent with wonder at a sense of oneness she'd never experienced before in her life? It would be so easy to let herself need Ben.

"Me, either," she managed to say airily, starting the Jeep with a competent flick of the key and a touch to the gas. "And if I ever did, I'd want an ironclad legal contract, a prenuptial agreement, drawn up first. Wayne taught me that much about law, at least." She was impressed at how cynical and tough she sounded when inside she felt this soft and vulnerable.

They were quiet during the rest of the drive home.

Charlie fervently hoped that everyone would be asleep when they got there. She didn't feel like coping tonight with the knowing looks and loaded remarks Eliza might make. Or the horror when she saw what her dress looked like.

But Charlie's heart sank when she drove in. Pogey and Eliza were sitting at the screened-in table, and the Reef was lit up like a fairground.

When nothing was said about her rumpled state, Charlie was momentarily relieved. Instead, Eliza excitedly motioned them over to the newly finished cabin they'd been working on all week.

"Look at this. Everybody was out tonight, and our friend paid us a visit." The wooden steps leading up to the doorway were slathered in wet paint, a dreadful khaki-green color. The old sink they'd torn out was propped against the side of the building, as were other pieces of decrepit furniture they'd put in a pile to be hauled to the dump.

It seemed as if someone had painstakingly tried to replace every single thing exactly as it had been before the construction began.

"Any real damage besides the steps, or just more of this senseless mischief?" Ben's voice was angry.

"Nothing we could see in the dark. We'll have to go around and check in the morning," Pogey said.

"Where's Carol?" Charlie looked around.

"Kimo sort of arranged things so she was in his car after we all had dinner. He said he wanted to talk with her," Eliza said blandly. But she couldn't pretend disinterest for long. She shot Charlie a broad wink.

"Pogey, let's get the flashlights and walk along the beach to see what we can find," Ben announced. "It's probably useless by now, but we'll have a look, anyway."

The men left, and Eliza trailed Charlie into the house. Under the glare of the overhead bulb hanging in the kitchen, Eliza suddenly stopped in the middle of a sentence. Her eyes grew wide as she assessed Charlie's appearance from top to bottom and back again.

"Not one smart remark, Liza," Charlie warned dourly. "It's late, and I'm exhausted." Eliza's right eyebrow soared at that remark, and Charlie blushed crimson. "I'll have your dress cleaned as soon as I go to town."

Eliza had a wide, self-satisfied grin on her elfin face. "I wasn't going to say a word." She was silent for two seconds, then burst out gleefully, "It worked, didn't it? My master plan for the seduction of the American male, playboy-surfer variety. Man, I ought to take out a patent. What part exactly did you—?"

"Liza—" Charlie leveled a narrow-eyed stare at the younger woman "—I'm in no mood for one of your inquisitions. I'm going to have a big glass of water, and then I'm going to bed."

"How about herbal tea instead?" Eliza put the kettle on and made them each a cup.

As Charlie sipped at the tea, she sighed and debated. "What do those magazines you read say about the life span of, uh, meaningful relationships, Liza? The average ones—like how long do they usually last before one partner or the other gets bored or something?"

"Four to six months," Eliza replied knowledgeably. "And after it's over, they say that six weeks is ample time to recover from even the most major breakup. You have to go through a 'separation trauma,' as they call it. There's a whole list of things to do, and you go through stages. If you concentrate and really work at it, in six weeks you're back on track again, just like new but richer for the experience.''

"Let's see, we'll be here for about four months," Charlie calculated, finding a pencil and a scrap of paper, unmindful of Eliza's fascinated interest.

"We should finish this job just before Christmas," Charlie mused aloud.

Eliza nodded eagerly. "Add six weeks and that takes you till the middle of February. There's not a whole lot doing in January, anyway, so that's probably an ideal time to recover, when you're not in the middle of a heavy job.''

Treated this way, matter-of-factly plotted with a beginning, an inevitable ending and a course to follow for recovery, the idea of continuing an affair with Ben was tempting.

Face it, Charlie, she lectured herself silently. *Ben has tempted you since the moment he fell through the roof, and after tonight—*

"Just one thing," Eliza suggested thoughtfully. "You have to be sure you're doing this for all the right reasons, that you aren't fooling yourself deep down with the idea that you'll get married and live happily ever after. That's how lots of women trick themselves into heartbreak. You've got to take a really mature point of view, to be realistic.''

Charlie thought of Ben's horrified response when she'd asked him how he felt about marriage. "No problem. This is realism all the way," she assured Eliza.

"Perfect. Boy, is this going to be fun to watch," Eliza said eagerly.

Charlie rolled her eyes in exasperation. "Liza, this isn't a spectator sport, you know." She realized uncomfortably how much she'd revealed already. "Besides, this whole conversation is completely theoretical," Charlie announced primly. "And now I'm going to bed.''

"I think I'll stay up and use some of this theory on Carol. You never know; maybe the same formula I gave you will work for her.''

"Carol's different, Liza," Charlie warned sharply. "She's not tough, and she could really get hurt. Don't you even dare tease her."

Eliza looked amazed and injured. "Don't you think I know that? Carol's the 'love and marriage and kids' type. She needs a family of her own. But she's never going to bend enough to let Kimo even suggest it."

Charlie thought that was probably close to a fair prediction. Carol had built a wall around her emotions, which even warm and loving Kimo would be hard-pressed to scale.

Charlie yawned and stood up. "Night, Liza."

What had happened to Charlie's own protective wall tonight? Ben had tested it, and it had toppled. Certainly Carol could get hurt in this jousting contest of romance. But couldn't Charlie be hurt just as badly?

"What about you and Pogey, Liza?" Charlie turned in the doorway and looked back at the redhead complacently drinking another cup of her herbal tea. "Any sparks there?"

"Nope." Eliza shook her curls in positive denial. "We're friends. He's a neat guy, and he's done fascinating things, things I'd love to try. He and Ben rode motorcycles over the Swiss Alps once. Wouldn't that be a blast, Charlie?"

Motorcycle riding appealed to Charlie about as much as surfing. "Just another diversion in the life of the American playboy," she commented cryptically. "If your life bores you, risk it." She yawned widely and headed for bed.

"Pogey says Ben is the best friend he's ever had," Eliza called after her. "So he must have something going for him besides money."

Charlie tried to ignore the implications of that suggestion. It was becoming more and more urgent that she keep Ben safely inside the stereotyped character sketch she'd drawn of him the day they'd met. Yet times like tonight, when he told her of himself as a little boy hiding in a greenhouse, of a family that sounded loving and zany, he started to become in her eyes a warm, feeling, all-too-ordinary human being. One who'd stirred in her the wondrous response she'd felt on the beach. A man who could really be a friend as well as a lover.

Ben Gilmour was much more, and much less, than she expected. He was more thoughtful, understanding and generous with his loving than she'd imagined any man could be.

He was much less one-dimensional than she wished he were for the sake of her heart.

AUNTIE LANI'S LUAU turned into the best party the women had ever attended.

Lani arrived home on Saturday morning, routed everyone out of bed and set them to work. She was driven to the Reef in a rusty red station wagon stuffed to overflowing with relatives recruited for the party.

"This is Kimo's sister, Lona, and her husband, Jim," Lani announced. "Jim's making huli-huli chicken for the luau."

Jim was of medium height, but his girth nearly equaled his stature. He had the typical Hawaiian mop of wildly curling black hair and a wide, happy-go-lucky grin that all his children seemed to have inherited.

His wife, Kimo's sister, was tiny, dark-skinned, pretty and much more serious than Jim or Kimo, but her infrequent smile lit her face with sweetness. Her midnight-black hair swung long and silky down her back.

Voices called back and forth. Lani turned her radio to her favorite rock station. Children ran in and out of the surf as the sun rose higher in the sky.

Charlie spent the morning doing what she could to correct the past night's mischief. The painted steps were there to stay, she finally admitted. There was no easy way now to remove the paint and stain them naturally, as she'd intended. Lani listened soberly as Charlie told her about the mischief, and her lips compressed into a narrow line.

"If I had been here, it wouldn't have happened" was all she said.

"I just wish Pogey and I could get our hands on this guy, whoever he is," Ben said. "We'd teach him a lesson in respecting other people's property."

Lani shot him a strange look. "There are always two sides to a story," she said sternly. "Never blame the volcano until you know what makes it erupt."

She marched back to the cookshack and started organizing dinner.

That night there were children sleeping in every spare bed.

"There isn't one damned corner in this whole place for two people to be alone," Ben muttered in disgust.

The next morning another vehicle filled with relatives arrived, this one an old half-ton truck. The inevitable coolers of food and beer were unloaded. More cars arrived with more people.

Ben had been quiet all day, only his eyes conveying to Charlie that their loving was as fresh in his mind as hers. Charlie watched curiously as Ben played with the children like a favored adopted uncle.

Kimo drove in late in the afternoon, and his gaze scanned the crowd like a homing device until he spotted Carol's blond head bent over the tubs of chicken, basting it with the special sauce Lona had prepared.

Laughter filled the Reef's spaces as the soft tropical darkness began to thicken. One of the recent arrivals began to strum a guitar, and someone else picked up the lazy melody on Lani's ukulele. Many of the people spoke the musical, flowing language of the islands, and Charlie marveled at its soft, repetitive syllables.

"Languages sound like the people who speak them," Ben remarked in her ear. It was close to what Charlie was thinking, and she gave him a surprised smile.

She'd changed into a gauzy, blue-green shirt, cool and long enough to double as a dress, or almost. Its tapered bottom hung mid-thigh, and she rolled the sleeves up her forearms and left the collar unbuttoned. Ben's appreciative gaze told her she looked fine, with her curly mane tied casually back with a scrap of leather lacing.

He took her hand when the food was finally ready. There was pali punch made with rum and pineapple juice. There were lomi-lomi salmon tomatoes and Oriental meatballs, served as pupus, or appetizers. There was huli-huli chicken and delicately baked pork and Polynesian rice and teriyaki beef. There were baked fish, and fruit of every color and flavor, piled high on a carved wooden salad plate. There was mai tai soufflé and Hawaiian sundaes with macadamia nuts for dessert.

"Our food is an adventure," Lona told Charlie as they filled their plates to overflowing. "It mixes flavors and recipes from all the ethnic groups that make up Hawaii."

The food was delectable, the rum punch potent, but somehow Ben couldn't enjoy either one. After only a few mouthfuls, he felt full. He'd led Charlie to a seat beside him on one of the many blankets spread on the sand, and he glanced over at her. She was neatly, hungrily, devouring a tender piece of chicken. Ben stared, fascinated by the way her full lips moved, the open, honest way she chewed and swallowed.

It was the same uninhibited way she'd given herself to him on the beach, no artifice, no small, coy displays of reticence or false modesty.

She caught him staring and smiled curiously, biting into the hot, sweet bread Lani had baked.

Ben could still feel the rasping roughness of her hands on his back, the tender softness of her concave belly against his, the entrancing, velvet delicacy of her thighs clasping him in a desperate embrace as her inner muscles quivered and clenched in a manner he couldn't think about without longing to experience it again.

And there was the problem.

Ben had never had to arrange his life to suit the needs of anyone else. The women he'd had affairs with in the past were only too pleased to arrange their lives to suit him, grateful for the remnants of time he found to spend with them.

But Charlie?

He was beginning to suspect that an affair with Charlie would be anything but easy. To begin with, there were these hordes of people around the Reef all the time. There was the fact that Charlie made it plain that her job came first. Being with him wasn't one of her top priorities; she'd made that crystal clear when he'd asked her to stay the night at the cabin. So when was he going to get her alone again? Soon. He'd pondered the problem all day.

He took a piece of melon in his fingers and held it out to her.

"Bite?" He watched in fascination as her lovely mouth opened, took the fruit and closed accidentally around his forefinger. He shuddered with delight.

"Charlie. About the other night. I can't just forget about it and go on as we were before. I want you now, more than ever."

She calmly went on eating.

"I want us to go away together for a while," Ben said.

"We can't," she said firmly. "You don't have to work, but I do. The carpenters, my father, they're depending on me, Ben. Look what happened here when we were gone for just a few hours. It took a whole day to undo the damage." She gestured in disgust. "It's just not a good idea to get any more involved than we are already."

Her reasoning infuriated him. So did her practicality. "Damn it all, Charlie, this is important. A week or two won't make a big difference. We'll fly to Maui or the big island or— Hey, there's this place I love on Molokai, a cottage set in the middle of a forest glade with a waterfall and a pool at the bottom, with nobody around for miles. I'm the supervisor here at the Reef, so if I say it's okay to take a couple of weeks off, then—"

It was the casual way he dismissed her work and her obligations; or was it the implied time frame he seemed to set on their affair that bothered her even more?

A couple of weeks. He'd done all this before; she was certain of that. How else did he know about such a perfect hideaway, for instance? He probably ran on his own schedule for relationships, too. This many days together—and then time allotted to let her down easy, and on with the next diversion. She ignored the neat schedule she'd drawn up herself.

Slamming her plate down on the grass, she exploded. "There's no point in hoping you'd understand responsibility. Well, I can't just take off at your whim, and that's that, Ben. One of us has to think about time and cost overruns on this job. I'm not in your league; I'm not a jet-setter. It's time we both realized that." Her chin jutted out in its usual mutinous fashion, and she started to scramble up, her short shirt dress slipping up so an edge of pink bikini panty showed for an instant, driving him mad. He grabbed her arm in a grip that made her wince.

"Shut up and listen to me, you stubborn, narrow-minded witch," he ground out between his teeth. "If you won't take a well-earned holiday, then I'll find ways of being with you right here. You want me just as much as I want you, so stop fighting me and we'll figure out ways and means."

Of course he could find a way. A sudden calm certainty made him loosen his grip and slide his arm up and around her shoulders, temper gone as suddenly as it had appeared.

"In the meantime, help me up. I want to hear the story Lani's telling. Knowing Hawaii's history, I'd guess it's probably about some queen or other. This place was nearly ruined by strong-minded, stubborn, opinionated women," he declared, retrieving his crutches and leading Charlie over to the grassy slope where children, and adults, as well, were lounging and listening as Auntie Lani's rich, dark tones floated into the night.

"Until a smart king came along and took charge," he added under his breath.

Lani's rich voice seemed a part of the breeze, the surf, the mysterious thick blanket of darkness shrouding the island before the moon and stars rose to prick the velvet blackness here and there with glimmerings of eerie light.

Ben found a spot and drew Charlie down beside him, settling her into the crook of his arm, his lips tickling her ear as he explained, "It's the story of Hawaii's most famous king, Kamehameha, back in the 1700s."

"The chiefs of Hawaii were afraid of the child, and they ordered him killed," Lani was relating, her voice thrillingly low and filled with tension.

The guitar player struck dramatic notes at points in the story, and Jim was tapping out a hypnotic rhythm on a gourd drum he called an ipu.

"The infant was hidden in a basket and covered with olono fibers, so the evil chiefs never found him. His name, Kamehameha, means 'the Lonely One.' He grew to be a great king. It was during the reign of Kamehameha that the white man first came to Hawaii, bringing change to our people. Kamehameha knew that progress was necessary, but he feared for the loss of the old ways, the old customs, like our hula."

The moon slowly appeared and flooded the beach with silver light, and a figure danced into the circle formed by the listeners. Black hair flew, bare feet stamped the sand, and hips whirled feverishly in counterpoint to Lani's words.

It was Lona. Her shyness and retiring manner were gone in the proud way she commanded the audience. Her graceful hands described rain falling, the sun appearing; her hips hinted at the sexual prowess of the king. That she wore blue denims and a T-shirt with a hibiscus flower trailing across it didn't detract in the least from the breathtaking beauty of her hula or the magic of Lani's story underlining it.

Kimo had been describing hula to them one evening not long ago.

"Hula is the heartbeat of our people," he'd explained. "There is hula for life, hula for death, hulas for joy or sadness. Because the early Hawaiians had no written language, hula and chanting became their literature."

Their power and beauty were obvious. Between them, Lani and Lona captivated their audience.

"The winds of change blow across our islands," Lani warned in summation. "We must do what wise Kamehameha said; we must bend with the winds, relinquish our past without forgetting it, adapt to a new era. If we cling too much to the past, Kamehameha cannot rest. If we forget our roots, Kamehameha cannot rest. The spirits of the king and his warriors will walk among us, as night marchers, until we learn to balance the parts of ourselves and our heritage.''

The guitar had joined the ukulele, and now the drum took over. Lona became a whirling, gyrating mass of graceful arms and wildly swaying hips and hair.

"We must treasure the past and welcome the future," Lani cried once, and once again, and between one note and the next the story and the dance were over, and everyone clapped in appreciation.

Charlie sat motionless in Ben's embrace. If only life were as clear-cut as Lani made it seem. If only one could find the path between past and future, happiness and sorrow.

She let her gaze wander thoughtfully beyond the chattering, joking group, out to where the ocean rolled gently up the stretch of lonely beach and the moonlight cast ghostly shadows over the lagoon.

She frowned suddenly, straining to see.

Was there a figure out there, now moving swiftly away? Even as she tried to be sure, it seemed to slip behind the dark pile of lava rock far down the beach and disappear.

Charlie snuggled closer into Ben's embrace. There was nothing out there. Everyone was here, laughing, singing, eating again.

She'd simply thought she'd seen one of Auntie Lani's night marchers.

Charlie smiled softly at her own foolishness, and Ben tipped her chin and kissed her, and sea and sky and stars came close together.

Chapter Eight

Sweat was dripping in a steady steam down Charlie's forehead, trickling over her cheeks and making her eyes sting as she tried to fit the trim on the doorway. Nothing had gone right all day. She silently formulated the worst curse words she could think of as she extracted a finishing nail from between her lips and placed it exactly where it should go, delicately balancing the hammer above the nail.

"Hi, d'you know where Ben Gilmour is? He's living here now, isn't he? Hey, this is a big change from his beach house, y'know what I mean?"

The hammer came down a shade too hard, and the nail bent in the middle. Charlie had heard the car drive in and ignored it. Since the luau four days ago, there'd been a lot more cars coming and going at the Reef.

Lani's relatives, all friends by now, dropped by at odd times of the day and evening. And it was amazing how many of these relatives were young, handsome men who made a point of chatting with Eliza or smiling, lushly curved young women who found excuses for chatting with Pogey.

This racy red convertible was much too exclusive to belong to Lani's unassuming relatives, however. These polished, expensive-looking sophisticates in their foreign car were jet-setters, Charlie labeled swiftly. Another few drops of sweat dripped off her nose, and she rubbed them away with a careless gesture, leaving a trail of dirt on her forehead and nose.

"We're old friends of Ben's. D'you know where—"

Charlie removed the mouthful of nails, gave the luscious spokeswoman a cursory nod, then opened her mouth and bellowed at the top of her lungs.

"Ben? There's somebody here to see you." She turned back to the trim and the hammer and nails, but it was impossible to ignore the greetings going on in the background.

"Hi, Debbie; how did you guys find me here? How are you? It's been weeks—"

Charlie made another attempt at fitting the trim over the slightly uneven edge of the rough board, doing her best to ignore the conversation behind her and the ridiculous emotions it conjured up in her to hear Debbie coo, "You poor thing, look at your leg. No wonder you haven't been surfing. We've missed you, Benjie."

Benjie? Charlie snorted, muffling the sound with a blow of the hammer. But Ben sounded less than relaxed as he suggested, "What do you say we wander over and get Lani to make us some coffee? The carpenters are working here, and the noise—"

"These women are carpenters? And they're working for you? Benjie, you sly devil. Now isn't that just like you, to find a bunch of women carpenters?" They made it sound like carpenters were oddities in some exclusive private zoo Ben owned. The voices faded, and Charlie turned her attention back to the trim. What did she care what people like that thought of her or her work, anyway? The burning in her throat was probably nail poisoning.

Eliza and Carol, with Pogey's able assistance, had started on the second and third cabins that morning, and they were covered in plaster dust. They dismissed the visitors more readily than Charlie could.

"We need the gooseneck to yank up those rotten floorboards," Carol explained, "and probably the hydraulic jack, as well. Can you come and have a look, Charlie? The subflooring in there isn't as firm as it was here." Charlie reluctantly laid the trim to one side. It was the last piece of its kind at the Reef. Wrecking it would mean a time-consuming trip to Haleiwa to the lumber supply yard, she reflected, leading the way to the cabins under construction, where they found Pogey intently observing the noisy scene now taking place in the cookshack.

"Looks like Ben's past has come back to haunt him," he remarked, and then flushed when he realized Charlie had heard him.

Fifteen minutes later, she crouched down and carefully fitted the last finishing nail in the last length of trim around the doorway. It fit perfectly now at top and bottom, and she tapped gingerly on the nail with her hammer.

"Charlie's the boss of the crew. Charlie, Debbie wants to meet you," she heard Ben say right behind her.

"Oh, that's so cute, being the boss of a girl's construction crew."

Charlie's hammer hit the nail with undue force, and she watched in horror as the entire length of trim, after an hour's painstaking work, split neatly up the center.

Slowly she rose to her feet to acknowledge the introduction Ben was making, longing to use her hammer on him, as well.

Her fingers were trembling with rage as she reached out to grip charming Debbie's pink, squeaky-clean hand in her own stained, rough grasp. Charlie did her best to control her nerves by squeezing just a shade too hard, making sure a lavish portion of her grime came off on Debbie.

It was moderately satisfying to watch the other woman's obvious distress as the greasy dirt smudged both her hands, and when she reflexively wiped it down herself, her white shorts, as well.

She was surprisingly good-natured about it, however. That made Charlie even angrier, for some reason.

"Is your name really Charlie? That's so cute. What happened to make that thing on the doorway break apart like that? It must be a blast, building things out of wood. I wouldn't know how to start. I never was good with my hands."

"It's really nice you came out to keep Ben company," Charlie said sweetly as the rest of the group assembled. "It's boring for him here, with nothing to do. I'm afraid we working girls don't have much time to sit around and amuse him."

Her glance skidded across Ben's suddenly frowning face. "It's a pleasure to meet you all," she lied. "Why don't you visit again as soon as you can? Poor Benjie's stuck here every single day with his broken ankle, and he'd be so pleased at having company." She gave Ben an innocently open smile. "Isn't that so, Ben? You'd love more company, wouldn't you?"

The red roadster had hardly bounced its way out the driveway before Ben confronted Charlie, eyes blazing and jaw thrust out belligerently.

"What the hell's the idea, arranging baby-sitters for me? The last thing I need is that crew hanging around here every day."

Charlie pointedly turned her back and became busy measuring the doorway.

Ben scowled ferociously. "Charlie, I don't know what gets into you sometimes. I've been avoiding that crew, and now you've got them believing they're doing me a favor by hanging around." In utter frustration he scrutinized Charlie's shoulder blades, fighting down an urge to reach out and grab her, to swing her around so he could see the expression on her face.

She was busily pulling nails out of a piece of wood around the door frame, and she began to whistle under her breath, pointedly ignoring him. He turned his attention to the door frame. "You know, you should've used a thicker piece of wood and it probably wouldn't have split like that. Or maybe your nails were too big," he advised absently, watching her struggle with a stubborn portion of broken trim.

She whirled on him, fists clenched around the handle of the hammer, and the wild venom in her eyes made him stagger back a step on his crutch. "Just leave me alone, you—you know-it-all. What makes you think you can go around telling everybody how to do his job and how to live his life? You're not an expert at either one. And as for your playmates, Benjie darling, well, maybe they'll keep you out of my hair."

"You, Charlie Cossini, are the worst-tempered woman I've ever come across in my life. You need to be turned over somebody's knee and thoroughly paddled."

He stomped off down the beach in a rage. If she wanted him out of her hair, that's exactly what she'd get. You wouldn't catch him chasing after a woman who didn't want him. That wasn't Ben Gilmour's style.

He was sick of her constant needling about his life-style, too. Just because he didn't nail things together didn't mean he couldn't make a suggestion, did it? He was so angry with her, it took a full hour before he realized that perhaps her furious words had revealed a lot more than she intended. Why would she get that mad if she really didn't care?

A small smile flitted across his grim features, and he settled more comfortably into the tide hollow of the huge rock formation situated half a mile down the beach from the Reef.

Maybe she was a little jealous of him, after all. But uncertainty wiped away the smile as soon as it appeared. Who the hell ever knew with Charlie?

Ben nodded politely at the three Shinto priests in their flowing gray robes as they glided past on their regular evening walk down the beach and nodded again at the tall, thin man with the blazing sky-blue eyes who accompanied them, who seemed to march instead of just walk along the sand.

His eyes were almost as blue as Charlie's, Ben mused. But not as deep a blue, he decided. No one had eyes as deeply blue as Charlie. The color in hers seemed to spill over into the whites, as if there were too much of it to be contained.

Her eyes had opened at the final moment that night on the beach, wide and startled and shining into his in the moonlight, and he'd never felt quite that way before with anyone. He'd actually felt humble.

He was beginning to suspect he'd never feel that way about anyone else, and where did that leave him when the affair ended?

And what affair? Incident was more like it.

Surely other women would begin to attract him again, he reassured himself, even though at the moment he certainly had no desire to experiment, the way he'd always had before Charlie came along. The fact was, nothing was as it had been before Charlie came along.

"CHARLIE, YOU GO AND FIND that man of yours," Lani ordered. "Tell him dinner will be ready in twenty minutes. I saw him hightailing down the beach. And don't you scowl like that. Your face is going to stay that way one of these days."

Charlie considered refusing and then thought better of it. Nobody ever seemed to win an argument with Lani, and it was too hot to try. Besides, Charlie had thought over what she'd said to Ben, and much as it hurt to admit it, she figured she owed him an apology. It wasn't his fault her work had gone badly.

Much as she hated admitting it, the plain truth was that she missed him, and he'd only been gone for an hour. Liza had better have her facts straight about this time span for romance. It must get easier on the far end of the schedule.

Charlie had hastily showered after work and put on her faded blue bikini with an old white shirt of Gennaro's over the top. Everyone went swimming each afternoon and evening, so swimsuits were worn almost like a uniform. In her usual fashion, she left her hair to dry in the breeze, as she headed down the beach in search of Ben. When she found him, he was seated on some rocks, looking out across the ocean.

"Ben? Lani says dinner will be ready soon."

Ben glanced up when she spoke, looking directly into her eyes, one heavy eyebrow cocked questioningly. He didn't move from his perch on the smooth black surface of the rocks.

She felt her cheeks flush, and she wanted to look away, but she held his gaze defiantly. Obviously, he was going to be as difficult as possible.

"Ben, I'm sorry I hollered at you," she began stiffly.

"You damn well should be, too. If that's how you treat your friends, I'm surprised any of them stick around." His voice was guarded, demanding more of her than her stubborn nature wanted to offer.

She went on looking at him, his long, strong legs outlined against the dark rock, his marvelous body bare except for brief trunks. The lavish faded brown hair was tumbled wildly by the hot wind, the muscles in his chest and shoulders outlined as he propped himself on his arms. He was a magnificent, virile man. Not just any man. He was the man she'd willfully chosen in this island paradise to be her lover.

But was he also her friend? She remembered how tenderly he'd held her when she told him about her mother and about her family. How he insisted every night now in rubbing those lotions he'd spent a fortune on into her hopelessly chapped hands, clumsily massaging them into every pore despite her embarrassment and the mild teasing Eliza gave him.

He was easy to talk to, he was thoughtful, she found him stimulating to argue with, and he made it plain he cared how she felt and what she thought.

He refused to let her bully him.

Yes, she decided with wonder, Ben was her friend.

"Well?" he demanded haughtily, inching his way to the edge of the rock. "Are you going to promise never to holler at me unfairly again?"

He slid onto the sand, balancing easily on one leg, intrigued with what she'd say next.

A slow, cocky grin tilted her full mouth upward, and she shook her head forcefully from side to side.

"Nope, because it wouldn't be the truth. Hollering is second nature to me. But if I'm wrong, I always apologize afterward." She squinted up at him belligerently, the breeze lifting her mass of curls and blowing them across her face. "Will that do?"

He reached out to brush a strand of thick burnt-honey hair from her eyes.

"If you add this to the apology, I suppose it will do," he growled, and in an instant she was squashed against his chest, and his lips were covering hers in a passionate kiss, his tongue sending shudders of desire coursing through her.

She was joltingly aware of how little clothing they both wore, her bare body touching his, intersected only by the merest bands of thin fabric at strategic intervals.

Her body reacted with sensual memory, immediately flooding with warmth as his tongue traced the outline of her lips, darted in and retreated before she was ready to release it. His arms loosened from her back, and his hands traced fire down her buttocks, lifting her into his hardness and heat, making her tremble with the promise of delight.

"Charlie, you make me crazy," he mumbled against the softness of her neck, tracing her ear with his lips, nipping at her earlobe with his teeth. "You're the most cantankerous, obstinate, irresistible woman I've ever met."

She wriggled against him, loving the smell and feel and hard desire he emanated, and he groaned and buried his face in her throat.

"You're also a vicious tease."

The wild, urgent wanting she stirred in him surged and threatened to flare out of control. He gently moved her away, glancing ruefully down the beach to where Eliza and Carol were splashing in the protected basin formed by the reef.

He took her head between his hands, threading his fingers through the tumble of her curls.

"I give you fair warning, woman. I'm going to make love to you whenever it's remotely possible, and as often as I'm capable, in every unlikely spot I can find during the next weeks. And every time you open that mouth of yours to holler or complain, I'm going to kiss you until your face looks exactly the way it does now, all rosy and soft and breathless." He planted another kiss on her lips. "Understood?"

It was the best warning she'd ever had. She stretched up and placed her lips softly on his in agreement.

"You got yourself a deal, Gilmour. Now let's go eat, I'm starving."

CHARLIE WAS SOUND ASLEEP that night when the tapping began on her window. She surfaced slowly into wakefulness, aware of the rhythmic sound, unable in her sleep-drugged state to figure out where it came from. Finally, she sat up, blinking, and the three soft taps on the windowpane came clearly.

Without making a noise, she reached under her pillow and drew out the heavy wrench she'd kept there since the night the window had been broken. Like a wraith in her short white sleep shirt, she advanced on the open window, hoping the thundering of her heart wasn't as loud as it sounded to her.

This prowler was in a for a surprise.

The window was open about a foot. Charlie stealthily grasped the bottom of the sash, and with all her strength heaved it the rest of the way up to the top. It made a loud rasping sound in the stillness, and she boldly took a stance in front of the opening. Brandishing the wrench, she faced the prowler, and Ben came within a hair breadth of falling backward off the extension ladder he'd coerced Pogey into propping up for him.

"It's me; don't shoot," he managed to gasp, and quick reflexes plus a death grip on the windowsill were all that kept him steady. "Charlie, would you for God's sake put that wrench down? Quietly?"

What had started out as one of the more romantic impulses of his life could also mark the end of it if she insisted on using that thing.

"What time is it?" she asked, blinking stupidly at him, holding her weapon casually at her side. "What are you doing out there on a ladder, Ben? I thought you were a rapist or something."

"Charlie, I'm going slowly back down this goddamned device, and when I get to the ground, we'll talk about it. Okay?"

"Why didn't you just use the stairs?"

"Because all the doors in this house are locked up tight, and I thought I'd do my Errol Flynn number and kidnap you out the window without waking up the entire neighborhood and announcing my evil intentions to Carol and Eliza, and probably Lani, as well. I conveniently forgot why the hell I despise ladders and that climbing with only one good foot and two strong arms should be an Olympic event. I also forgot you'd probably have a gun or something else under your pillow."

Even whispering had a tendency to make the ladder quiver. He added abruptly. "I'm going down now," and started his laborious descent, with Charlie watching from above.

The moment he was off the last rung, she swung lithely out the window opening and scampered down the ladder, realizing halfway down that all that was between her, the night air and Ben's upturned gaze was a pair of scanty pink panties and her thigh-length nightshirt.

Well, it was quite dark. She put a bare foot into the dew-wet grass and turned questioningly to Ben, now propped on the crutch he'd tossed on the ground.

He reached over and ran a finger down her face, over her forehead, down the delicate length of nose, over the full, curved lips, the stubborn chin and the line of her throat. When he reached her collarbone, he made a left turn, and his finger paused and lingered where her tender, soft nipple grew hard and eager under his touch.

"I warned you" was all he said, and she followed him eagerly to a secret, secluded place by the rocks on the soft sand, where he'd somehow hidden a blanket.

"D'you think we'll ever get to make love in a real bed?" she asked much later, her whisper mock plaintive in the thick darkness, cradled and covered and protected by his strength and warmth, complete and limp from his loving.

"I've heard it's a privilege here in Hawaii, that you have to practice a lot before you're good enough to rate a real bed, with sheets."

"Well, if we're going to have to train for it—" she sighed with mock weariness and, reaching up, stroked her hands down his length "—we'd really better get at it. Time's wasting."

The night grew deeper, and still they couldn't bear to part. He wrapped his big, warm body around her like a cloak, and they fell to playing the game of "what if."

"What if you could do whatever you chose, without worrying about debts and your family and your carpenters?" he asked.

She answered without having to think, and he smiled tenderly. It was this certainty in her that captivated him, this certain knowledge of what she was, even of what she dreamed of becoming.

"I'd go back to school and learn to be a practical architect. I'd bid on jobs for low-rental housing units, those ugly cement blocks of houses cities build, and I'd find a way to make them beautiful. It wouldn't be difficult," she mused, and looped her arms around his neck, resting her head on his chest, feeling the lovely, even rumble of his heart under her ear. "They spend so much money making them ugly; I'm sure you could spend less and make them beautiful."

It was the quality of the darkness here that encouraged dreams, she decided. It had an endless property, as if it were a world in itself, with no relationship to daylight.

Out over the Pacific she could hear the eternal breaking of the mighty waves on the reef, but the darkness showed only faint specks of stars, and tonight the moon was hidden by clouds. The palm trees rustled mysteriously, and now and then one of the strange bird sounds blended with the other noises, never obtrusive, part of the fabric of the darkness.

Ben cuddled her closer, and she inhaled the smell of their bodies, their loving, mingled with the smell of seaweed and salt air.

"What if you could be anyone you chose instead of being Benjamin Valentine Gilmour. Who would you be?" she half teased, realizing how stupid the question must sound to a man in his position, with unlimited supplies of money and not a care in the world. What, after all, was there left for him to want? Who would he care to be except himself?

But Ben surprised her.

"I'd be a guy I once met up in Canada called Herman Bennington. We were on a fire-fighting crew in the Rockies, and Herman and I ended up hiking out of a canyon just ahead of the fire. We got to know each other in a way we wouldn't have otherwise, and he told me all about this twenty acres of land he'd homesteaded in a place called the Chilcotin. He loved that place in a way I didn't fully comprehend at that time, but I understood enough to envy him. I lead a sort of rootless existence, and it's what I choose. But he'd found a chunk of earth where he belonged, where he could look out at his own land and feel at peace and never want to leave. The Hawaiians have a name for that feeling. They call it *aloha ainal*, sort of a kinship with the land."

"Did you ever see him again?" A tenderness had quivered within her at his words. This was a Ben vastly different from the privileged-beachboy image he liked to present to the world.

His strong hand caressed her arm and shoulder idly, testing the textures of her skin, smooth as polished ivory everywhere except on her hands. He took one narrow, rough paw in his own, rubbing a thumb across its chapped and callused surface. Was that lotion helping at all?

"Herman Bennington? No, I didn't. He invited me to come and visit him, but I'd planned to go on a walkabout with Pogey around then. One thing led to another, and I never got back."

He'd never dared go back, he realized now. Something about Herman's settled life had made him feel restless and empty. Homesick.

Even remembering now made him feel that way. How had Charlie managed to dredge that scrap of memory up, anyhow? She had a knack for making him reveal things he'd half forgotten.

Her body was that of a graceful sea nymph under his hands, long and slender and passionate. He bent and kissed her for a long time, and the uneasy memories faded as his body leaped in answer to the woman in his arms.

IN THE MORNING, when Charlie woke long past her usual hour, she leaped out of bed and raced to the bathroom, jumped in and out of the shower, in a fury of haste. How could she have slept an hour and a half beyond the start of the day? Muttering in disgust, she dragged a wide-toothed comb viciously through her hair, flung on her tattered denim cutoffs and a wrinkled cotton shirt and scampered down the stairs, frantically wondering how to explain this disaster to her carpenters.

Lani was crossing the yard, an emerald-green length of tapa cloth knotted carelessly over her huge breasts. "Good morning, lazybones. Come to the cookshack; I'll make you breakfast," she ordered, but Charlie shook her head anxiously.

"I'm late, and there's a shipment of tile arriving, and the carpet man was supposed to come and lay the rugs in the finished cabins," she babbled on distractedly.

Damn Ben, anyway, she fumed. This was a direct result of his keeping her down on the beach until nearly dawn. She glanced guiltily at the side of the main house where her bedroom window was, looking for the ladder, but it had disappeared. Glancing toward the two cabins currently under construction, she noticed that Carol was methodically nailing the new flooring in place. In the other cabin, Eliza's head appeared over the half-removed wall, and she waved cheerfully. Pogey measured boards and cut them precisely with the power saw. A delivery truck from the lumberyard was just disappearing down the driveway.

Charlie took all this in, slightly dazed. How could everything seem to be progressing in some sort of order when she, the foreman, the boss, hadn't been there to supervise?

Lani scowled ominously when Charlie glanced her way again. "Get over here and eat something to keep up your strength. You get skinnier every day, and men like some meat with their bones, contrary to what you young women think." Lani sniffed, herding Charlie ahead of her and pointing imperiously to a chair by the outdoor table where she promptly poured out a huge mug of coffee from the pot always kept on the stove and leisurely set to cooking one of her famous four-course breakfasts.

Charlie sank into a seat, added cream and sugar and sipped her coffee in a daze of confusion. She had never, ever, even once, been late for work before in her entire life. It was inconceivable, the next thing to a mortal sin—probably one of the few sins she'd never even contemplated committing.

Yet everything was progressing as it should, and exceptionally well, she admitted grudgingly, assessing each cabin with sharp-eyed care. Her gaze lingered on the door frame she'd struggled with and wrecked the day before. It was now professionally finished. One of the carpenters had obviously gone into town this morning, picked up the strip of trim for the cabin door and meticulously nailed it in place.

Lani banged down a platter in front of Charlie with eggs, bacon, french toast and three kinds of melon. She poured herself a giant mug of coffee and lowered herself into the chair reserved for her, a sturdy, comfortable canvas lawn chair with reinforced legs.

"Eat," she ordered.

She gave Charlie a long, speculative stare and then scolded, "One thing you must learn; nobody is irreplaceable. In some ways, that's good. Doesn't hurt you to sleep in once in a while, give those workers of yours more responsibility."

Lani paused, drinking her coffee in deep, satisfying drafts, and it was several minutes before she added thoughtfully, "Trouble is, the same rule applies to people. Nobody is irreplaceable. If men and women don't love each other enough, there's always somebody else happy to take over. Lots of wahines interested, oh, say, in that Ben, for instance.'' Lani drained her coffee cup and sighed with pleasure. ''I don't suppose many would be very good at climbing ladders, though,'' the wicked woman added innocently. Charlie's face slowly became magenta, and Lani threw her round head back and laughed and laughed.

THAT MORNING just before dawn, Ben had enlisted Pogey's help to quietly remove the ladder from the side of the house. Pogey was tactful, not making any of the ribald comments he might have under the circumstances.

''Surf's good this morning,'' he remarked instead, carefully putting the long extension ladder back in place beside the tool shed and squinting out at the dark, rolling ocean. ''Why not come along with me to Sunset Beach, see the guys, do your morning swim there and we'll have breakfast at Ali's, like old times? We'll be back here in plenty of time for me to start work.''

Half an hour later, Ben hopped out of the water, collecting his crutches and toweling himself dry before sprawling onto the damp sand. He stared morosely out at the huge, rolling breakers crashing in on Sunset Beach.

Far out, in the rosy glow of red morning, light was beginning to spread over the horizon. He could just pick out Pogey, confidently knifing his way below the crest of a gigantic wave several hundred yards offshore, expertly twisting and adjusting his body to accommodate the whims of the unruly ocean and still keep himself upright on the minuscule purple surfboard, half hidden by roiling water.

It was a duel between man and nature. Ben had heard that Hawaiians challenged the mighty surf on boards such as these before the first white men arrived on Hawaii's shores.

Surfing was more than just a sport. Learning the demanding art had consumed Ben. He remembered how his chest had been rubbed raw at first just from paddling the board out to the surf. Then he'd repeatedly been tossed like a twig into the waves for days until one memorable morning the intricate ballet of man and board and water took shape within him, not in his head but deep in his bones, in his pores, a primeval gut knowledge that couldn't be taught, only felt and recognized and responded to with sinew and muscle and nerves. He'd found himself inside a tunnel of water, able to slide and climb and maneuver at will, speeding or slowing his flight as a porpoise or sea otter might, at one with a medium unsuited for man's survival, yet mastering it.

It had been intoxicating, a triumphant victory he couldn't wait to repeat each morning, honing his technique, his skills, alone with the elemental ocean.

Ben lay back and closed his eyes, the morning sun still not strong enough to warm him, and he shivered. When had he lost that consuming desire to conquer the waves? When had the idea of surfing every day first started to bore him?

This morning, instead of longing to be out there with Pogey and the others, a vague sense of unease had crept over Ben, a restless, bored impatience with a life centered around surfing.

Always before when restlessness overtook him, he'd simply found a new playground, a new challenge, another pretty woman in another place.

But right now he didn't want any of those things. His body ached pleasurably from the hours he'd spent loving Charlie, and all he wanted was another night with her, and another after that. He certainly didn't want another woman. He'd hardly begun to know Charlie, maddening as she was.

He didn't want to leave Hawaii, either. There was a feeling about the islands he'd never had before about any of the other places he'd been. He felt a deep sense of belonging. But there was something gnawing at him, something deep and disturbing growing inside him like Lani's yeast dough, warm and spongy, unformed but filled with promise....

"Hey, Ben, ready for breakfast? I'm starving, and the other guys are coming in now," Pogey called, and Ben rose quickly, retrieving his crutch from the sand.

Three hours later, Ben sat waiting in the Haleiwa clinic for his doctor to check his cast. Pogey had dropped him off on his way back to work at the Reef. He flipped aimlessly through the collection of dated magazines in the waiting room, glancing here and there at headlines.

Volcanoes, earthquakes, famine. Business takeovers, high-level conferences, mergers. Strictly Mitchell fodder. His brother read at least four weekly news magazines and three financial newspapers a day lest some elusive bit of information escape him.

A human-interest story caught his eye about a man in Vancouver who'd developed a strain of yeast that could feed on sugar by-products and produce cheap protein to be used for livestock feed. Ben read it twice, his botanist's training intrigued by the idea.

"Ben? Step in here and I'll have a look at that ankle." The doctor was young, and Ben liked him. Ben glanced around and then furtively ripped out the beef-sugar story and tucked it into his wallet.

"That's healing really well. I think we can do away with the crutch and the cast now. You can start putting more weight on it, and in a couple of weeks it should be good as new."

Feeling like a kid suddenly turned loose on a bike without training wheels, Ben limped out into the heat of the afternoon, having to adjust all over again to another change in balance.

Now he wanted to celebrate his liberation from the weeks of crutches and cast, so he limped down to Rosie's Cantina. There was always somebody in Rosie's arguing about something, and he used to enjoy whiling away an afternoon over draft beer and conversation.

He left after an hour. There'd been another big layoff at the local sugar mill, and the atmosphere at Rosie's was all doom and gloom. The diminishing markets for pineapple and sugar, two of Hawaii's basic industries, and the resulting concern about the economy had even the easygoing crowd at Rosie's upset.

Ben's sleepless night was catching up with him. The Reef would be a noisy bedlam this time of day. And the unaccountable mood that had plagued him all morning was still there, making him want to be alone until it passed. He stopped at the pay phone, deposited a coin and yawned as he waited for Kimo to answer the phone.

"Haleiwa Police Department, Captain Nakanani speaking."

Kimo generously let Ben sack out in his small apartment on a quiet street in the village, near the park. The three tiny rooms were filled with books and maps about Hawaii, both modern and ancient. Ben stretched out on the bed under a lithograph that covered one entire wall. It was a fiery depiction of the eruption of one of Hawaii's volcanic mountains, back in the 1800s. It was titled, "Kamehameha Making Peace with the Goddess Pele."

The mighty king, wrapped in his cloak of yellow feathers, was tossing a bundle into the very mouth of the volcano. What the heck could it be? What did they feed volcanoes, anyhow?

How could Kimo sleep peacefully with that going on a foot above his head?

Ben tumbled gratefully into oblivion.

When he awoke three hours later, the astonishing idea was fully formed. All he had to do was see if he could make it work. He felt as if the aimless boredom of the past weeks had blown away with the fresh Hawaiian breeze, leaving him with a vast freedom and sense of purpose.

Excitement made his hands tremble as he extracted the torn bit of newsprint from his wallet and impatiently waited for the long-distance operator to reach an inspired stranger in Vancouver, Canada. A botanist, like himself, who'd found out what to do with sugar by-products.

Pineapple had by-products. What would grow from pineapple residue? Ben didn't know, but he intended to find out.

Chapter Nine

"Charlie, have you listened to a single word I've said?"

Eliza's voice buzzed around Charlie like a persistent bee.

"Sorry, Liza. I was daydreaming. Say again?"

The women were lying on the sand, side by side, turning lazily now and then to toast every area of skin bared by their scant bikinis. Saturday afternoon was well advanced, and the week's work had been satisfyingly completed.

"I said," Eliza repeated patiently, "that Pogey and I are going over to the big island of Hawaii tonight, and we'll be back late Sunday. Pogey's friend has a small plane, and he's taking us with him this evening. I'm telling you so that when you come out of this trance you're in, you won't set Kimo and the entire police force on my trail, thinking I've been kidnapped by the night marchers of Reveille Reef."

Charlie snorted. "Lani and her night marchers. I asked her how the heck they learned how to paint and why they'd even be bothered glopping that awful color on my beautiful wood, but all Lani does is give me that superior gaze of hers."

She sat up and rubbed more coconut oil onto her thighs. She was browner than she'd ever been in her life. They'd now been in Hawaii almost nine weeks, she calculated.

How long would this tan last after she got back to winter in Bellingham? A cold feeling of loss interfered with the warmth of the sun's rays, and she forced it away, lapsing again into the thought patterns that had distracted her for the past two weeks.

The renovations were going exceptionally well. All the cabins were done now except for the one occupied by Pogey and Ben. This week they would move into one of the finished units, allowing work to begin on the final cabin. After that, there was the major project of the main house. The job was turning into a great success. There was a fair chance they'd finish ahead of schedule.

"Where's Ben these days?" As usual, it was Eliza who voiced the question that was uppermost in Charlie's mind. Ben had been conspicuously absent all day, every day, for the past fifteen days. Plus seven hours, twenty minutes, Charlie added in her head. Ever since the morning after the ladder caper, he'd been gone from the moment Pogey returned from surfing until dinnertime, or even later. And Charlie hadn't a clue where he was or what he was doing. He was evasive, distracted and loving all at the same time.

"Where is he, Charlie?" Eliza persisted.

Charlie snapped, "How should I know? The man's a free agent, and I'm not his keeper, so don't hound me about where he is, okay?"

Eliza sat up, too, pushing her purple sunglasses onto the top of her riotous red curls and widening her eyes dramatically at Charlie.

"Ever thought of just asking him, sort of casual like, so you could keep from biting our heads off every time we mention his name? You're not exactly strangers, the two of you," she added knowingly, and Charlie blushed to the roots of her tied-back hair.

Of course, Carol and Eliza guessed what was going on with Ben. He may have been gone all day, but he was emphatically on the scene every night.

He'd fulfilled his warning so thoroughly, Charlie passed her days in a relaxed euphoria. He was ingenious at spiriting her away or finding a reason to visit the company's guest house or tempting her to walk with him on the beach in the moonlight. Except they ended up loving instead of walking. And instead of diminishing, her attraction to Ben was increasing every hour.

Thankfully, Carol came to Charlie's rescue.

"How come you're going away with Pogey, Liza? I thought you told me you were just friends."

Carol winked over at Charlie. Eliza was perpetually grilling one or the other of them about the men in their lives. Obviously, she felt Eliza deserved a dose of her own medicine now.

Carol was blossoming, Charlie noted. The sun had bleached her blond hair to gold-tipped silver, and it lay like a close-fitting cap on her well-shaped head. She had good, clear skin that was thick and creamy and tanned a buckwheat-honey shade by the rich sunlight. Her warm brown eyes were wise and thickly lashed, gentle and deep, and her large body was lushly curved.

After the first week at the Reef, she'd given in to heavy pressure from the other two women and shyly relinquished her old one-piece maillot swimsuit for a bikini Eliza had bought on sale in the village and then decided was too large for her. It was a simple triangular affair, in shiny brown fabric, and it emphasized the lovely proportions of Carol's tall frame, making her incredibly long, curvaceous legs seem even longer. Carol might have relented about wearing the bikini, Charlie mused, but not for one moment had she changed her attitude toward Kimo's determined courting of her. In that area, Liza's badgering did absolutely no good at all.

Yet despite her evident rejection, Kimo never gave up. He was at the Reef faithfully every day, and every day Carol steadfastly refused his invitations to go out.

Liza flopped back onto her mat impatiently and pulled her glasses down over her eyes.

"But Pogey and I are just friends," she insisted in an aggrieved tone of voice. "Just because we're going over together doesn't mean we're staying together. Well, we are, at Pogey's friend's cabin, but the whole thing is strictly platonic." She tugged at the ridiculous white scraps intended to be a bathing suit and announced judiciously, "I don't believe in casual affairs for myself. I made a value decision when I was sixteen that I'd wait until I found the right man; then I'd marry him and have two point five babies and a one-piece plastic bathroom you can hose out."

Carol was sitting up on the other side of Liza's prone form, and she met Charlie's wide-eyed expression of disbelief with one of her own.

"You mean you lectured and advised Charlie that night on how to go about having an affair and you've never, ever, had one yourself?"

Eliza nodded complacently. "Sure, because it was exactly what Charlie needed. There's no one rule for everybody in this game, and Charlie was turning into a frustrated, shrieking shrew. She doesn't want marriage and all that stuff. An affair was right for her. Besides, you don't need to have done something just to give good advice about it. And I read a lot."

"That's a great comfort and relief to us, Liza," Carol said dryly, and both she and Charlie had to laugh at their friend's audacity. Only Eliza would dare call Charlie a shrew and get away with it, to say nothing of lecturing on subjects she knew nothing about.

They were still smiling when Kimo drove in, with Ben beside him. The brawny men wore shorts, with brilliantly patterned unbuttoned shirts exposing their bare chests. Carol became quiet, averting her eyes as Kimo casually spread another mat and stretched out beside her on the sand.

Ben unceremoniously flung himself prone beside Charlie, and to her chagrin he drawled, "Hello, beautiful," closed his eyes and instantly fell asleep, cradling his head on his forearm close to her side, his relaxed fingers barely brushing the naked skin of her leg.

She'd been with him at the beach house the previous evening, but as always, conversation came second to the magical thrill of his arms and lips on hers. The stolen hours, filled with loving, passed like minutes.

They'd come back here in the early-morning hours, but when Charlie awoke and looked for him this morning, he was gone. Pogey explained vaguely that he'd driven Ben into Haleiwa before he went surfing, and Charlie had felt a sense of loss.

She'd wanted to have breakfast with him, the way they used to. She'd wanted to share a pot of coffee, a swim, a stolen hour or two before she tended to Saturday's chores.

Just as she wanted to talk with him now, to banter and laugh and explore ideas lazily while she had a few free hours to relax and it wasn't the middle of the night. And all he could do was fall sound asleep.

She watched him sleeping, his tangled hair soft and tempting to touch, his strong features vulnerable despite the short stubble on his cheeks that suggested he hadn't shaved yet that day.

He was always meticulous about grooming. What was so interesting about his mysterious absences these days that he even forgot to shave?

Was it another woman? Jealousy stirred until she resolutely forced it away. What Ben did away from her was his business, right? Right.

And surely no human male, however virile, could spend his nights as Ben was and turn around and spend his days doing the same thing with another woman. Could he?

Charlie felt the now familiar clench of uncertainty in her stomach. It was so ironic. At first, all she wanted was that Ben leave her alone during the day, to do the job she was hired to do without the distraction of questions, criticisms or suggestions.

Yet now it seemed the more she wanted of Ben, the less she had of him. She'd realized this last week how much she missed him, that she actually would have welcomed one of his less informed suggestions or even one of his annoying interruptions with cold drinks and conversation.

When had the affair she'd plotted so meticulously gone awry? Ben was the same carefree, directionless playboy he'd been when they met. She felt the same disdain for his life-style, the same contempt for a life without purpose.

But Ben, the man? What did she feel about him?

She stared unseeingly out beyond the sheltered waters of the lagoon to where the rolling breakers of the Pacific were thundering in to crash in mighty, smashing crests of foam and sound on Reveille Reef, and she finally admitted to herself there was a good possibility that she had fallen in love with the man who snored gently a bare few inches from her leg.

How could she have done such a thing? Surely there was a law in the universe that prevented carpenters from Bellingham from falling in love with playboy princes?

She lightly traced the thickness of Ben's eyebrow with a finger whose nail was split to the quick, the result of a duel yesterday with a rough cedar board. She examined the long, strong fingers on Ben's hand. Apart from several strange purple and blue stains—ink?—the hand was smooth and unmarked by signs of labor. She laid her own callused, damaged palm next to his.

There you have it, Charlie. Visible evidence of the irreconcilable differences between his world and your own. Never the twain shall meet.

She felt as if cedar slivers had penetrated her heart.

Carol had left the group and was wading into the lagoon. In a moment, her tall figure slipped into the blue-green water, and she began to swim.

Kimo, too, ran down the sand and into the water, throwing himself under and disappearing. He surfaced out near the reef, and in a lazy, strong crawl headed for the barrier between the quiet waters and the boiling surge of the ocean. He pulled himself onto the lava rock and stood staring out at the breakers, a huge figure even at this distance.

Watching him idly, Charlie saw him begin moving up the rough surface of the reef, saw him turn and call urgently to Carol. She began to swim quickly toward the reef, but Kimo didn't wait for her to arrive.

As Charlie curiously watched, Kimo began to run along the reef, reaching a point where the high surf was at its most frenzied, and suddenly he crouched and flung himself into the heart of the immense wave now cresting above him.

"What's going on out there?"

Eliza had sat up and was watching Carol, who had pulled herself upright on the rocks and was moving cautiously but purposefully along the sharp coral surface. Charlie, with a faint sense of unease, rose and walked to the edge of the lagoon, and Eliza followed.

"Carol would never try swimming out there, would she? And Kimo's told us the ocean's dangerous when the surf's this high. What d'you think they're doing?"

Ben's voice from right behind her made Charlie jump. He was staring out at the scene, a frown creasing his sleepy face.

"Did Kimo take a board? Is he surfing?"

Charlie shook her head, and now she saw Carol scurrying for the farthest edge of the rock barrier. Ben cursed vividly and tore the loose shirt from his body, stripping off the shorts to reveal the narrow band of swimsuit he wore underneath.

He waded clumsily out, and soon was stroking rapidly and strongly toward the reef.

The next moments were laden with tension and an unbearable sense of helplessness as the two women peered anxiously out at the strange scene taking place hundreds of yards and millions of gallons of water away.

Ben reached the reef, but his ankle made his progress along it slow. At last, he reached Carol, and she agitatedly motioned out into the caldron of water where Kimo had last appeared.

For one terrible instant, it looked as if Ben were about to jump into the forbidding face of the waves, as well, but then he hurriedly anchored an arm around an outcropping of dark stone and hung for a moment suspended between a rising wave and the reef before heaving Kimo up beside him.

The wave reached its zenith, and for terrifying seconds Charlie held her breath, the spume hiding the people in its mist.

Then she saw the three figures, drenched but together, slowly making their way along the rock to where the lagoon provided protection from the worst of the waves. Kimo seemed to be clutching something against his chest with his right hand, helping Carol along with the other hand, and he slipped carefully into the water this time instead of diving in for the return trip to shore. The trio waded slowly up onto the beach, and Eliza and Charlie raced over with towels and questions.

"Kimo spotted a dog and went in after it," Ben explained briefly, and Charlie could see that Kimo was clutching the smallest, wettest-looking dog Charlie had ever seen. The furry, quivering mass hardly seemed to breathe, lying limply in Kimo's grasp. The huge policeman, already recovered from his bout with the waves, took the beach towel Eliza proffered and gently wrapped it around Carol's quavering shoulders.

"Let's go up to the cookshack and get you dry and warm," he suggested, seeming to forget the puppy in his concern about Carol.

But the tall woman at his side reached over to run a hand over the bedraggled dog's head, taking the towel from her own shoulders and carefully tucking it around the animal, and Charlie saw the expression of longing and love that came over Kimo's face as Carol stood close to him, her attention riveted on the shivering animal.

Kimo gently laid the dog in Carol's arms.

"A gift from me and the sea," he said lightly. He tipped a broad forefinger under Carol's chin, tilting her head up so he could look into her eyes. "His name's Happy," he added softly. "Anybody'd be happy belonging to you."

Carol stood absolutely still, looking fully into Kimo's face.

"Thank you," she whispered, and just then the dog gave a pitiful sound and promptly vomited seawater all over the two of them.

Perhaps it was the memory of Kimo's straightforward statement that spurred the demon in Charlie that night. An aching emptiness had grown in her as she thought of Kimo's words to Carol, loving words, spoken by a man filled with purpose, a man who knew who he was, knew what he wanted out of life.

The group had fussed over Happy until the animal showed signs of recovering from his near-fatal adventure. Kimo thought it probable the dog had fallen from the deck of a boat somewhere out beyond the reef. It was miraculous the tiny thing had survived at all in the turbulent ocean, and if Kimo hadn't been foolhardy and brave enough to risk the waves, the dog couldn't have lived even another few minutes.

Charlie was standing beside Ben, laughing over the first staggering, drunken steps the animal was taking, exactly like a sailor who'd been too long on a rolling deck. Eliza excused herself, saying she had to pack for her trip, and Kimo was obviously loving every minute of the unrestrained admiration Carol exhibited for his rescue of the dog. Kimo needed time alone with Carol, Charlie decided, and she wanted time alone with Ben.

"Care to come for a walk down the beach?" Charlie softly murmured into Ben's ear. It was probably the first time she'd asked him to be with her. Ben always did the asking.

And he refused. He didn't meet her eye, just awkwardly muttered, "Sorry, Charlie, I've got things to do this afternoon, but we'll go out for a late dinner. Okay with you?"

Then he hurriedly changed into jeans and a fresh shirt, and shortly after that, while Charlie watched balefully from the kitchen window of the main house, a large gray Lincoln purred into the driveway, and Ben limped over, climbed in and was gone. The woman driving the Lincoln wore sunglasses and a business suit. Charlie felt ridiculously deserted, abandoned, betrayed.

"Kimo's taking us into Haleiwa to visit a vet he knows just to be absolutely sure Happy's really all right," Carol announced, cradling Happy in the crook of her arm. She added shyly, "Then I think we're going out for a pizza." She glanced at Charlie's downcast face and kindly added, "Why not come with us? Kimo wouldn't mind."

Charlie almost laughed at that. Poor Kimo had spent weeks of patient effort for every moment he ever succeeded in being alone with Carol. He'd burst a blood vessel if Charlie suddenly said she was accompanying them.

"Ben's coming back soon, and we're going out to dinner."

For over an hour, Charlie walked and fumed and tried to make order out of her chaotic thoughts, failing miserably. The realization that she loved Ben seemed to have exhausted her reasoning powers for one day, leaving her confused and angry no matter how far she pushed her legs up and down the beach.

Pogey and Eliza called a cheery goodbye a half hour later, just as Charlie was toweling herself dry after a shower.

"Have a good time," she yelled down to them, and then she heard Pogey's small car pull out of the driveway. She ransacked her drawer for underwear, realizing she hadn't done her laundry yet this week, and finally settled on a pair of orange bikinis one of her sisters had given her that had 'Monday' scrawled across them and a navy bra that should have had matching panties but didn't. When she tugged her white jeans on, she realized the orange underpants shone right through, which she might have ignored except that the 'Monday' logo was clearly visible, as well. She took off the slacks and decided on a cotton knit dress in bright yellow, which was clean because she never wore it.

Now the dress was fine, but the navy bra showed. She solved that by taking the bra off and doing without one, ignoring the way her breasts were subtly outlined under the thin fabric.

Eliza and Carol usually helped her dress, and she felt irrationally annoyed and angry at them for abandoning her on one of the few occasions when, for some reason, she actually cared how she looked. Nervously, she contemplated her hair in the mirror. How did Eliza pin it up for her in that simple fashion?

Twenty frustrating minutes later, she tore it down in a frenzy and nearly scalped herself brushing it out, and then she scrubbed off the attempt she'd made with pencils and shadows to duplicate Eliza's ability with makeup. She swiped on some tawny lipstick, wiped most of it off, managed to darken her eyelashes without blinding herself and found her one pair of brown high-heeled sandals.

Conscientiously, she rubbed a generous amount of one of Ben's lotions into her hands, uncomfortably aware that the last time she'd fretted this much about what she looked like had been for Wayne. And, she reminded herself, look how that had ended.

What had become of her fine resolve to live her life her own way, to be her own boss?

She wandered into the kitchen and ran a glass of water from the tap.

It was Lani's day off, and she was alone at the Reef, all alone, for the first time since she'd arrived. It was a strange sensation, eerie and a bit frightening. Who or what was really responsible for the things that happened here? When everyone was around, she never stopped to really consider the mysterious intruder, but now she peered out nervously at the grassy clearing. It was evening already, and the sun had disappeared.

She wasn't really frightened, she told herself, but she'd be glad when Ben arrived. He'd be here in twenty minutes. She wandered through the quiet rooms and finally went outside to wait.

She was sitting at the table in the cookshack, the naked electric bulb shining over her, when Ben drove in forty-five minutes later. The same sleek car that had collected him earlier now delivered him back. The car smoothly turned and drove away. It was too dark to see the driver.

"Charlie, I'm sorry I'm late. I had to talk to these people, and I couldn't break away any earlier."

He came into the circle of light, and she studied him petulantly. He didn't look at all contrite. He looked excited and happy. Tired but exhilarated. He bent and planted a kiss on her hair, and she felt like punching him in the stomach. While she'd been waiting in this spooky, deserted place, he'd obviously been out having fun.

When had she started being the type of woman who sat and waited for a man, anyway? a tiny mutinous voice queried.

Ben didn't even seem to notice there was no one else around. He washed up and put on fresh clothing, while she again waited. Finally, she led the way stiffly over to the Jeep, and he climbed in beside her. He seemed to take for granted she would drive, although without his cast he was perfectly able to drive also. Well, Charlie thought malevolently, Ben must have a whole stable of women to drive him around.

"Where to?" Her tone was curt.

"Do you mind if we just go somewhere kind of quiet? I'm beat," he said with a sigh, sliding down into the bucket seat and rubbing the back of his neck.

She bounced recklessly over the ruts and wheeled onto the highway. "It must be exhausting, all right, working so hard at amusing yourself," she muttered.

He glanced over at her set chin, the white-knuckled hold she had on the steering wheel, and he sighed heavily. Charlie was in a bad mood, and he suspected it was a result of his secretiveness over the past weeks.

He couldn't blame her. He should just tell her. Why did he keep putting it off?

"Did Pogey and Eliza get away okay?" He hid behind small talk, trying to figure out exactly what he ought to be telling Charlie.

He could tell her that for the first time in his entire life he was involved in something that consumed him, challenged him, demanded every ounce of concentration and ingenuity he could muster. Would that sound suspiciously like a small boy bragging about what he was going to be when he grew up? Ben had few illusions about Charlie's opinion of him. She'd told him often enough.

"Yeah, they left a couple of hours ago. Eliza was excited about seeing more of the islands while she's here."

He pretended interest in where they were going to be visiting, his mind far away.

The executives he'd met that afternoon from Hawaii's largest pineapple company had expressed intense interest in his work, but he didn't fool himself into thinking that what he wanted to try would have a hope in hell of succeeding unless he had financial backing. Money.

Ben sighed. So far he'd used his own savings to buy lab equipment and all the paraphernalia necessary for his experiments. But now he wanted to begin production on a large scale. The potential was enormous, but it meant finding factory space, hiring men, buying more equipment. Money. And that, of course, meant Gilmour Developments, and Mitchell.

"So what quiet place to eat did you have in mind? I'm hungry," she stated haughtily.

"Let me think about it for a minute. Just keep driving down the coast."

Delaying tactics. He'd delayed talking with Mitchell, too, but finally, after today's meeting, he realized it was now or never. So he'd phoned and booked a flight to Seattle, one that left early Sunday morning. That way he could grab some sleep and be fresh to beard Mitchell in his den on Monday.

After that he'd made arrangements to meet his affable but unambitious botanist friend from Vancouver, the man who'd shared his own research, generously giving Ben's experiments a head start. Ben was going to try to convince him to become a partner in the fledgling company. Then he'd fly back to Oahu as fast as he could not only because of the business but because of Charlie, too.

What was this reluctance about leaving Charlie, even for such a short time? He'd avoided examining the ever-increasing passion he felt for her because the rest of his life had become so uncharacteristically busy, its demands so acute. But always, during the hours spent hovering over his sporophytes, the endless testing, the search for buildings suitable for his purposes, in some deep, secret part of his being, he held the thought of her, of how she felt in his arms, how she sounded in moments of passion, even how she looked when she was furious and blaming him. Like right now.

"There's a new place up past Sunset. Let's try that." He gave her directions, and the silence grew oppressive between them.

He ought to tell her. But what if Mitchell turned thumbs-down on the whole idea and Ben couldn't go ahead with his plan? Growing exotic mushrooms on a large scale with the residue left from pineapple processing needed a bit of imagination, and Mitchell unfortunately had none.

And lovely, practical, pragmatic Charlie? What would she think of the whole thing?

The Jeep flew along the road, rocking him with the reckless way Charlie took the many corners, bouncing them both over ruts and potholes.

"That's it, just up ahead on the right. There's a wooden sign by the driveway."

He'd feed her first; they'd have a bottle of wine. Then he'd tell her, he promised himself. Dealing with business people left him drained, and trying to deal with Charlie in this mood was even worse than the damned executives.

She was a difficult woman. A tired smile crossed his face. She was everything Ben had never imagined in a woman. That's what captivated him.

She parked, and the moment they walked in through the green shrubbery and he saw the flaming palm-oil torches of the building, designed to look like a Polynesian hut, Ben knew he'd made a mistake in his choice of a restaurant.

They were greeted with loud, welcoming, raucous voices as soon as Ben opened the door. At a large, round central table, a half dozen of his former surfing buddies and their dates were having an uproariously good time. Ben remembered, too late, that word of a new eating establishment would pass through the surfer community like a flash fire and the healthy, always-hungry young people would flock to try it out.

His glance picked out Debbie Lou and her date, a short man wearing a three-piece suit, shirt collar open and filled with ostentatious gold chains. He looked out of place among the more casually dressed surfers. A sick sense of foreboding crept over Ben as several male heads turned their way, zeroing in on Charlie before they accidentally discovered him by her side.

"Ben, old buddy, get your broken bones over here. Where the hell you hanging out these days, anyhow? How's the leg? Hear about Shatsi winning the prelims at Sunset?"

Immediately, waiters were summoned, two more places were set, and greetings and introductions were made.

Charlie and Ben reluctantly joined the party.

Charlie smiled and nodded, feeling alien among this fast-quipping, sophisticated group. The women gave her that quick, assessing once-over that pinpointed how little her dress and accessories were worth. Their eyes took in the frothy mass of unformed hair, the naked face, and flickered to Ben, lingering there before returning momentarily to her. By the quirk of an eyebrow, a tilt to a professionally made-up mouth, they signaled their dismissal.

Not in our league, the message read. *Not one of us.*

Where do you suppose Ben found her?

The men were vastly more interested. Their forthright eyes correctly read the fiery blue of her eyes as passionate, dropped lustfully to the long, bowed upper lip, slid to the firm, unbound breasts enticingly outlined under some kind of clingy stuff and in the blink of an eye knew precisely how her narrow waist surrendered to delicately swelling hips and long, elegant, bare legs. They admired her spun-sugar, tof-fee-bright hair and smiled at her.

There wasn't a single tanned, handsome young male who didn't immediately covet Charlie, Ben surmised accurately.

There wasn't a woman present who wouldn't trade the man she was with for suave, rich Ben Gilmour, either, Charlie guessed shrewdly.

"Hey, you guys, you won't believe this, but Charlie's a carpenter," someone announced.

Debbie's date, who was Murray somebody or other, watched and listened, putting a proprietary arm around Debbie's shoulders, which she shrugged away from to gig-gle and whisper in Ben's ear.

Murray didn't look especially pleased.

Ben wasn't pleased, either. Annoyed and bored, he pointedly involved Murray in the conversation and turned away at the first opportunity to talk with one of the surf-ers.

But Murray interrupted rudely, and Ben realized the man had had too much to drink. His eyes were slightly blood-shot, and his speech sounded aggressive. He leaned over and pawed at Ben's shoulder, demanding his attention.

"I'm a business consultant, from Arizona," he an-nounced importantly, leaning much too close to Ben and fixing him with a bleary stare. "What do you do for a liv-ing if your gal's a carpenter?"

"Nothing concrete at the moment." Ben's response was offhand. He was desperately trying to figure out a way to get out of there fast. The waiter appeared at his elbow, and he was forced into ordering, so they'd have to stay until they finished eating, anyway. He scowled into his water glass.

"What do you mean, nothing? Everybody works, don't they?"

Some demon stirred in Ben at Murray's sneering tone.

"Work?" Ben drawled the word as if it had four differ-ent letters. "Hey, man, I don't work. I'm the last of a dying breed, the great American playboy. Never worked a day in my life."

He expertly swirled the expensive golden liquid the wine steward had just obsequiously poured into his stemmed glass, sipped, rolled it on his tongue and judiciously gave a superior nod.

He'd deliberately spoken loud enough that Charlie couldn't fail to hear, and out of the corner of her eye he caught the disgusted look she shot his way.

It infuriated him that she didn't even realize he was being sarcastic. He forgot he hadn't told her that he was presently working twelve hours a day, harder than he'd ever worked herding sheep or fighting fires.

He was jealous, too. He was well aware of the interest she sparked in the other men at the table, the way their eyes lingered on her.

She was his, damn it, and the least she could do was give him her tacit support in this interchange bombastic Murray had started. And plainly she wasn't about to.

She apparently believed what he was saying because she believed he actually was a playboy.

Suddenly the entire situation escalated for Ben from merely annoying to incendiary, and Murray didn't recognize the danger.

"Well, you're in good company here in old Hav-aw-wee, playboy," he drawled contemptuously. "Far as I can see, this whole place is full of playboys who live off the rest of us." He took a long pull at the amber liquor in his glass. His voice was righteous and condemning, if slightly slurred, when he added, "The natives here are lazy and ignorant, and hardly any of them've ever done a good day's work in their lives."

He mistook the sudden charged silence all around the table for interest in his portentous speech, even raising his voice a shade when he added, "Hell, if it weren't for the tourists and the military, I'll bet these islands would revert right back to naked orgies."

The lovely Hawaiian woman gracefully serving their table suddenly turned her back and walked away. The surfers, all of whom had friends who were Hawaiian, and some of whom had native blood themselves, seemed to freeze into a stony expectancy.

"You know, Murray, honey, I'm part Hawaiian," Debbie said into the silence, and Murray shifted uncomfortably.

"Well, present company excepted, of course," he said heartily.

Charlie sat motionless, stunned by the man's ignorance. She turned to tell Ben she wanted to leave, and to her surprise, Ben was already on his feet.

"The people of Hawaii are among the finest on earth." Ben's quiet, earnest words dropped into the pool of silence. "I'm proud to be classed as one of them. My advice to you is: Go home, haole." His eagle-eyed gaze and steely voice had the attention of half the room.

Then Ben picked up the bottle of wine beside his plate and calmly tipped it over the man's carefully styled hair. The foaming liquid poured out over his suddenly florid face, down his neck with its gold chains, onto his expensive suit and down to his highly shined shoes.

Too stunned to react quickly, Murray sat under the torrent of wine for long seconds while the onlookers hardly breathed.

He staggered up at last, choking and hollering, "Why, you creep, I ought to—"

"Ought to what?" Ben's low voice was satin over steel. "Our hosts in this restaurant are Hawaiian. My guess is they agree with me that you ought to leave." Ben's hand hung casually at his sides, but Charlie could see the way the iron muscles in his upper arms tensed and the careful way he shifted his feet to give him the firmest stance.

She was both thrilled and appalled at the scene, fiercely proud of Ben's dignified words, horrified that he was making them the center of attention of the entire restaurant.

Murray hesitated, taking in Ben's expressionless features, the width of his powerful shoulders. Then the man snatched up a linen napkin, mopped at his hair and clothing and ordered, "C'mon, Debbie. This guy's a goddam lunatic. Let's get out of here."

But Debbie shook her head and stayed exactly where she was until Murray finally shoved his way rudely among the tables and disappeared out the door. Then she burst into noisy tears and ran into the ladies' room. Ben tossed a handful of money on the table and took Charlie's elbow.

"Sorry to wreck the party. See you guys around," he said tersely, and steered Charlie out of the restaurant.

The night was balmy, the sound of the ocean peacefully part of the background, the torches flaming into the darkness.

Charlie's heart was thundering when she finally found the keys. Ben took them from her and started the Jeep with a roar.

Adrenaline was pumping through his veins. What the hell had happened to him in there? He'd met plenty of Murrays in his life, and he knew perfectly well how to defuse them without resorting to something like that.

But a feeling of grim satisfaction lodged in his gut. The scene had drained some of the tension out of Ben, relieved some of the helpless frustration he experienced around people whose minds were locked into narrow attitudes.

Charlie. He turned to study her, remembering his sense of betrayal at her acceptance of his joking words in the restaurant. And he realized, also, why he hadn't yet told her of the change his life had taken.

The main reason, naturally, was ego. Charlie would immediately assume he'd recognized the error of his ways, all because of her. He knew her well and had no illusions about her modesty. She'd be insufferably self-righteous about his salvation, and he'd feel like drowning her in the surf. But he could handle that.

The real problem was much more complex. He wanted, he needed, this woman to accept him for exactly what he was, what he had been, whatever he would become.

With no criticism, no barbed remarks, no scathing looks. He wanted her to like—love?—him. He handled the word gingerly, nervous of it. He just wanted her to accept him the way he was.

Ben Gilmour, my man, no changing necessary.

He didn't want to examine why this should be important to him. It simply was.

"That was quite a display, Ben."

Apprehension flooded him at her tone of voice. He'd never realized Charlie could actually sound prim, as she did now.

"You realize you brought the whole thing on yourself, bragging about not working, while he obviously saw himself as a high achiever. He was a revolting character, but all the same, you goaded him."

Goaded him? Ben felt like baying at the moon in utter frustration. He should have decked the sucker instead for the way he'd oggled Charlie, if nothing else.

"Your aimless life-style isn't exactly something to brag about," she added judiciously, thinking of the way those women had looked at him.

Avaricious, lusting, useless female ornaments. If he hadn't poured wine on that idiot, Charlie might have ended up punching one of those polished females right in the chops before the night was over.

But she sure wasn't going to tell Ben that. He'd been smiling back at them, preening himself and enjoying the attention.

"What difference should it make to anybody what I choose to do with my time? It's my life, and I can use it however I want." He sounded angry, and she was perversely pleased.

The last straw had been overhearing that supercilious remark he'd made about working. Over the past weeks, he'd kept on and on at her about her "antiquated work ethics," her "type A compulsive personality," her refusal to put pleasure ahead of the job.

Then, when he finally realized she meant it and wasn't going to change, he'd simply turned elsewhere for entertainment.

And whether Charlie admitted it or not, his assertion stung. Somewhere inside she'd never really believed him to be that shallow.

"You're absolutely right, Ben. You're perfectly free to waste your life in any fashion you choose." She sounded sarcastic, and she didn't care. "I'm certain any of those women back there would be delighted to help you waste it." Anger and outrage, fueled by the feeling she'd had in the restaurant of being an outsider and a misfit among his friends, blossomed the more she dwelled on his recent behavior.

He was furious now as they sped down the road. "Bossing a construction crew doesn't qualify you to make suggestions about my life, Charlie."

Suddenly she was irrationally convinced that he was using her as a pastime for his evenings, while some real love interest occupied his days. That had to be it. Why else would Ben wander back to the Reef, exhausted and preoccupied, later and later each evening?

He was using her because she was convenient. Damn it all, nobody used Charlie Cossini. After all, she'd decided like a mature woman on beginning this affair; she'd drawn up the rules and guidelines. It was her own problem that she'd somehow allowed herself to fall in love along the way, and being around Ben, waiting for him each evening, finding herself in situations like the one they'd just left, took away the feeling of control Charlie needed in her life.

The thought was like bile in her throat, but she forced herself to face it. Perhaps the time had come for her to end this. It was ahead of the schedule she'd planned, but there'd been overruns in areas she hadn't foreseen. She swallowed several times to get rid of the annoying lump in her throat and made up her mind.

"Listen, Ben," she burst out, and he brought the Jeep to a crashing halt on a pull-off area of the highway and turned off the motor. "I think we should get some things straight here. The differences in the way we think aren't going to disappear, and both of us agreed this was a casual affair we're having, so why are we fighting?''

Ben tried to remember when he'd agreed to a casual affair. This didn't feel very casual to him anymore. He started to say so, but she interrupted.

"It's been fun, but I think it's time we stopped fooling ourselves that we have much in common, beyond, besides..." Her voice was starting to tremble, and she cleared her throat angrily. She couldn't let herself start to cry. "Besides fun," she ended with a gulp.

"Fun? Is that what this has been for you, just fun?" Ben was aghast at her summation of their relationship. "Charlie, how can you sit there—"

Ben quite abruptly heard his own words, his aggrieved, injured tone of voice, and knew, in a painful moment of insight, that he'd heard them in one form or another many times over the years. They were an echo of all the futile arguments women had used on him when he made a version of the speech Charlie had just concluded.

She'd switched roles on him, as he might have expected Charlie would. She was giving him the brush-off he'd perfected. And he, Benjamin Valentine Gilmour, was all but begging a woman—this damnable, infuriating woman, at that—not to leave him out in left field alone.

Where's your pride, Gilmour? The lady's trying to bow out gracefully. But a bitter anguish started in him, and his voice was grim when he quietly asked, "Is that what you want, Charlie? You want out of this relationship we have?"

Relationship. How mature and sophisticated a word to describe a recurring explosion, comparable to the eruption of one of Hawaii's volcanoes. She forced herself not to throw her arms around him and tell the truth about how she felt and what she wanted.

Common sense stopped her. What would it result in except this same ending, several weeks or months postponed, more painful still for being delayed?

Get real. Do it now, Charlie. Time's wasting. Your heart's being sawed in half, and the sawdust is making your eyes water.

"Yes," she lied. "Yes, that's what I want."

Already he'd retreated far from her, although he still sat rigidly upright beside her in the Jeep.

"I'll be away next week, anyhow," he said formally. The effort nearly choked him. "We'll talk it over after I get back, see how you feel then. I'm leaving early tomorrow, so maybe we should get back home now. I need to pack a few things. Unless you're hungry? We didn't get much to eat."

Time. He needed time with her, and he'd figure out what to do.

The last thing he'd planned to do tonight was pack. He'd planned to take her in his arms, kiss her senseless, love her again and again. He'd planned to share his dreams with her. Why was she doing this to him? To them?

Utter desolation swept over her at the offhand way he mentioned a trip. Where could he be going on such short notice? Was he going to the hideaway he'd begged her to visit with him? He must be. If it were another kind of trip, surely he'd have mentioned it casually before now.

That was it. He'd planned a—what did they call it? A liaison.

A new anger swept her along as he started the motor and headed inexorably toward Reveille Reef.

"I don't think anything else needs to be said. And no, thank you. I'm not at all hungry."

How long before you died from not eating?

How long before you died from a broken heart?

Chapter Ten

Ben was in Mitchell's glass-walled office high above Seattle's Pioneer Square at nine-fifteen on Monday morning. By nine forty-five, Mitchell had turned down Ben's request for financial backing politely, logically and reasonably.

"Using pineapple residue to grow mushrooms could turn out to be a great secondary industry in Hawaii," he said, leaning back in his expensive swivel chair and peering nearsightedly out the smoky glass wall, fingers pressed against one another to form a tower in front of his well-shaped nose. "I have no doubt that it would be beneficial to the local economy, as you suggest. It's innovative and an interesting idea. But it's rather farfetched as a viable business investment. As chairman of the board, I have a responsibility to our investors; you understand that. This, er, brainstorm of yours is not something I think Gilmour Developments should get involved with at the present time."

Ben soundly cursed the day his father had turned control over to this pompous accountant who also happened to be his brother. Dad was an adventurer in his way. He'd at least give Ben a fair hearing. Mitchell had listened with a condescending half smile and asked exactly one question.

"What do you plan to call this endeavor, Ben?"

"The Fungus Factory." The name had just the right touch of impertinence to it. It had a nice T-shirt sort of ring. No three-piece suits for the executives at a business with that name. Mushrooms, after all, were an unpretentious breed.

"Yes, well, I'm sure that's appropriate," Mitchell sniffed.

A short, wiry man bustled in with a silver carafe of hot coffee, poured two cups and left again. Mitchell's secretary. Ben guessed having a woman in that role would be too much of a distraction. Mitchell would likely have to start noticing a difference between the sexes, and who knew where that would lead?

How could this dry, serious, endlessly boring man be his brother? Ben studied Mitchell curiously while the coffee ritual proceeded, wondering for the millionth time if the tall, spare man behind the desk ever became excited about anything except stock market quotations and the price of Gilmour shares.

He sure as hell wasn't excited about Ben's briefcase filled with tests proving the validity of the pineapple-mushroom research, the additional reports from the botanists at Hawaii University whom Ben had asked to confirm his test results or the professional cost-return projections Ben had sweated over. He'd barely glanced at the signed confirmations from numerous island restaurateurs guaranteeing they would buy both exotic and ordinary mushrooms—consumed voraciously by a large Oriental population—from Ben.

Ben shivered, even in the cocoonlike warmth of this luxurious office. November in Seattle wasn't anything like November in Hawaii, and he had an overwhelming desire to get this over with and return home. Patiently, he tried again, knowing as he did so that Mitchell wouldn't change his mind.

He silently blessed Aunt Stella for coming up with plan B.

After a fruitless half hour, Ben rose and gathered his papers into the battered briefcase. Mitchell grew expansive. "Well, little brother, it's great to see you even if we can't do business this time. It's just too risky, this little scheme of yours, and the market's soft, as I'm sure you realize. How about lunch, say, one o'clock today? We can catch up on each other then. Unfortunately, I've got a meeting in ten minutes, so—" Mitchell spread his hands in helpless acceptance of the sacrifices that being chairman of the board of Gilmour Developments involved.

"So do I, unfortunately." Ben grinned ingenuously at his brother. "I just happen to be able to attend the monthly shareholder's meeting for the first time in years. Oh, and Aunt Stella's coming, too. It'll be like a family reunion, all of us together like that."

Mitchell instantly went from complacent to suspicious. "That's absurd. Why, Stella never attends these meetings, at least not since the time she got it in her head to waste company money on that project in Hawaii you're supposed to be supervising."

"Well, she's coming today. With me." Ben closed the thick oak door behind him with a delicious feeling of expectancy.

Stella was still a major shareholder. Between the combined weight of her shares, Ben's and his mother's, Mitchell didn't stand a chance. Ben fingered the telegram he'd received from their mother the night before giving him full authority to vote her shares in favor of the project. Stella had planned her campaign well.

Eighty minutes later, the Fungus Factory was alive and well, funded by Gilmour money over Mitchell's protests. Mitchell was not a good loser. He'd stiffly declined Ben's offer to join them for a victory lunch.

Stella, on the other hand, was so excited she seemed to shoot sparks into the air around her. She was a large lady, not stout but big-boned and wide-shouldered, made up of interesting angles and planes, with green eyes much like Ben's own and an outrageous grin that made her look like an overgrown leprechaun.

She settled herself in the chair Ben held for her in one of the trendy small restaurants along the waterfront, giving their flustered young waiter a flirtatious wink. She ordered a huge luncheon, which Ben figured would probably have given any other seventy-four-year-old lady fatal indigestion, accepted the offer of a drink before eating and ordered a tall white-rum-and-Coke. Sipping it with relish, she turned shrewd eyes on Ben, waved away his thanks for her help and demanded, "Now, young man, I want all the details about this renovation of mine you're handling. And don't give me those damned cost overruns Mitchell bores me with. I want to know the real guts of the thing. Talk, boy, talk."

Ben did. He studiously avoided mentioning Charlie for all of five minutes, but Aunt Stella knew a diversionary tactic when she encountered it.

"And who's Charlie?" she demanded the moment he took a breath.

Ben felt the strange, annoyingly familiar sense of unrest, deep loneliness and frustration wash over him that came every time he thought of Charlie.

"She's the boss of Cossini Construction. She's the most impossible, stubborn, single-minded woman I've ever come across in my life, and I should charge you hazard money for making me deal with her."

Stella took another good slug of her drink, and an interested gleam appeared in her eye.

"How old is this Charlie?"

"Twenty-six. She's—" Ben gulped his beer with desperate haste, ordered another and then proceeded to fill the ten minutes before lunch arrived, and the half hour after, with a full, detailed account, heavily censored in places, of his maddeningly chaotic dealings with Charlie Cossini. He inadvertently painted a vivid portrait of days at the Reef complete with Lani and Pogey and their mysterious night walker scattered amid the atrocities he'd suffered at Charlie's callused hands.

Stella ate her way efficiently through deep-fried zucchini strips, marinated prawns and a large order of linguini, until it finally dawned on Ben that he'd talked his way right through lunch. "Stella, I'm sorry for going on like that."

"Nonsense. Aunts are designed for listening. This crowd sounds like just my kind of people, too. I remember Hawaii, and Reveille Reef, vividly." She stared at her cheesecake for a second, and then, with a resigned sigh, she pushed it away and reached for her coffee cup.

"Your Lani is right, you know. The Reef is haunted."

Ben looked skeptically across at his aunt, and she nodded at him, her eyes filled with memories.

"I know you young people get tired of stories about the war years, but they were a crucial time in the lives of people my age. The war altered our perceptions of the world and of ourselves as well as what we believed in." She sipped her coffee again, adding more cream before she went on.

"Reveille Reef is haunted because it was a haven for us in the midst of terrible chaos. The army sent officers there for a rest before returning them to duty in the Pacific. I was an army nurse, you remember, Ben, assigned to troop ships carrying the wounded. Even now, as an old lady, I remember vividly the time I spent at the Reef, the softness of the air in the mornings, the birds singing, the everlasting surf pounding in and lulling me to sleep. The utter simplicity of sun and air and sand."

Stella set her cup down and reached across to place a strong hand on Ben's fingers, resting on the snowy tabletop.

"And the wonder of love. The Reef is haunted by memories, Ben. It was a magic place, a place where lovers stole precious days from bedlam."

"Lovers?" Ben lifted an eyebrow at his aunt. She'd never married.

Stella snorted. "Lovers, of course, lovers. Why does every generation believe they've invented the word? I spent stolen days with my lover at the Reef, and I've always been glad of that. He was killed—toward the end of the war."

Ben looked at his aunt, seeing her differently than he had before, seeing the fine young woman she must have been. Her eyes were filmed with tears, and love for her welled inside him.

"Stell, I'm—"

She held up a palm commandingly. "Don't you dare tell me you're sorry for me. I've had other lovers in my life, more than enough of them, and now I adore being old. It gives me license for eccentricity, you understand." She winked roguishly at Ben, and he grinned. "It's your turn now," she added stoutly, and he stopped grinning and shook his head in protest, but Stella paid no attention.

"There's always one other person who's exactly right for you. One person who spoils you for any that might come afterward. There's one golden time in your life when you find the other half of your soul. It happened to me at Reveille Reef." She was serious now, more serious than Ben had ever seen her. "I have a hunch it's happened to you, as well, young man. Don't be too blind to recognize it. I want to come and meet your Charlie when the mess of construction is all cleared away. I don't do messes anymore."

It took a moment for Stella's casual pronouncement to sink in. When it did, Ben shook his head harder in emphatic denial, attempting a laugh.

"Hey, Stell, you've got it all wrong. I just finished telling you that Charlie is one woman I don't need complicating my life."

Stella summoned the waiter with an imperious wave and ordered a small glass of blackberry liqueur, savoring its sweetness sip by tiny sip.

"I've always thought you were the smartest of my nephews, Ben. Don't disappoint me at this late date."

"YOU," LANI PRONOUNCED, pointing an accusatory forefinger at Charlie, "are making me good and mad. You need a dose of something, so don't stand there arguing with me. Drink it. All you've done all week is tell me you're not hungry and then go and run like a crazy thing up and down that beach." She fixed a worried look on Charlie. "You don't even holler at everybody the way you usually do," she accused, handing the tall glass of dark liquid firmly back to Charlie and watching, arms akimbo, as Charlie gulped it down and gagged.

"My gosh, Lani, what was in that stuff? It's lethal." Her windpipe burned as the concoction descended slowly to her stomach.

"It's a folk remedy," Lani said complacently, rescuing the glass from Charlie's numb fingers. "It's good for constipation or headache or aching limbs or upset stomach."

What about a broken heart? Charlie seriously considered the question but decided not to ask.

She'd known that first, awful night after Ben brought her home that her decision to end what was between them would be hard. But hard was one thing. Hard was difficult; hard was bearable. This was something else again.

What she'd anticipated had no relationship whatsoever to this raw agony that assailed her when she awoke early each morning, the pain that gnawed at her every moment of every day.

She missed Ben with a loneliness she'd never known before, as if part of her body were missing. More than ever she recognized how deeply she loved him, and now she desperately wished she'd at least told him so.

What did it matter whether he responded? Charlie's basic sense of honesty insisted now that it had been deceitful of her not to openly tell Ben how she felt and let him take it from there.

Neither of them had spoken of love. Like wary gladiators in some curious contest, they'd whirled through passion and conversation, laughter and argument, sharing the most intimate of acts and avoiding emotional honesty. They'd shared their bodies, and much of their thoughts, with each other. They'd lived here at the Reef close together, eating at the same table, yet withholding an essential part of themselves.

Lani's potion was giving her a stomachache, Charlie decided. Besides that, it was actually hotter than usual this afternoon. The air was heavy, although the usual blue sky had disappeared behind thick gray clouds.

Listlessly, she undid her tool apron and called to the other women, "C'mon, you guys. Let's go for a swim while it's so hot. We can always work later, when it cools off."

Eliza's flushed, sweaty face poked around the corner of the men's barracks, which was now under development.

"You mean that? Boy, Charlie, I used to figure you were related to Simon Legree, but lately you've changed a lot. I'd love a swim, and I'll bet Carol would, too."

At that moment, Happy, Carol's puppy, trotted out the door of the cabin with a mangled object in its jaws, which used to be Carol's best moccasin.

"Happy, you bad dog," Carol chided, and the other two women groaned at her indulgent tone. The truth was, all the women doted on the tiny animal, although Carol was the worst. She was like a mother with a child who can do no wrong. Happy cavorted through the days, and Carol patiently cleaned up after him, rescuing the array of objects he collected and chewed, and loved him to distraction. The interesting thing was that she'd shyly started to respond to Kimo, too. It was as if loving the mischievous little dog had unlocked some barrier within Carol.

Was there a similar barrier within her, Charlie wondered, keeping her from freely expressing how she felt? Surely adults should be able to communicate better than she'd managed with Ben.

And where, exactly, was Ben? The few days he'd said he'd be away had now stretched to a full week and a day. Had he found a new pastime to occupy him, a new diversion with which to fill his days? Charlie was beginning to wonder if Ben would return to the Reef at all.

What if he didn't come back? And what if he did? Had anything really changed?

The women hurried into their suits and made their way down to the beach, laughing at Happy. He raced ahead of them and threw himself heedlessly into the water, yapping excitedly all the while.

Charlie waded into the shallows. A medium-size wave broke over her legs, and immediately following it, a much larger one. The surf was really up, as Pogey would say. Out beyond the reef monstrous hills of green rose, crested and smashed down on the protective rocks, sending sizable repercussions into the protected bay. Charlie ducked under the surface, wet herself thoroughly and gave up the idea of swimming.

She spread a towel on the cement breakwater that separated the sandy beach from the grassy beginning of the resort's lawn and sat down, propping her head over to rest it on her knees and closing her eyes.

She felt tired, and a swim would have been revitalizing, but she refused to swim if there were waves of any size, preferring to wait until the lagoon was smooth as a millpond.

Eliza took a spot to Charlie's right.

"You asleep?" she inquired.

"Nope."

Charlie's lack of enthusiasm for conversation didn't deter Eliza.

"Kimo taught Carol how to dive into the waves and use her body to ride along the crest of them. Look, she's getting good at it."

Charlie raised her head and squinted out to where Carol was playing in the frothy turbulence inside the lagoon. Happy sat on the sand and yapped plaintively, but for the moment Carol ignored him as she practiced.

"You should get Ben to teach you. Pogey's offered to start me on a surfboard, but I don't feel ready yet."

Charlie wished Eliza wouldn't talk about Ben. Surely she realized Charlie didn't begin to share Ben's passion for surfing, his enthusiasm for challenging the ocean. It was just one more minor difference between them to add to the master list she'd compiled and reviewed countless times already this week.

Eliza didn't seem to notice or mind Charlie's silence, however.

"Maybe you and I could give it a try together when Ben gets back. Say, Charlie, where the heck is Ben, anyhow? Is it some big secret or something? You don't talk about it, and Pogey either doesn't know or isn't telling."

"Ben Gilmour's whereabouts are of no interest whatsoever to me," Charlie stated haughtily. "I have no idea where he is, and I don't care." It would have sounded fine if her voice hadn't quavered that way.

Eliza pursed her lips and whistled. "Wow, sounds like you two had a snorter of a fight."

Charlie gave up. Once Eliza pried this much out of her, there would be no peace until the redhead had satisfied her boundless curiosity.

"We didn't have a fight, Liza. Well, not much of a one. We mutually decided to end the relationship. We're...we're not compatible."

"Charlie, stop talking like a divorce lawyer for a second and explain this to me in plain English," Eliza demanded. "Not compatible? What's with not compatible all of a sudden? C'mon, Charlie. All those nights you two spent together and now you decide you're not compatible?"

Charlie was in danger of losing what little patience she had left.

"Damn it, Liza. The nights weren't the problem. They were the reason I got myself into this mess in the first place. It's the way Ben is that's the problem."

"So how is he? Explain."

Why hadn't Eliza taken up criminal law? Anybody would confess anything after an hour around her just to get her to shut up and lay off.

Less than patiently, Charlie's list of Ben's failings were enumerated for Eliza, and Charlie listed them on her fingers.

He was irresponsible. One long, scratched forefinger settled in Charlie's callused, narrow palm.

He was a self-styled playboy. The second finger, with the hangnail, joined the first.

He had no goal except keeping himself entertained and therefore no ambitions for his life. The third, bare, ring finger had a scraped knuckle.

He didn't know, or want to know, one end of a saw from another. Her fourth finger had a blood blister on the tip from a bout with a hammer.

He was fickle and probably promiscuous. She used her thumb to illustrate this damning point. It was in reasonable shape, considering.

He was dishonest about being promiscuous. Charlie started on her other hand.

Charlie wasn't jealous, but she couldn't stand dishonest, promiscuous people. That counted for two more fingers at least, and she felt a surge of almost uncontrollable rage at the idea that he would pull such stunts on her.

The final, irrevocable flaw was that Ben was rich. She gave up hopelessly on numbering with her hands, because in Charlie's opinion that overwhelming catastrophe probably was the root cause of all the other problems. It was a full ten-finger disaster, for sure.

Apart from gesticulating, she reviewed the list in a reasonably calm, mature fashion for Eliza, a convincing printout of all the reasons to forget Ben had ever been a part of her life.

"Y'know, you and Carol are driving me nuts. I just get one of you sorted out and the other one falls apart. Here I'm feeling all smug because I caught Carol kissing Kimo the other night—I mean, really kissing him—and I'm all elated because maybe her romance is getting off the ground, and bang. I turn around and find out you're having some kind of mid-life crisis and breaking up with Ben, for heaven's sake. And for nothing," she added plaintively, throwing herself backward onto the grass in exasperation. "I've got a good mind to tell Lani the whole story and see what she thinks."

Charlie grabbed Eliza's arm in a viselike grip. "Don't you just dare. If you breathe a word of this to her, so help me, Liza, I'll hint to her that you have a mad passion for that cousin of hers she keeps trotting out, the one with the glasses who breathes heavy," Charlie threatened, shaken out of her lethargy. Auntie Lani's folk remedies were one thing. Auntie Lani on the path of a broken romance would be something nobody in his right mind would get involved with.

Eliza nodded thoughtfully. "You're right. She'd probably get Kimo to lock you both up in the local jail, in one cell, until you came to your senses." Eliza rubbed the marks Charlie had left on her arm. "Maybe that's not such a bad idea."

Despite the less rigorous schedule Charlie demanded of them, the carpenters had finished the cabins that week, on late Thursday afternoon.

Charlie walked halfway down the driveway, turned and took stock of the resort, comparing it to what it had been when she first saw it, months before, from this very spot.

One by one, Eliza, Carol, Pogey and Auntie Lani joined her, and as a group they silently admired their handiwork.

Each of the outlying buildings was covered in golden cedar siding, roofed with darker cedar shakes. The roofs extended beyond the walls, creating a protective overhang for the large screened windows that allowed a view in nearly every direction from each cabin. Three wide cedar steps led invitingly up to each new front door.

The effect was earthy and inviting as well as charmingly private. The multitude of trees and burgeoning foliage that isolated the buildings acted as a backdrop for the natural materials Charlie had used. The buildings, which had resembled nothing so much as a sad row of discarded, windowless boxcars, were now attractive living spaces sure to please anyone fortunate enough to rent them. Lani's cookshack had become a roofed, open-air enclosure equipped with a brick barbecue, a modern range and an immense refrigerator as well as stainless-steel sinks and cupboards. The sides could be easily enclosed with sliding panels if necessary, and screens kept the bugs out.

Every glass surface sparkled in the sunshine, mostly because Lani had insisted on washing all the windows till they gleamed. There was no sign of construction clutter—Pogey had cheerfully gathered up all the waste materials and carted them to the nearby dumpster.

The carpenters were now ready to start work immediately on the main structure. It looked like a poor relative compared to the cabins.

Despite herself, Charlie longed to have Ben by her side at this moment to share the overwhelming sense of accomplishment and pride she knew the others shared. Reveille Reef at last looked as if someone loved it.

"Doesn't the word *reveille* mean awaken?" Pogey, hands on hips, surveyed the pleasant scene, obviously proud of his part in its restoration.

Lani nodded emphatically. "Looks just like the whole place has come awake after a long sleep," she commented, and the words brought tears to Charlie's eyes. So much more than just the buildings had come awake here.

The women moved into the lovely new cabins that evening. Carol and Eliza chose to share one, and Charlie decided she preferred to have one to herself.

She wasn't good company these days, reverting as she did to long periods of introspective silence. Carol and Eliza seemed to understand.

Being the first to inhabit the cabins they'd created was an added pleasure for the carpenters.

That night Charlie lay in the strange bed, breathing in the smell of cedar and the indefinable odor of spanking newness the room exuded. The renovations made her realize once again how much pleasure her work gave back to her, and she wanted to share the thought with Ben. He'd understand.

She thought longingly of Ben, wishing things might have been different for them, wondering when she'd see him again; a kind of resignation came over her, and she reached an understanding.

It had been wrong of her to want Ben to change, she now realized. She'd fallen in love with him exactly the way he was. She should have been smart enough to enjoy and respect his individuality.

If she had another chance with him, she'd tell him so.

She fell asleep repeating a phrase her father had often used when everything seemed to have gone wrong.

"Tomorrow's a new day," Gennaro would state. "Every tomorrow we get another chance."

Charlie awoke to fog, thick and cottony, seeming to press against the sliding glass of the patio door in the bedroom. And like an eerie thread through the gray mist came the sound of the bugle and the notes of reveille. Here and there, the musician missed a note or two, as if his attention were not entirely on his playing. But then the melody would recover, the high, clear tones hauntingly poignant and commanding.

When the melody ended, he repeated the ending twice over, as if reluctant to let it float away.

Without stopping to cover her nightshirt with a robe, Charlie thrust her feet into her worn blue Adidases and raced out the door of her cabin, down toward the ocean.

Seconds later, she stood on the beach, straining to pinpoint the direction of the eerie music through the claustrophobic thickness of the morning fog, not understanding why it was imperative to locate the bugler but knowing that it was and that he was near.

It was barely dawn, she judged. The fog was so thick she couldn't see the reef, or even the resort, from where she stood. Blindly, she closed her eyes and concentrated on the notes, which soared and floated once again, and then she took off at a heedless trot into the mists, heading down the beach to where the sound seemed a shade louder.

Panting, she suddenly burst into an area where the fog seemed to create an open room in its midst. It was the exact place where she and Ben had once made love, a depression containing a smooth mass of lava rock and fine sand. Charlie stopped running abruptly, and her heart nearly leaped out of her chest, because near the rock stood three figures, and one of them held a battered bugle cradled in his arms.

Flanked by thin priests from the Shinto mission, he was a tall, gaunt man in army fatigues. His eyes were blue, but their shape was Japanese. He was taller than the other two, and he didn't wear their long gray robes. He had on some sort of army surplus gear over his skeletal frame, a khaki green shirt and trousers, with well-polished boots on his feet.

He was looking straight at Charlie, his face expressionless.

She was conscious suddenly of her wildly tossed, uncombed hair, her thigh-length nightshirt and the ridiculous contrast of running shoes on her feet.

"Good, er, good morning," she stammered inanely, and the priests bowed their heads in formal greeting, but no one said a word. The tall man stood immobile, and Charlie had the eerie feeling he wasn't really seeing her, after all, with his unblinking blue gaze.

His look went through and beyond her, seeming to penetrate the fog.

Charlie stared at the trio, and she suddenly felt a complete fool. What had she thought she'd say once she found her bugler, anyway? Thank you? I've enjoyed your music?

Feeling like an idiot, horribly aware of her state of undress, she took two slow steps backward and found herself enveloped again in fog as if the clear space where she'd been two seconds before had disappeared. The trio had been engulfed in the mist as if they'd never existed.

Frowning into the haze, Charlie hesitantly walked ahead again, and as her feet went down the incline, the hollow room in the mist appeared as if by magic. But now it was entirely empty, and although she listened carefully, Charlie couldn't hear even the men's footsteps moving away.

Plunging into the wall of mist, arms pumping up and down in time with her thundering pulse, she raced as fast as she could back to Reveille Reef, not stopping until she was safely inside her silent cabin with the door firmly slammed behind her.

Sinking into a chair, panting, she tried to laugh at herself. First she'd spent weeks trying to prove there was a bugler. Then, when she found him, she ran like a maniac without even asking his name.

Good going, you fruitcake, she chided herself. *Who's going to believe you when you tell them a tale like this?*

She swallowed hard.

Who was there to tell? It was Ben she'd argued with about the bugler. They had a bet on it, she remembered.

If the sound had proved to be a recording, Charlie owed Ben. Slow tears welled into her eyes and dripped down the tip of her nose unheeded. The forfeit for the bet was naughty and personal and delightful to pay, whichever one of them lost the wager.

But both of them had lost long before Charlie learned the truth.

They'd lost each other.

Chapter Eleven

The fog finally cleared by midmorning that day, but then it began to rain, a drizzle at first, soon becoming a steady, soaking downpour that drenched the carpenters and left them shivering.

"Good thing we didn't strip the roof off first thing," Carol commented as they struggled to get the rotten old asphalt siding off the exterior walls of the house. Charlie stripped her gloves off and tossed them away in frustration. She couldn't get used to wearing gloves for every job. Now there was no one to nag her about her hands, anyway.

Grasping a jagged piece of the ugly green stuff, she gave a mighty jerk and it came free, bringing with it a shower of dirt and small nails that rained down on her already wet head.

"I hate tearing things apart," she spat out, rubbing her scalp to rid it of the debris. "It's the worst thing about being in this job, having to do this dirty work." She thought a moment, then added, "Besides the wear and tear on your body. It's heavy, hard work for women."

Carol stoically grasped another chunk of the siding.

"Y'know, I've never heard you complain before. You used to drive me nuts by being always positive, never admitting you disliked any part of our work. If there was a dirty job like this to do and I hated it, I'd never dare tell you, because you'd just say something pious like 'A job's a job. We're getting paid for working, not complaining.'" She wrenched another strip loose and added warmly, "You're lots easier to work with now."

There it was again, Charlie reflected. Eliza had said something similar more than once this past week. The remarks forced Charlie to think about the change in her attitude since coming to the Reef.

Had she really been as authoritarian and priggish as she suspected? The irony of the entire thing was that the crew actually worked harder and accomplished more without her steady admonitions.

The telephone was ringing, and Eliza ran to answer.

"For you, Charlie," she shouted, and Charlie went into the nearest cabin to answer, adrenaline pumping as she hoped and feared it might be Ben.

It wasn't. It was her oldest sister, Gisella, and after an instant of plummeting disappointment, Charlie felt a rush of warmth and homesickness for her chaotic, loving family. She had to grin, though, at the course of the conversation. It was standard for every call they made.

"Charlie? Hi, honey, it's me Gisella. Yeah, it's good to hear you, too. The kids and Tony are fine, eating me out of house and home as usual. What time is it there, anyway?"

They sorted out the time difference for several sentences.

"What's the weather like? It's freezing here today; bet it's hot there" was the next gambit. They sorted that out, too.

"How's Papa?" Charlie asked anxiously. Her family didn't usually waste money on phone calls when one could write letters instead. Gisella's lilting voice was filled with excitement when she said, "Papa's fine—more than fine, actually. That's why I called." Charlie drew the receiver sharply away from her ear and grimaced as Gisella suddenly bellowed, "Don't you guys dare touch that cake; it's for the bake sale at the school." Then, now softly she said, "Charlie, you there?"

"Yes, I'm here. What about Papa?"

"Yeah, well, you remember Victor Torterelli, who used to own that bakery on State Street?"

Charlie was mystified. What did Victor Torterelli have to do with Papa?

"Yeah. No. Heck, I don't know. Gisella, would you please just tell me what's going on, without the subtitles?"

Gisella chuckled. "You never had any patience. Remember how you always poked a little hole in every single present under the tree 'cause you couldn't stand to wait for Christmas morning? I got so mad at you, having to know what was in my presents as well as your own."

Charlie screwed her eyes shut and warned, "Gisella, so help me—" And her sister giggled complacently and continued.

"Well, Victor died a couple of years back, and a month ago or more, Papa hired Rosalie Torterelli, Victor's widow. Yeah, well, she's the nicest person, plump and cheery and sort of bossy, nice bossy, you know what I mean?"

Charlie thought of Auntie Lani and nodded and grinned. Boy, did she know about nice bossy, all right. Gisella didn't wait for an answer, however.

"She sort of took control of Papa—well, as much as anybody ever could. You know Papa; he's as stubborn as you are. Anyhow, she's put money into the business with him, become his partner. You've never seen such a change in your life. She got Papa to open up the front of the store, put a sort of lunch counter there so people walking past can buy hot coffee and stuff. Then she sold off all those dusty old cans he had lined up on the shelves, got rid of all that moldy old linoleum, and she got him to put down a nice rug she had and put tables inside and added a big espresso machine. She makes submarines—yeah, sandwiches, big, long ones—homemade soups and muffins and cookies, and for the first time the place is making money."

Gisella paused for dramatic effect, and Charlie couldn't find anything to say. She tried to visualize the changes, and Gisella went on. "And you know what? Papa loves it. He's done all the carpentry work, and he actually enjoys feeding people, even emphasizes his accent." The sisters giggled. Papa could sound as if he just got off the boat.

"They're talking about expanding, maybe getting a pub license. I can't get over the change in him, Charlie." Gisella's voice was excited. "You know what? I think he's going to marry Rosalie eventually; best thing he could do. And he told me last night that if I was writing you, to tell you he doesn't need any more money for the loan, either. He was really proud of that. He sold the house. Did I tell you that? And he's paying off the whole thing with the proceeds." Gisella stopped again for breath, and Charlie silently shook her head, speechless. She felt overloaded with surprises, as if she couldn't react properly without time to consider them.

Gisella was off again. "Don't let on I called, Charlie, because I know he wants to tell you himself, but I had to phone and tell you. Isn't it wonderful?"

Gisella's voice softened wistfully.

"After all those years with Mama the way she was, all of us unhappy because of her, wouldn't it be a miracle if Papa found somebody to love him for a change? Somebody to get old with."

Ten minutes later, minutes filled with news about Rosa's morning sickness, Gisella's job as a meter maid, which she loved, Tony's success as a student of computer programming and what the kids all wanted for Christmas, Gisella suddenly said, "Oh, yeah, Sis, what's with this Ben Gilmour guy Dad's so keen on? He sounds first-class; it's about time you settled down and got married."

"Married? Gisella, you ought to write romances; your imagination is running away with you. How did Dad come to mention Ben, anyway?"

Puzzled, dazed, Charlie tried to remember exactly what she'd written about Ben to her father. She'd never hinted at anything, had she? She frowned, and the familiar ache returned to her midsection as she said casually, "Don't start this matchmaking stuff on me again, Gisella. The guy's my boss; that's as far as it goes."

Fortunately, Charlie's brother-in-law, Tony, grabbed the phone right then, teasingly holding Gisella off and asking about the carpenters' progress on the job. Gisella finally retrieved the phone long enough to say goodbye, and Charlie put the receiver down slowly.

She felt disoriented, as if all the constants in her life had suddenly shifted.

Papa had sold the house, and she hadn't even known.

She'd worried about her father for so long, felt weighed down by debts, ached inside for the seeming futility of his life. She'd even worried about coming here, wondered how Gennaro would fare without her for these months. And now it seemed a bossy woman called Rosalie had come along and filled the empty spots in her father's life.

Rosalie. Charlie had to grin at the name. It conjured up an Italian woman of a certain type—plump, smiling, generous and, yes, bossy.

Would Gennaro marry her eventually, as Gisella thought?

The idea brought the strangest series of reactions. After the first shock, Charlie found herself hoping fervently that it would work out that way. Her father deserved someone on whom to lavish the warmth of his loving nature, a woman who loved him in return.

Where was Papa living now? Gisella hadn't said. Where would all Charlie's belongings, the things from her room, be? Stored somewhere, most likely. A peculiar sense of rootlessness took hold of her, and it wasn't totally unpleasant.

Then the full import of what Gisella had said sank in. If Gennaro had paid off the bank loan, it would leave Charlie free to do whatever she chose to with both her time and the rest of the money she would realize from this job, a considerably large amount.

Money of her own, money not earmarked long in advance for bills, loans and mortgages.

It was a new experience, and it would take some thinking about. What did people do with plenty of money and no responsibilities?

Ben would have been the perfect person to help her decide, she thought sadly. Ben was an expert at knowing how to have fun. If only Charlie had paid more attention, she might even have been able to learn how. Goodness knows, it wasn't a skill she'd been born with.

Charlie went thoughtfully back to work, and the rain increased.

At three in the afternoon, Lani hollered at the workers to come in the trailer and have coffee and cake with her. The trailer was warm and dry. They stuffed themselves with fresh yeasty coffee cake dripping with butter and macadamia nuts. When the time came to return to work, Charlie gave the depressingly dark, rainy afternoon a long, reluctant assessment from Lani's front window and impetuously announced, "To heck with it. We're taking the afternoon off, guys. Why don't we go into Haleiwa, do the shopping and laundry, and I'll treat us all to a burger? You, too, Lani. Didn't you say you had to go for groceries, anyway?"

She hadn't explained her phone call to the others, but she felt like celebrating her father's good fortune.

Her suggestion was greeted by a rowdy cheer from Eliza and immediate acceptance by the others, except for Pogey. He explained that he had urgent business of his own to attend to and asked for a rain check on the burger, making the others groan at his pun.

He'd already driven off when Big Mama pulled out of the driveway with her cab filled with the women, and Charlie suddenly had a sharp moment of apprehension about leaving the Reef unattended. Ben's rigid rules had become a way of life, she mused.

Still, there hadn't been any vandalism for several weeks, and surely nothing would happen on such a rainy, dark afternoon. They'd only be gone for two hours or so, she reasoned.

The two hours stretched into four. Eliza decided to get her hair cut at the small beauty parlor, and afterward they had tacos and pizzas and beer at Rosie's Cantina. It was almost dark when they started back home to the Reef, and when they arrived, Pogey drove in almost immediately behind Big Mama, tooting his horn in cheery greeting.

"I'll unload for you," he offered, hefting two of Lani's grocery bags and striding with them over to the cookhouse. He took both low steps at one long stride, balancing on the wide top step to wait for Lani to open the door.

Charlie was reaching for another bag from the truck when the new steps gave way with a dramatic crash, landing Pogey and the split bags of groceries on the wet and muddy grass among pieces of broken two-by-two.

"What the hell—" he growled, staggering to his feet and bending over the slivered wood nearest him.

"Charlie, come look at this."

The steps had been half sawn through, on both sides, in several places. Charlie stared at the jagged saw marks in the half-light that was rapidly turning into total darkness, raising her eyes to meet Pogey's angry gaze.

"Wrecked," she said in a dazed voice. "Somebody wrecked them on purpose." She leaped up, hurrying over to the cabins. Out of the four, two other sets of steps had suffered similar treatment.

Lani said little as the carpenters assessed the damage. She stood looking down at the sawn steps, slowly shaking her great round head from side to side, her arms folded across her broad breasts, a frown creasing her forehead.

Lani burst out forcefully, "This has gone too far. All that work ruined for nothing. I watched Eliza and Carol build those steps—lots of work and measuring and time. This makes me mad. It's time this foolishness stopped once and for all." She stalked off to her trailer, but in another few minutes Charlie saw her walking purposefully toward the beach, wrapped in a waterproof cape.

"Lani's going to ask the gods for help in catching our vandal, I'll bet," Carol said in a weak attempt to lighten their mood. Pogey was phoning Kimo to report this latest damage, and the women made their way back to their cabins.

But Charlie found herself idly wondering why Lani would head off down the beach in the rain, and though she kept half an eye on the window facing the water, she didn't see the older woman return until well over an hour had passed, long after Kimo arrived and Charlie watched him inspect the damage.

Charlie didn't go out to talk to the policeman. Kimo had Carol's hand clasped firmly in his, and Carol was showing him everything he needed to see, Charlie judged.

They talked, and Charlie watched Kimo bend and give Carol a tender kiss before he left. Carol kissed back, too, Charlie noticed with satisfaction. A sense of deep yearning for the times Ben had kissed her made Charlie turn away hurriedly.

Lani appeared shortly afterward, welling up through the darkness like a frigate in full sale as the increasing breeze blew the rain clouds farther south and the rain cape bellowed out around her.

It seemed a long time to walk on such a miserable evening, Charlie mused. Several times, she'd wondered at Lani's attitude toward the vandalism at the Reef. Instead of anger or fear, Lani had always seemed saddened by it. As if it were a sort of tragedy instead of an infuriating annoyance.

Until tonight. Tonight Lani had been honestly angry.

Who was really behind the things that happened at the Reef? The incidents were so scattered, somehow so purposeless. Did Lani have her suspicions about the culprit's identity?

That brought the steps to mind, and their repair. Planning time sheets and materials, she went to bed, deciding to have a good talk with Auntie Lani in the morning about the whole affair.

But Ben came back the next morning, and Charlie forgot everything in the intoxicating pleasure of seeing him again.

Charlie's heart began to hammer crazily when she returned from her morning run to find the yellow Jeep in the yard, and her eyes centered on Ben's tall form standing in the cookhouse, talking earnestly with Pogey. He raised a hand in greeting to her, and Charlie waved back after a moment's surprised hesitation. The greeting he gave her was detached, almost remote.

"Hi, Charlie."

He wore a blue cotton pullover with a V-neck. His hair was getting longer, curling madly around his bronzed features. He was the most incredibly attractive man she'd ever laid eyes on.

"Hi, there, Ben." It took considerable effort to find the exact balance between casual friendliness and disinterest. What the hell was wrong with him? Why didn't he come over to greet her properly?

Maybe the memory of their parting was as fresh in his mind as it suddenly was in her own. And there was the huge uncertainty of where he'd been and who he'd been with gnawing at her. There was time and distance between them.

She felt hesitant, uncertain of how to proceed with him. Instead of running over to him the way she longed to, she gathered her pride around her and instead went in and showered, trembling with anticipation as she soaped and shampooed and dried, even sprinkling on dusting powder that he'd given her as she practiced what she'd say to him over breakfast.

Perhaps a casual greeting, an offhand "So, Ben, where have you been?" would be best.

She'd try for a nice, aloof sort of tone. Or should she say, "How was your trip?" Pleasantly, of course, but not showing much interest.

Or maybe— She was still formulating conversations in her head when she finally emerged, brushed and dressed in fresh jeans and a pink T-shirt, even wearing a touch of lip gloss and hastily applied gobs of hand lotion.

And like a stone weight, her heart sank into her shoes.

She might as well have saved her energy.

The yellow Jeep, with Ben in it, was disappearing with an impatient roar down the driveway, and in seconds even the engine noise had faded away.

It was just as if he'd never come back at all. He hadn't cared enough even to speak to her properly. He'd tossed her aside like a flawed piece of cedar with too many knotholes.

Rage and hurt and incredulous disbelief filled her and overflowed.

Charlie spent that day and several days afterward driving herself and everyone in her immediate vicinity to distraction. She was unreasonable, demanding, cynical and bad-tempered. She was bossier than ever.

She single-handedly rebuilt all the steps in a frenzy of rage and frustration, warning the other carpenters away when they offered to help, muttering oaths to herself in staccato Italian and smashing nails in with the hammer so hard they often broke off, making her even angrier and necessitating horrible sessions with the nail puller.

She threw her gloves in the trash bin in an orgy of martyrdom and succeeded in making her hands so sore she could hardly stand them. That, in turn, made her more short-tempered than ever, especially when Ben insisted on appearing and disappearing at irregular intervals, seeming to use the Reef and the lovely new cabin she'd set aside for him as nothing more than a place to shower, eat a hasty meal, if Lani caught him and insisted, and leave again. He didn't even seem to sleep at the Reef more than a few odd hours here and there, and when he was around, he acted like someone in a daze.

He talked to her in his new, distant way. He said intimate things to her like "Well, Charlie, how's it going? The place looks really fine, now the cabins are finished," and "Did you happen to see my running shoe? I left it just outside my door when I showered, and I think the puppy took it," and, "Looks as if it might rain." Remarks that made her want to hit him with a crowbar.

He acted as if they were the most casual of acquaintances, as if he had no desire whatsoever to be more than that—if, and when, she saw him at all. His visits to the Reef grew shorter and less frequent with every passing day as the week progressed, and the weather didn't help her mood at all.

She'd grown used to sunshine and warmth, perhaps interspersed with an occasional shower, but certainly nothing approaching what people in Bellingham might call "bad weather."

This week, however, the pattern began to change, not noticeably at first but gradually. The air was cooler, the sky often cloudy, but the most annoying factor was the wind. The trade winds blew incessantly, and the waves thundered in, so high they were hardly deterred by the reef.

The force of the wind was astonishing. Several times each day, a piece of plywood or building paper being used by Carol or Eliza in their work on the main house would suddenly be lifted by the force of the wind and carried away, with the carpenters in hot pursuit and Happy yipping at their heels. The articles would usually land somewhere down the beach or catch among the trees bordering the resort, but several times Charlie lost expensive materials far out in the angry surf, which made her temper deteriorate even further.

The huge orange tarp that had been covering the hole in the roof of the main building ever since that long-ago first day when Ben fell through it was snatched like a toy on Thursday afternoon despite the extra nails Charlie had hammered in just the day before as a precaution. It billowed and floated above the upturned, anxious faces of the carpenters, sank slowly till Carol was able to grasp a corner and then was capriciously ripped again from her grip by a powerful blast of wind.

The tarp had been an expensive item. Charlie raced desperately after it down to the shoreline, choking in the blowing gusts of sand, jumping as high as she could in a lunatic dance as the tarp flirted with her, dropping nearly low enough to grab before it soared out of reach once more.

When it made one final, sassy flip of a corner, she managed to catch it. But then she tripped over Happy, falling face first into the sand. The tarp slipped through her frantically grasping fingers and floated serenely far out to sea, looking like a giant's gaily colored kite as it danced away toward the horizon.

Charlie got up, brushed herself off and stomped back up to the resort in a towering rage, with Carol and Eliza close behind her. She berated Carol and Happy the whole way.

"That dog is nothing but a nuisance, Carol. I've had it with him. He chewed up half my tools, he wrecked my shoes, and he ate a perfectly good leather apron. Now this tarp. You had a hold of it, Carol. Why the heck couldn't you hang on? Or keep that lousy dog out of the way, at least? You know how much that darned thing cost me; you could have tried a little harder."

Charlie was full of anger, not at Carol but at everything in general and for Ben Gilmour and his maddening antics in particular. Carol was just a handy target, and even as she said the damning words, Charlie knew she was being unfair and petty with her friend.

Usually, Carol would have shrugged in her good-humored way and made a quiet rejoinder. Then Charlie would have felt ashamed of herself in five minutes and apologized, and things would have returned to normal.

Instead, Carol burst into a storm of noisy weeping, scooped Happy into her arms and ran into her cabin. Eliza gave Charlie an ugly glare and snapped, "You have no right to get on her case like that. What's the matter with you these days, anyway?" and ran after Carol.

Lani, who had the knack of always appearing at exactly the wrong time, gave Charlie the "look" and said, "I thought you were feeling better, but it seems not. You're too mean to believe. You need another dose of the remedy, girl."

She narrowed her eyes at Charlie and added wisely, "Or else you need to make up with that man of yours. What's wrong with you two, anyway? Don't either of you have any sense?"

Charlie was mortified. She mumbled something apologetic to Lani and hurried over to Carol and Eliza's cabin, feeling more ashamed of herself than she'd felt since grade-school days.

"Carol," she apologized wretchedly the moment she opened the door, "I'm so sorry. I'm in a rotten mood, and like a spoiled kid, I took it out on you. I love Happy, and you, too. I don't give a hoot about that stupid tarp; really I don't. Please forgive me?"

Carol was sitting at the small table under the window, head propped in her hands, the picture of dejection. An empty tissue box and a pile of used Kleenex littered the floor. She looked up, eyes still brimming, and gave Charlie a wan smile.

"I just needed an excuse to bawl, Charlie. It wasn't what you said at all." She hesitated and then blurted out, "Kimo asked me to marry him last night. There's no way I'm ever going to get married again, and I told him that, so we had a fight. He said I was a coward, that all I let myself love was Happy, and that he wished he'd never met me. I told him the whole thing had been his fault from the beginning and that I wished I'd never come to Hawaii." She gulped and wiped her nose.

Charlie sank into a chair across from Carol. She reached over and took Carol's hand.

"I know just how you feel," she said fervently. "Ben and I had this fight before he went away, and I was sorry, but when he came back, he wouldn't talk to me, and he still won't, and now I, I—" She felt herself beginning to choke up, and the sight of Charlie in tears made Carol start crying all over again.

Eliza, busy making coffee in the tiny kitchen, threw her hands in the air and produced a full roll of paper toweling from a cabinet.

"I don't believe this," she muttered, watching the other two women sniffle and tear off huge pieces to wipe streaming eyes and noses. "We're out of Kleenex, and this is my last roll of paper towels. You two are going to waste the whole thing because of mere men. I just don't believe this is happening to me."

She poured cups of coffee all around and drew up a chair, straddling the back and leaning her tanned arms on it.

"Look," she began cheerfully, her voice in its lecturing mode, "crying wastes paper and solves nothing, right?" She waited brightly for the programmed response, but the other two shot her killing looks and went on sobbing and blowing noses in an orgy of weeping.

"Look," she began again, "we have to finish boarding in the wall we tore out, right? Because if we don't, this killer wind is going to rip the whole house to a shambles. So what do you say we work like Trojans the rest of today and get up early tomorrow to get it all done? Then tomorrow night we can make ourselves gorgeous, pile into Big Mama and go to some fancy joint and have a regular gab session over a bottle of fine wine and good food. Among the three of us, we can find some solution to the messes you two have gotten into." She looked from one swollen face to the other, and a note of desperation crept into her tone.

"Hey, time's wasting. There's a job to do. Up and at it. C'mon, gang. All you have to do is put the whole thing on hold until tomorrow night. That's not impossible, right?"

Carol and Charlie slowly got up and took turns splashing cold water on their faces at the sink.

"Right," Eliza answered herself. Then in an undertone, she added, "Where did I put that *Cosmo* magazine with the article on recovery?"

THE EVER-RISING WIND was no more than a trifling annoyance to Ben. He'd spent almost every waking minute since his return from the mainland inside the long metal Quonset huts he'd leased from a defunct sugar grower, first supervising the meticulous cleaning process necessary to convert the long-deserted spaces into an optimum environment for his mushrooms, then struggling with and triumphing over the problem of effectively sterilizing his medium—pineapple residue—and keeping the huts at the constant temperature required for the fastest growth of his mushroom sporophytes. Then he was busy interviewing and hiring eager, intelligent help and finally, ecstatically, with his own hands, starting the first of the batches of spore that would quickly produce thousands upon thousands of pounds of precious pine-and-morel mushrooms to supply the voracious markets already phoning anxiously for tentative delivery dates.

By Thursday afternoon, as the force of the wind increased and the waves along Hawaii's miles of beaches thundered in like behemoths from the mouth of an angry, seething ocean, everything inside the Quonset huts was shining clean, moistly warm and silent with expectation except for the automatic clicking off and on of the switches and thermometers hooked to a central computer that controlled the environment automatically—and, of course, the muffled sighing of the wind.

The only thing left to do was wait and watch, and Ben had hired two excellent technicians, one Hawaiian, one Japanese, to do that for him. He suddenly realized he was exhausted, desperately in need of a shower and shave, and even more urgent, a mammoth amount of food.

More than that, a million times more than that, Ben was in need of Charlie.

He would have never believed a man could feel so lost inside without his woman.

At Kimo's insistence, he'd been using the policeman's apartment in the village for the past two days instead of driving to the Reef to shower and clean up or snatch a quick nap.

The last thirty-six hours had been a crucial time for the Fungus Factory. Ben had needed to be on the job almost steadily, and as Kimo explained, the apartment was empty most of the time between the odd hours Kimo worked and the time he spent courting Carol at the Reef.

Ben was avoiding Reveille Reef. He told himself he couldn't afford the time spent driving back and forth to the isolated resort, which was true. There was another reason, however. He was deliberately avoiding Charlie, following to the letter the master plan painstakingly drawn up by himself and Charlie's father, Gennaro Cossini.

Ben's impetuous trip to Bellingham the day after his conversation with Aunt Stella had been both enlightening and alarming. He reviewed it now as he stepped from the peaceful Fungus Factory hut into the howling wind. He remembered the sudden nervousness he'd felt as he pulled over to a phone booth by a garage in the small city of Bellingham that cold afternoon.

Gennaro Cossini had been listed twice in the Bellingham telephone directory, with a home number and another one that read, "Cossini's Deli." Ben gave up on phoning after a few hesitant moments of wondering what to say and instead copied both addresses on the back of an envelope and climbed into the stately car Stella had loaned him when he'd told her of his decision to make the two-hour drive north from Seattle to meet Charlie's father.

Stella's huge red Oldsmobile had Ben slightly intimidated, and he started its powerful motor and pulled into the small-town traffic with extra care. It was like driving a spaceship on wheels.

He smiled a little, amused at his own disinterest in operating the sleek vehicle. Charlie would adore driving this beast. Charlie loved machinery, another one of the incongruous differences between them.

"Differences are the spice between lovers," Stella had said.

It would be hard to find two lovers more opposite than he and Charlie, for sure. Stella had better be right. Ben had mulled that over as he checked street numbers, drawing up in front of a brick-fronted building just off a busy major intersection. A wooden sign announced, Cossini's Deli, and through a long, narrow window that was open to the street a smiling woman, with salt-and-pepper hair in a puffy short cloud around a plump face marked deeply by smile lines, was selling cups of steaming coffee and long, Saran-Wrapped sandwiches to passersby. Business seemed brisk; there was a short lineup.

Ben opened the wide wooden doors and went inside. There were a half-dozen small round tables, and the waiter was an extremely handsome middle-aged man, balding on top but with thick graying sideburns and a pronounced Italian accent. He served bowls of soup and huge chunks of what appeared to be homemade bread to the customers, with a friendly greeting or a joke for each table. He smiled in welcome, gesturing to a table in the corner, and Ben knew this had to be Charlie's father.

Gennaro Cossini and his daughter shared bluer than blue eyes identical in shape and color, and there was much of Charlie in Gennaro's smile.

Ben felt the knot of his earlier uncertainty twist his gut. It suddenly became immensely important that this tall, muscular man approve of him, and it was a totally new sensation for Ben.

It had been a long time since he worried about what someone thought of him, besides Charlie, of course. Now it seemed both father and daughter had this effect on him.

He'd nearly bolted then, watching Mr. Cossini wind his way slowly toward him. The old Ben Gilmour would have done a slow fade and headed for parts unknown in a situation as uncertain as this. Meeting a woman's father was nerve-racking. But Ben wasn't running now.

He settled firmly down in his seat and leaned back with an attempt at casual insouciance, doing his best to appear suave and unconcerned.

Suddenly Cossini was standing beside him, asking genially, "So, young man, what will it be for you?" His voice was deep and musical, its heavy accent adding warmth and charm to an impression of confidence and strength.

And Ben had slowly stood up, reached out a hand to the startled Gennaro and blurted out, "My name is Ben Gilmour, sir, and I want to marry your daughter Charlie."

It was as much a shock to Ben as it was to Gennaro. It was the first time he'd actually projected his love for Charlie to its final—inevitable, he could see now—conclusion. Of course he wanted to marry her.

Everything had gotten easier after that. Oh, there had been tense moments. Gennaro had been wary, as well he might, of a lunatic who walked in off the street and made such an announcement. But to Ben's relief, Charlie had actually paved the way by apparently going on about Ben at length in her letters home—mostly critical, Ben guessed, but it seemed Gennaro already knew a fair bit about him and had guessed the rest. Gennaro Cossini knew, loved and, surprisingly, understood his youngest daughter amazingly well.

After Gennaro's charming partner, Rosalie, had been introduced to Ben and realized what the men were talking about, she'd insisted they move to the tiny table in the back kitchen where they wouldn't be interrupted.

There, amid the smell of soup and steam, with a young teenage boy wearing a Walkman headset busily washing glasses in a corner and Rosalie hurrying in and out, they had measured one another, old male and young, taking stock and coming to conclusions.

Gennaro was a man strong enough to be gentle, but he was far from being anybody's fool. His love for Charlie glowed in his blue eyes each time her name was mentioned.

"My Charlie, you've talked to her about this marriage?"

Drawing a deep breath, Ben sighed. "No, sir, I'm afraid I haven't yet. You see—" And Ben succinctly outlined the past, present and hopefully the future of his relationship with Charlie, being brutally honest about himself and what his life-style had been until very recently and listing the circumstances he knew were sure to make Charlie decide against marrying him when he did get around to asking her.

"The fact that I'm financially solvent through no effort of my own is probably one of the biggest problems between us," Ben admitted ruefully. "Charlie's got this thing about earning your own money, being motivated and independent. I'm afraid she'll think this business venture of mine is just another temporary game."

"Is it?" Gennaro was direct.

Ben slowly shook his head. "After Charlie, this is the most important thing that's ever happened to me. For the first time, my life has direction and purpose. All I need to do now," he added ruefully, "is convince Charlie I'm serious about both the business and her."

Gennaro nodded thoughtfully.

"Any suggestions?" Ben watched the older man, gauging his reaction. It would tell Ben what Gennaro thought of him as a prospective son-in-law.

There was no immediate answer. Instead, Gennaro unearthed a bottle of wine from a cupboard in the corner, half filled two glasses he rescued from the boy at the sink and plopped one in front of Ben.

"My Charlie, she's a chip off the old block," he began, and Ben heaved an invisible sigh of relief. He'd rather have Gennaro for him than against him.

"She's stubborn, hardheaded, temper like the devil and proud." A twinkle came and went in the blue eyes, and he reached a hand out to gesture at the woman hurrying in and out of the kitchen.

"Rosalie, she knows all about such problems with a Cossini. You and her should have a talk someday soon." Another fact about his daughter occurred to him just then, and he added, "Charlie, you know, she's also one hell of a bad cook."

Looking like a man who had fulfilled his moral obligations with that pronouncement, Gennaro leaned back comfortably and crossed his ankles, meeting Ben's forthright look across the rim of the water glass holding his wine, one bushy white eyebrow quirked questioningly.

"She's the only woman I want to marry," Ben repeated evenly. "I'm just as stubborn and single-minded as she is, and one way or another I'll convince her she should marry me." He raised his glass to Gennaro. "I can always hire a cook." Then he finally realized why he'd come here to the man who'd known Charlie so much longer than he had himself.

He swallowed his wine, and leaned toward the older man. "But I can use all the help I can get in that regard, Mr. Cossini."

"Call me Gennaro."

He refilled the glasses to within an inch of the top. "You have to talk to my daughter. Of course, she's her own big boss. But I figure Charlie, she needs a man like you, whether she knows it yet or not."

Gennaro's blue eyes strayed to Rosalie's plump figure as she hurried out the swinging door with a plate of muffins in one hand and a fresh bowl of butter in the other. "This thing between a man and his woman, it can be hell, or it can be heaven." Sadness crept over his handsome features. "Charlie, she saw too much of the bad kind when her mother was alive. It's made her scared to try."

He looked at Ben appraisingly for several moments, then nodded to himself, and a cunning look came over his features, not unlike an expression Charlie herself had at times.

"You'd be a good husband for that girl of mine, Ben Gilmour. In spite of all that money. Now, here's what I think you should do."

THE "CLOSED" SIGN on Cossini's Deli had been in place for several hours before Ben and Gennaro came unsteadily out the door and practical Rosalie loaded them both into Stella's car. She drove them home to the apartment Gennaro was renting, scolded them roundly for drinking so much wine, made them supper and then discreetly went home herself.

For the next five hours Gennaro told funny-sad tales of his little tomboy daughter, dragging out an old picture album to show to a fascinated Ben.

Gennaro ended up pouring them another glass of wine each, and then another.

They both had formidable hangovers in the morning.

DRIVING TO KIMO'S, Ben reviewed for perhaps the hundredth time the suggestions Gennaro had made. They still sounded good, based as they were on hard, male common sense and Gennaro's knowledge of the workings of Charlie Cossini's mind.

"Don't just tell her about the mushroom farm," Gennaro had instructed. "Take her there, show her the finished product, make her see you as a success. She needs concrete evidence, Charlie does."

"Draw up a marriage proposal in logical, practical terms, listing all the details, and go over it with her, point by point, like a business document, like a proposal for building a house. Charlie always said she needed her contracts in writing.

"Don't chase after her," Gennaro counseled. "Men have been chasing her since she was thirteen, and she never once looked at any of them. The reason she got involved with that no-good lawyer," Gennaro claimed, scowling fiercely, "was because he was just smart enough not to chase after her. Keep her guessing. She likes a challenge.

"Let her stew for a while. Don't hurry anything. Give her a chance to miss you good. Absence makes the heart grow fonder.

"Once she agrees to getting married, do it right away. Don't give her a chance to change her mind."

The last suggestion was the easiest: "Be good to my little girl. Love her long and well."

Ben braked to a stop, watching idly as a piece of a roof tile lifted off Kimo's building and sailed away in the wind. The wind was nearly a hurricane, ripping off roofs.

In a burst of frustrated longing, Ben smashed his fist down on the wheel. He couldn't wait much longer. He needed Charlie in every single way a man could need a woman. Through the haze of exhaustion and hunger, he came to a decision. Pushing his weary body through the wind to Kimo's front door, he decided tomorrow was it.

Tomorrow he'd launch his full-scale campaign, draw up the marriage contract, drag Charlie bodily to see the Fungus Factory, overwhelm her with his business success, sweep her off her feet and have witnesses present when she agreed to marry him.

He thought of Auntie Lani and the others at Reveille Reef, and a wry smile twisted his unshaved cheek. Witnesses were definitely available any hour of the day or night, no notice required. The Reef was an absolute hotbed of witnesses.

But he'd better phone Charlie right now, tonight, and make a definite date to see her tomorrow afternoon. Charlie was unpredictable as hell; she might not even be around tomorrow afternoon.

And after his all-out effort, if she still balked? Ben knew exactly what he'd do.

He'd take her somewhere private, lock the door and make frenzied love to her until she finally gave in. Tired as he was, his body reacted with aching, yearning intensity to that delicious idea. He almost hoped she'd balk.

Tomorrow, Charlie Cossini, he warned her silently as he let himself in and flopped down on the bed for just a second before he showered and phoned.

Tomorrow, my callused angel—Charlie, how I love you.

He'd get up in a minute and jot down notes for the marriage contract.

He'd get up and make reservations at a fine hotel for the best suite they had just in case he had to revert to plan B and seduce her into acquiescence. He'd phone Lani and clue her in so she could help behind the scenes. He'd get Eliza to pack a bag for Charlie.

He'd— The wind surged and sighed, the loose roof tiles flapped, the windows rattled and Ben closed his eyes for one precious second just to properly visualize his beloved's rebellious, stormy face—and how it changed and grew softly rosy when he kissed her.

He slept, in a drugged stupor, until the next afternoon.

Chapter Twelve

The arrival of three unusually attractive young women to the covered portico of the Turtle Bay Hilton Hotel wasn't that unusual an occurrence, although shapely young females were guaranteed to create an appreciative stir among the male doormen, bellhops and parking attendants stationed there.

But the arrival of Charlie, Eliza and Carol early Saturday afternoon created something akin to a riot.

"Maybe we should park Big Mama in one of these lots away from the hotel?" Carol suggested a bit anxiously as Charlie, lip between her teeth in concentration, herded the recalcitrant truck off of Route 83 and onto the long, tree-lined driveway leading to the Turtle Bay Hilton.

The parking lots that Carol indicated were a discreet distance from the prestigious entrance, with its uniformed attendants, but even here Cadillacs, Mercedes and BMWs preened themselves in ostentatious evidence of wealth.

But Charlie guided her outsized steed single-mindedly toward the main entrance. "It's raining, none of us have on coats, and you two worked hard on this hairdo of mine," she said firmly, emphasizing her words with hard, frantic pumps on the brake as she finally lurched to a full stop under the canopy. Big Mama shuddered, backfired and subsided. An attendant in a formal suit approached the truck gingerly, and Charlie stuck her head out of the open window and gave him her most charming smile.

"We're here for dinner and to do some shopping. Would you park her for us, please?" The rusty doors opened, and the women slid down in an enchanting flurry of long, curvaceous legs, giggles and rustling peacock shades of whispering silk. As if by magic, two more attendants appeared to gallantly assist the women and shoot covert, unbelieving looks at the massive bulk of Big Mama, with her feminine streaks of pink, blue and yellow spray paint covering her rusted hulk of a body.

Charlie handed over the keys. "Open the throttle and pump hard on the gas. Also the steering's a tiny bit loose."

The women disappeared into the glass-roofed expanse of the lobby, and the growing crowd of hotel employees flipped a coin to see who had the privilege of trying to park the mastodon that was Big Mama.

The newest attendant somehow lost the flip and came heart-stoppingly close to wiping out two huge pillars and landing himself and the truck over the cliff into the wildly breaking ocean before he managed to lurch around the corner and get the truck parked where it would be out of sight of arriving guests. There, in the middle of the staff lot, he abandoned her gratefully.

Coming back had been a big mistake, Charlie decided, eyeing the huge bird cage in the lobby and remembering every second of her evening here with Ben. Even the parrot made her nostalgic.

Why deliberately remind herself of him? Obviously he had no problem forgetting her. It had been three days now since his last hurried visit to the Reef.

"I'll be in touch this weekend," he'd told her then. And like a fool, she'd waited for him, always listening for the phone under the noises of frenzied hammering and voices calling.

The main lodge was nearly completed. In a marathon effort, the women and Pogey had finished the walls this morning. All that remained was the roof and the final finishing touches inside, mostly subcontracting work. The job was ending, and an emptiness grew within Charlie as she moved slowly past the bird cage, following the other two women as they excitedly scouted out the boutiques and intriguing small shops in the Hilton's cavernous corridors.

Carol bought a long, patterned length of crimson cotton fabric that formed a dress when wrapped intricately and tied above the breasts. "Lani wears this sort of thing all the time," she remarked. "It's called a pareau. She'll teach me how to tie it."

Eliza was trying on a wide-brimmed straw hat. "Lani gave me a big lecture about how none of us should be out tonight, because a bad storm is coming. *Ino*, I think she called it. Big trouble. Anyway, she was all nervous and on edge." Eliza studied her image in the display mirror, shrugged and took the hat off again.

"I think I can live without a hat like that. It emphasizes my freckles and round face." She tilted her head to the side and frowned, her green eyes puzzled and concerned. "Don't you think Lani has been acting weird lately? I catch her muttering away to herself, as if she's in an argument or something. She stomps off down the beach at all hours of the day and night. And today she was downright jumpy and irritable. That's not like her at all."

Charlie had to admit she'd hardly noticed, but then, she'd been so irritable and distracted herself over Ben Gilmour, it was no wonder.

"Anyway, let's hope she's wrong about the storm. Big Mama has no side windows, and that rope holding the roof on is loose. Even the light rain on the way up here was bad enough," Carol said as she led the way out of the boutique. After another half hour of browsing, Charlie said firmly, "Enough shopping, you've spent all your pay. Let's go find food. I'm starving."

They were seated by a friendly girl in a bright Hawaiian print dress in the glass-roofed, sunken dining room, and again it caused an unbearable pang of loneliness in Charlie to be here without Ben.

Instead of getting used to being without him, the ache of missing him was growing worse every minute, Charlie concluded morosely. If it kept increasing in relation to time expended, she'd be nothing but a ball of misery and wet handkerchiefs by the time she left Hawaii.

She shuddered at the thought of leaving the islands. How very much at home she felt here, with the rolling Pacific all round and the sunshine and the blue skies.

Sunshine and blue skies had been noticeably absent the last few days, however. The wind had even blown the phone lines down this morning.

She gave the waitress her order, and as the other two also ordered, Charlie gazed beyond the dining room and out at the increasing wind and rain buffeting the glass walls. The sound of the storm was muted by the thick glass and the soft Hawaiian music being played for the diners' pleasure by a smiling trio with guitars wearing incredibly brilliant Hawaiian shirts.

Inside, all was sophistication and quiet graciousness and pleasant music, while out over the Pacific ominous clouds clotted above a bruised-looking horizon, as if a giant fist had punched the sky and given it a shiner. Purple, green and sickly yellow were all fading drunkenly into dismal dark gray, and the wind was increasing.

Charlie gave a moment's anxious thought to the ten-mile long, winding drive home to the Reef and then deliberately brought her attention back to the table and her friends. They'd managed the drive here. Big Mama would certainly get them home.

The food was every bit as delicious as she remembered, and twice the women had to refuse the discreet offer of company over dinner from tables of good-looking, eager men. They sent back the men's hopeful offerings of fine white wine that had accompanied the invitations, and Charlie ordered a bottle in self-defense. After all, this was a celebration of sorts.

When the wine steward had gone through the elaborate tasting, nodding and pouring performance, she raised her glass in a toast.

"Well, carpenters, the Reef is all but done. One more week should see us to completion. Here's to another successful project by Cossini Construction, and to many more in the future. I think we're a winning combination." She glanced around at the male attention centered so blatantly on their table and added saucily, "We mustn't be that hard to look at, either."

They drank, but the atmosphere had subtly altered among them. Carol was tracing the rim of her glass on the thick white cloth in a preoccupied circle, and Eliza's face was flushed with more than her usual rich color.

They ordered a dessert filled with chocolate, whipped cream and nuts, and Charlie looked thoughtfully at her companions as they spooned up the rich concoction with less than their usual enthusiasm. It wasn't like Eliza to be subdued, and Carol seemed downright worried tonight.

"Okay," Eliza pronounced with an air of finality as they sipped coffee. "We're here for a therapeutic group-encounter session to determine what comes next in our lives. So I'll start off by telling you what's happening in mine." She reached across the table and surprised Charlie by grasping her hand and giving it a fierce squeeze.

"Hawaii's been the best experience I've ever had," she said softly. "Living at the Reef, getting to know Lani and Kimo and Pogey made me realize how many different people and places are out there, waiting to be explored before I settle down someday with the man of my dreams." She ducked her head, uncharacteristically shy all of a sudden. "Pogey and I are friends, good platonic friends," she emphasized, making the others smile. Eliza didn't notice, however. She was frowning at her coffee cup, and she went hurriedly on. "He's invited me to go along on a mountain-climbing expedition in India right after Christmas, and I really want to go. But Charlie, I don't want to leave you and Carol and the company, either. As you said, we're just starting to get it all together. Besides, I feel you two are like, well, my sisters." Tears shimmered on Eliza's mascaraed lashes, and when she looked up, huge, fat drops spilled over and ran down her freckled cheeks.

Carol and Charlie stared at her in amazement. Eliza never, never cried. She always said it wasted tissue and solved nothing. Carol found a crumpled Kleenex and handed it over, and Charlie struggled to find the right words to say to Eliza. It had been so natural to project a future for Cossini Construction. Could Hawaii and Reveille Reef represent an ending for her company instead of a beginning?

It was a frightening possibility.

"Liza, for heaven's sake, don't cry," she began, and the trace of familiar impatience in her voice seemed to bring normalcy back to the three of them. "None of us is married to the company. We can remain friends whether we work together or not, and if you want to go off to climb mountains, then I think you should go." She added stoutly, "Actually, all of us need a holiday. This job was a tough one." *In so many ways,* she added silently.

Carol and Eliza were watching Charlie intently, measuring her words.

"But don't you need steady work for the company to pay off that debt you worry over?" Carol asked. "Can you afford to take time off?"

Charlie quickly outlined for them the happy story her sister had relayed about the change in her father's life and fortunes.

"So all of a sudden the pressure's off," she explained. "I even have money in the bank for a change instead of an overdraft." It was still such a novelty, she had trouble believing it herself.

Eliza had regained her aplomb. She said triumphantly to Carol, "There, see? There goes your last excuse for not marrying Kimo."

As Carol tried to shush her, Liza explained excitedly to Charlie, "Carol thought it would be disloyal and unfair of her to stay here and get married and break up the company after the way you worked to get us all jobs when we were down and out. It was the exact same feeling I had about going off mountain climbing. But if you're free of pressure over money, then she's free, too, right? We all are, right?''

Warmth and humble gratitude for friends as loyal as these two made Charlie swallow from the lump in her throat.

``Right,'' she confirmed huskily. She met Carol's eyes and attempted a wink. ``You're nuts to put work ahead of romance, Carol. Maybe you better phone Kimo right now and tell him you accept his proposal,'' she teased, and watched in amazement as Carol put her napkin firmly on the table and stood up.

``I'll see if the phone lines are fixed yet,'' the tall woman agreed, her lovely features suffused with rosy color. ``I've really given him a bad time, haven't I?'' she added wonderingly. ``Now, where's the public telephone?'' She walked off, determination in her stride.

``Wow,'' Eliza enthused. ``She may be a slow starter, but once she makes up her mind, look out.'' She turned her probing eyes on Charlie.

``Well, boss, where does this leave you? And when did you start putting romance and work in the proper order?''

Charlie attempted a laugh, but it sounded hollow. ``I told you, for the first time in my life, I just may take a holiday. I haven't even seen the rest of the islands, and I'd like to explore them before I go home to Bellingham.''

``Alone? Without Ben?'' Eliza always managed to hit a nerve, Charlie reflected, nodding an answer. She had a positive talent for it.

``That's just plain stupid,'' Eliza announced vehemently. ``You're in love with Ben Gilmour, and now you're just going to leave as if nothing ever happened between you?''

``Liza, that's just what you suggested I do in the beginning, don't you remember? You advised having an affair until the end of the job and then taking a few weeks—six, I remember you suggested—to get over him and get on with life. Well, that's exactly what I'm doing.''

Eliza waved a dismissive hand in the air. ``I only said that because you were being so boneheaded about him. You're not that superficial, Charlie. Don't you think I know that?

I never dreamed you'd take me seriously. I mean it was plain as the nose on your face that you were falling in love, and so was he, and you needed some kind of shove to keep you from running away. You are in love with him, aren't you?''

Charlie fought the agony of emotion twisting her heart to shreds. ''Yes,'' she admitted quietly, ''I'm very much in love with him.''

Eliza studied her intently. ''What happened to all the buts?'' she demanded. ''Before, you would have said, 'I love him, but—' and then listed a whole pile of dumb things. Like 'but I'm never getting married.'''

Charlie shrugged. ''They stopped being important somewhere along the way. Right about the time he stopped caring about me, I guess I smartened up. Too late.'' Her voice was desolate. ''I'm a lot like you, Liza, after all. I want a husband who loves me, two point five kids and a bathroom I can hose out once a week.''

Eliza snorted. ''For a smart lady, you sure are dumb, Charlie. You've never even told him how you feel, have you? How do you know he doesn't care anymore? Did you ask him? Did you even try to make up after that fight you two had? No.'' She shook her head in disgust. ''You don't have to sit around waiting for him to come to you, you know. Why don't you make him a proposal, like you did when you wanted him to give us the job at the Reef? Men like Ben respond to logic. You fought for what you wanted then. How come you're not fighting now? Take control, for heaven's sake. Live with him, marry him, fight with him— whatever. But don't sit around like a martyr.''

At first, Charlie glared at her red-haired friend. Then honesty took over. She knotted her hand into fists, reluctantly admitting that what Eliza said was absolutely true. She, Charlie Cossini, had acted like a sap by whining and moaning instead of taking action. As soon as she accepted that, her mind seemed to slip back into gear and begin to operate as it ought to have all along.

''I could make him an offer, like a business contract,'' she began to plan aloud. ''I could list the advantages of living with me." She thought for a second, then added, "Of marrying me. I want an ironclad contract, down in black and white. Permanent."

She frowned at the darkening window wall, not seeing the angry turbulence steadily increasing outside.

"Let's see.... I make him laugh, and he hates to drive, and I love it, and—"

There was the spiraling beauty of their lovemaking. No question about that being an advantage. But what else? Well, there must be lots of other advantages, and she'd list every one.

She'd make him an offer he couldn't refuse. And if by some stubborn chance he dared to say no at first, then she'd get him alone and—the blood rose in her cheeks as she imagined the delicious methods she'd use to coerce him into agreement. Maybe she should reserve a room right here in the hotel, just in case?

A line of half-forgotten poetry came to mind: "There is a tide in the affairs of men, which taken at the flood—" *Ben Gilmour,* she vowed silently, *this is flood tide, and I'm grabbing it. I'm grabbing you.*

She saw Carol winding her way back to the table, her face ablaze with joy.

"She's a knockout, isn't she?" Eliza said. "Look at the stunned looks on those men's faces. She's like an amazon come to life. She must have gotten hold of Kimo."

The intensity of Carol's happiness made urgency rise in Charlie. She had to get things straight with Ben, and right away.

Leaving a generous tip on the table, she headed decisively for the cashier's desk. "C'mon, carpenters. This dinner's on me. Now, let's get this show on the road."

That was easier said than done, however.

At first, Big Mama wouldn't start. She hunkered rebelliously in the back lot, ignoring the frantic efforts of the half-drowned doorman and Charlie. After a conference, the doorman courteously held an umbrella over Charlie, and she opened the hood and wiped Big Mama's plugs dry, but the umbrella turned itself inside out in the ferocious wind, nearly upsetting the patient man holding it. Charlie was drenched and exasperated when the motor finally sputtered and caught.

Even then, Mama sounded ill. Her innards made gurgling noises, and her exhaust backfired rudely all the slow way down the hotel's driveway.

Carol and Eliza huddled miserably inside the breezy cab as Charlie steered a haphazard course through the wild night. Mama's broken side windows funneled in the rain and wind from the worsening storm, and her windshield wipers worked at half speed. The tied-on roof slapped up and down, and the rope holding it looked frayed. When they reached the highway turnoff, the ten miles to the Reef suddenly seemed an impossibly distant drive.

Charlie felt a moment's apprehension about the wildness of the night and the all but deserted roadway ahead. She idled the engine before making the turn, undecided.

"Want to go back and wait out the storm at the hotel?" It was only fair to pose the alternative to her passengers. Both women shook their heads, however.

"This is probably just a storm front; it'll be gone by the time we get home," Carol said.

"We're not made of sugar; we won't melt in the rain" was Eliza's comment.

"Kimo's going to meet me at the Reef in an hour," Carol explained, and added, "He's bringing Ben along. Ben's looking for you, Charlie."

Charlie engaged the gears and optimistically pointed Big Mama in the right direction.

They crawled along the deserted highway, soaked by the rain coming in the window, pouring down through the rust holes in the roof.

The roof was worrying Charlie. Tied on as it was, it rattled ominously in the gale force wind, threatening to part company with the rest of the truck. How far had they come? The gauges didn't work at the best of times. Perhaps four miles, with another six to go? Charlie's arms ached from wrestling with the steering wheel along the narrow, winding road.

"What's wrong with the headlights?" Eliza's voice was high and thin.

The feeble beams piercing the rain-swept darkness faded, grew bright and faded again. At the same time, Big Mama's motor coughed. Charlie pumped the gas frantically, but the truck gave one more feeble jerk, the headlights died, and there was just time to coast over to the shoulder of the road before Big Mama expired completely.

Nobody said a thing. There were no cries of "What will we do now?" and Charlie felt a surge of affection for her carpenters as she vainly tried everything she knew to get the motor started again.

It was hopeless. In another few minutes, she gave up in frustration.

Without the growl of the motor, the howling wind and streaming rain seemed much louder and more ominous than before. They must have stalled within a few hundred feet of the beach, because the crashing sound of breakers was part of the noisy chorus of the night. The truck actually rocked with the force of the wind, and the utter blackness all around seemed almost to have texture, so intense was the darkness.

Carol's voice broke the stillness. "At times like this, I wish I still smoked," she said plaintively, and that broke the tension. Eliza giggled, and Charlie said reassuringly, "Somebody's sure to come along soon and rescue us."

But they'd waited for what seemed like ten minutes longer than forever before headlights finally appeared behind them.

Eliza rolled her window down and waved an arm out the window excitedly, and the approaching vehicle rolled to a stop behind the stalled truck. Charlie felt a wave of relief wash over her, but it was followed by sheer panic as the interior lights in their rescuer's car blinked on and she could see the men inside.

"Oh, no," Eliza wailed, and Charlie silently agreed.

The car was an old pink Cadillac. Inside were four young, brawny Hawaiians. Charlie recognized the driver as the wild-haired young man who'd come to install the telephone at the Reef, stripped off his clothing down to his swim trunks and narrowly escaped a fistfight with Ben. These were Kimo's prime vandalism suspects and the last four men in the world Charlie would have chosen to rescue her.

The men were getting out of the car, unfolding gigantic, muscle-bound bodies into the storm, and the sound of their laughter carried over the wind and rain. They were huge, wet and ominous-looking.

Charlie's voice quavered slightly as she instructed her frightened companions. "Let them make the first move. We'll take them by surprise if they try anything." She gulped and tried to steady her voice. One of the men was nearly at Eliza's window. "Go for the eyes and groin. Be brave, carpenters." Her voice quavered despite her best efforts. Eliza's side door was being opened, and a wildly curling mass of black hair on top of a dark-skinned face appeared.

Eliza cowered back in her seat, and a tiny squeak of terror escaped her.

The face was split by a wide, white grin. The voice was deep, musical and friendly. "You ladies sure picked some kind of night to break down. What seems to be the trouble?"

For the next forty minutes, the four men—Ed, Aki, Ty and Jim—all with unpronounceable Hawaiian surnames—tried valiantly to get Big Mama going again. They worked under her hood, getting themselves and an impressive array of tools dripping wet in the process.

When Charlie and Carol got out to try to help, Aki insisted they collect Eliza and go and wait in the luxury of the Cadillac.

"Here's the keys; you can start her up and keep warm. The radio works," he advised the abashed women. They accepted without argument and avoided each other's embarrassed glances as they climbed gratefully into the warm, dry car.

"Good thing Liza didn't go for his eyes right off the bat," Carol murmured.

At last, the unlikely knights gave up on Big Mama and hurried back to the Cadillac.

"Looks as if that truck's gone into cardiac arrest," Jim joked, squeezing into the back seat beside the women as Aki, Ty and Ed squashed together in front, shaking themselves like shaggy dogs and shedding raindrops everywhere.

"She'll have to have major surgery, and we need more tools. You women are the carpenters from Reveille Reef, aren't you? You probably don't remember, but Ed here put your phone in a while back. He told us what you were doing down there to the buildings."

Charlie was grateful for the darkness that hid her embarrassed blush at the memory of the less than cordial way Ed had been treated that day. But the men seemed to bear no grudge. Ty turned half around in the seat and asked curiously, "How's the old place coming along, anyway? We'll drive you back there now, and tomorrow we can tow your truck down to Ed's garage and see if we can fix her for you. Looks like she might need a new fuel pump." He laughed cheerfully. "Among other things."

The powerful Cadillac purred to life under Aki's sure touch, and in moments Big Mama was left far behind.

The man kept up a spirited conversation, asking specific questions about the renovations and revealing in the process intimate knowledge of Reveille Reef.

Charlie listened closely, letting Eliza chatter on about the changes, answer ingenuous questions about the eventual clientele who would rent the units, explain why three women would become carpenters and enthuse over how they all liked Hawaii.

Could these men, kind and harmless as they seemed, be responsible for the strange happenings at the Reef? Charlie tried to imagine it being possible and failed. Full of youthful high spirits, they certainly didn't sound like criminals, for all their obvious knowledge of the Reef. They wouldn't terrorize the place in such a senseless manner and then show generous kindness to their victims, would they?

Questions raced through Charlie's mind, and she only half listened to the conversation until Aki casually said, "Have you guys had any trouble with old Tom Tanaka-Martin?" He was confidently negotiating the narrow, treacherously dark route toward Haleiwa.

"Who's that?" Eliza asked curiously.

"Tall guy, thin, shaves his head, wears old army clothes?"

Charlie remembered in a flash the pocket of fog and a tall, thin man with a shaved, bony skull, carrying a bugle.

She listened intently as Ed laughingly added, "Old Tom haunts the Reef; you must have seen him. He's part Japanese—lives with the priests at the Shinto mission down the beach. He's not quite all there. We used to use the beach all the time, and he seemed to think we were army officers or something."

Aki added matter-of-factly, "Tom gets kind of crazy sometimes; thinks the war's still on. He calls the place 'the club,' and he figures he's in charge of it, the way he was when the army used it for R and R."

No Trespassing, Charlie thought.

Carol must have reached the same conclusion Charlie did just then, because she reached a hand and caught Charlie's arm and gave it an excited squeeze. Was the answer to the riddle at Reveille Reef that simple?

"Tom figured the club was his baby, see. He used to cut the grass, sweep out those old cabins, repaint the steps all the time. Remember when he insisted on giving you a haircut, Ty?"

Ty grunted in disgust, and the other men laughed uproariously as Charlie pictured the ugly khaki paint on her cedar steps.

Jim said, "Old Tom's kinda weird, but he's harmless. The priests at the mission try to keep an eye on him, but he used to sneak away on them, times when he figured the war was still going. Guess it was hard on him those times, being half Japanese, in the Allied Army."

Jim's voice was thoughtful. "Yeah, sorta like being haole to both races and not belonging anywhere."

The men were suddenly quiet—embarrassed, perhaps, by Jim's remark. Charlie knew they had probably roared around in this souped-up Cadillac and shouted, "Haole, go home," much the way the gang of youths had shouted at her and Carol and Eliza when they'd first arrived. Young, healthy, secure in their belonging.

The same way she and her friends had roared around the streets of Bellingham, she thought, not so many years before, smugly dividing the world into "us" and "them."

And Tom Tanaka-Martin? Where would he belong? Was he simply trying to establish a place of his own, where he felt secure, by keeping the Reef the way it had always been?

Charlie knew, with a deep certainty and a sense of exultant triumph, that the mystery of Reveille Reef's mysterious saboteur had just been solved quite accidentally. She couldn't wait to tell Ben. She couldn't wait to see Ben.

"Did you ever hear this Tom play the bugle? He's pretty good, especially when it rains," she commented.

Before anyone could answer, the Cadillac was bumping down the driveway to the Reef.

Their arrival was chaotic. The moment the car stopped, Kimo and Ben both erupted from the men's cabin, their expressions almost comically menacing when they realized the women were in the car with the four men.

"C'mon, everyone, let's go warm up with some of Auntie Lani's coffee," Eliza insisted as they all piled out of the car. Charlie gasped and tried to catch her breath in the gale, and the wind nearly tore the car door from her hand. But Ben grabbed it, wrapped a corded arm around her protectively and escorted her into the cabin.

Everyone piled haphazardly into the cookhouse, and Ben slammed the door shut, using the full weight of his body against the force of the wind, turning to glare a challenge at the four young Hawaiians with Charlie.

Eliza, as usual, solved the problem with her tongue. "Big Mama broke down miles away, and these great guys rescued us," she announced blithely, making introductions with polished ease.

Kimo's expression altered almost comically from menace to gratitude as Eliza elaborated on her story, and he wrapped a propietary arm around Carol's shoulders, extending his other hand to an embarrassed Aki in a friendly handshake when Liza finally ran down.

"Thanks for taking care of my fiancée," he growled. Then he went on worriedly. "We've been catching weather reports on the radio, and I'm afraid we're in big trouble here. A hurricane expected to pass north of Midway Island turned and is now threatening us with gale-force winds and extremely high tides. The water's washing right up past the cement breakwater, as far as the lodge." Kimo's broad face creased in a worried frown. "The buildings are in danger of being washed away. The waves are already too high for the reef to deflect, and they're rolling up and hammering on the lodge's walls. The deck supports are already gone, and it won't be long before the whole building goes. There's nothing to protect the cabins, either, unless we do something."

Horrified at this destruction of her work, Charlie gave a choked cry and immediately started out the door to see for herself. The door slammed back as if a giant had kicked it, and the wind filled the room.

Charlie gasped as Ben's hand caught her arm, hauling her back inside and shutting the door with difficulty. His voice was harsh, but there was a tenderness in his eyes. She didn't have time to dwell on its meaning just then. She was well aware, however, that his hand slid down until it found her own, spreading her fingers and slipping his between them in a warmly intimate, reassuring embrace that made her absurdly happy.

"Nobody's going anywhere until we figure out a plan, Charlie. In a storm like this, buildings aren't the only things in danger. Those waves can pick a person up like a toy and drag him out to sea."

The door opened again, letting in an unbelievable burst of rain and wind, and Lani sailed in like a stalwart ship with all sails furled, her long cape wrapped around her, its hood pulled down almost over her nose. Directly behind her stood Pogey, and he greeted the women with obvious relief.

"We were going to have to man a search party if you women didn't show up soon," he commented. He and Lani both looked relieved at having the four big Hawaiians on the scene, as well.

"We just tried phoning the Department of National Defense. All the phones are out," Lani announced, calmly removing her cape and immediately checking the level of coffee in the huge enamel pot.

For a time it seemed the excited voices inside almost rivaled the storm in intensity and volume. Everyone talked at once, and it took several minutes before anyone became aware of the steady banging on the door.

When it opened, the noise of voices died away as an emaciated figure seemed to tumble inside, pushed by the force of the wind. He might have been one of Lani's night walkers come to life, so skeletal did he appear in his ancient army uniform and polished forage boots.

An eerie stillness fell over the warm room, and only Lani sounded normal when she said quietly, "This is Tom Tanaka-Martin, from the mission down the beach. Hello, Tom. What are you doing out on a night like this one, old friend?"

He looked even thinner and older than he had that morning on the beach, Charlie thought, fascinated by the figure before her, seeing him now in the light of what she'd learned and feeling an overwhelming compassion for him.

There was no vagueness clouding the blue eyes, as there had been the morning she'd met him in the fog. He was a man with a purpose.

He nodded familiarly to Lani and seemed to assess the crowded room. The young Hawaiians greeted him with sober respect, and Charlie felt another surge of warmth for them, because this strange man could easily be a comic figure with his moldy green army clothing and that rapt zealot's light burning in his sunken eyes. If only she had had a chance to talk to Ben, tell him what she'd learned about Tom. She ought to hate the old man for all the harm he'd caused to her buildings, all the extra time and work he'd created with his mischief. Instead, she could only feel this absurd protectiveness, this understanding and pity for the confused old figure.

Tom instinctively singled out Kimo and Ben as the commanding officers of the group, and he almost stood at attention as he spoke directly to them, his voice high-pitched and reedy but powerful and urgent.

"The club will be destroyed unless we sandbag the breakwater," he stated with authority. "We have to build a wall and deflect the water until the tide goes down. It happened once before, and we saved the buildings. I can show you where the sandbags are kept. Come, we have to hurry."

Ben studied the old man for a moment, glanced at Kimo inquiringly, and they both nodded. There was something odd about him, but his idea was sound. "C'mon, everybody. It's worth a try."

The storm was frightening in its intensity, the noise of the ocean and the wind making conversation all but impossible. They staggered after Tom, and at a half run he led the way to a shack half hidden by underbrush in a far corner of the property. Charlie had considered using it for storage, but its location was inconvenient, and she'd left it untouched during the renovations.

The sand-filled canvas bags had been there for years. And when Ben picked one up, the covering split and the contents spilled out. Hawaii's salt air and humidity had done their damage, and the bags were rotten and useless.

"But they were new just a few months ago," Tom insisted, and Ben shot him another long, curious look.

Then understanding and compassion flickered across Ben's face as he recognized the truth about Tom, and he led the way back into the shelter of a cabin, his hands gentle on Tom's arm.

Ben took charge. "Kimo, there's hundreds of sacks, old sugar sacks, in the warehouse behind the Fungus Factory. I don't think anybody will care if we break in and take them. Nobody's using them."

"I'll get them for you. I've got to get back to the police station right away, I'm on duty tonight, and this storm will cause a million problems," Kimo explained. "If I can, I'll send over some of my guys to give you a hand, and I'll also get in touch with National Defense. Ed, Aki, you two follow me in Ben's Jeep. We'll load the sacks and you can bring them back here."

Then, oblivious of the others jammed into the small space, Kimo gently took Carol into his arms and held her for an instant.

"Take care of Carol for me," he said to the men, and then he hurried out. Eliza met Charlie's eyes and held up a thumb in triumphant glee, and Lani noticed and beamed like a lamp. At least one thing was going right.

But nothing could detract for long from the howling, pelting chaos of the elements. Even from inside the cabin, Charlie could hear the monstrous crashing of water battering at the main house, wave after wave destroying what it had taken Cossini Construction months to build. It would be at least an hour, maybe more, before Ed and Aki returned, before they could hope to start fighting back at the rush of water. How much damage would already be done in that length of time? Too much, she whispered desperately. The lodge, at the very least, would be destroyed.

All of a sudden Charlie understood exactly how Tom must feel about the Reef, because she, too, felt it. There was something magical about this place. She'd fallen in love here, both with Hawaii and with Ben. She couldn't wait around and see it wrecked.

"Liza," she called. "Those sacks the insulation came in, and the other ones, the heavy plastic bags from the rugs and the empty cans from the drywall. Where are they?"

The discarded containers were in the huge trash bin, and when she and Eliza flung them down to the others, the wind did its best to snatch whatever it could away from grasping hands. But they salvaged a great many between them. They were less than ideal, but they were the best there was until more suitable bags arrived.

"Good thinking, honey," Ben complimented her, and Charlie felt she could whip the waves single-handed if he only kept on calling her honey.

With everyone's eager help, a frantic but well-organized sandbagging brigade was formed, and by the time Aki and Ed sped in with the sugar bags, a crude but effective wall was being constructed. So far it was only a joke to the awesome grandeur and power of the battering waves, but with each added row, the water had to rise that much higher to thunder against the foundations and walls of the lodge.

The time would soon come, Charlie told herself as she scooped up sand in the thick darkness and filled bag after bag after bag, when man's wall would deflect nature's waves. It had to.

She needed the reassurance, because she was absolutely miserable. Her ears, her eyes and her nose felt as if they were filled with sand, and like everyone else, she was soaked to the skin. It was hard to breathe in the tearing insanity of the wind, hard to even move without being blown over. Her arms had ached and finally now were blessedly numb. She felt as if she were a figure in some artist's conception of Dante's *Inferno* as the wind howled like a live thing around them, scrabbling there in awful darkness on the edge of the sand and the sea.

"You okay, love?"

Ben hollered it into her ear over and over, and always she nodded stalwartly.

There was deep satisfaction in beating back the water, and there was comfort in knowing that Ben had kept close watch over her during the long hours they'd worked here, never allowing her to move more than a few feet away from his side. In the midst of the turmoil, Ben was taking care of her as well as he was able, and Charlie sensed it.

Just wait till I get you alone, she warned him silently.

Another sackful handed to Carol, transferred to Ben—
And another and another.

Reinforcements arrived sometime during the endless
night, surfer friends of Pogey's and strong young policemen sent by an anxious, overworked Kimo. The ferocity of
the storm had created havoc on this northern end of Oahu.

With the arrival of the new volunteers, Lani stopped filling bags and started making pots of coffee and hot soup in
her trailer. The electricity had been off for hours, but the
trailer was fortunately equipped with cylinders of gas for
cooking, and practical Lani had lanterns stored away.

The blackness of night was pierced by gray dawn so
gradually the exhausted workers hardly realized the change,
until Ben, taking a filled bag, which seemed to weigh a ton,
from Charlie and passed it to Ed, realized he could discern
the faces and forms of the people nearest him in the chain
of filling, carrying and placing.

Beside him, Charlie's slender body crouched low in the
sand, one dirty hand automatically holding the neck of a
bag open while she used a short spade to shovel it full. Her
hair was an unbelievably tumbled mass, wet and bedraggled and hanging in soaked strands over her forehead. There
was no longer any color to the faded jeans she wore—they'd
taken on the muddy shade of the sand, and they, too, were
wet. She tipped her head back as far as it would go, her exhaustion evident in the gesture, and Ben gave a low curse.
Why hadn't he forced her earlier up to the trailer, made her
go and get dry and rest?

Then a tired, grin flitted across his mouth. You'd think
he'd have learned by now that he couldn't force this woman
of his to do anything. He seemed to hear Gennaro's voice,
wise with years of knowing his daughter.

"Charlie," he'd said acceptingly, "she's her own big
boss."

All Ben could do was cherish her, just the way she was.

A few feet from her, Tom lifted a filled sack and labori-
ously made his way to where the man-made wall rose a good
five feet above the breakwater, stretching a hundred yards

in either direction. Tom laid the bag carefully on top of the others and stumbled wearily as he returned for another.

Ben watched the routine, eyes sore from salt spray and sleeplessness. His ankle, still sensitive and quick to ache, felt as if it were on fire, sending jolts of hot pain up his shin.

The wind was still screaming through the palms, and now and then huge fronds broke off and tumbled dangerously down. But the force of the waves was diminishing noticeably, and the rain had stopped.

Ben limped over to Tom and put a hand on the wet sleeve of his army jacket. This guy, Ben marveled, was one tough old bird. He'd worked throughout the night, steadily carrying, stacking, coming back for another load. How old was he, anyhow? Too old to work like this.

"You must be exhausted," Ben said. "I sure as hell am. How about coming up with me for a bowl of Lani's soup and a cup of coffee?"

But Tom stubbornly shook his head.

Ben gave up and instead went to Charlie.

"Come or I'll carry you," he warned wearily. "You're going to collapse unless you have something to eat and drink, and so am I."

Maybe when Tom saw the two of them admitting fatigue, he'd give up, too. The old man's face was haggard and drawn. But he went on stolidly filling, lifting, placing. Charlie hadn't moved at Ben's words, either.

"Charlie?" Ben demanded, reaching a hand out to pull her up.

She rose to her feet like a marionette, jerky and unsure whether her legs would still work. Ben put a strong arm around her narrow waist, steadying her, and she gave him a bleary grin of thanks. Together they trailed up the bank, and Charlie savored the strength and warmth of Ben's arm supporting her, his hand resting on her hip. Her weary body slumped into his, and he half carried her along, his hip pressing hers.

She stopped between one stride and the next and turned half around in his embrace when she heard Happy barking excitedly. The dog shouldn't be out. Where was the mischievous animal? Carol had carefully locked him in the cabin before they'd started the sandbagging, Charlie had held the door for her against the wind.

But there he was, down beyond the line of sandbags, ecstatically yapping and bouncing along the beach, just as if this were any other morning, his ridiculous little tail whipping from side to side with joy.

"Happy," Charlie screamed. "Happy, get back up here. Come here," she ordered frantically.

A choppy wave rolled up to the puppy and wrapped him in its froth. It ebbed, and Happy was tumbled in its backflow.

Charlie cried out again, and before either she or Ben could move, Carol screamed and went sprinting down the beach, leaping the sandbag barrier in one easy, graceful motion of her long legs, running hard as Happy tumbled end over end, helplessly rolling through the water.

Ben's hand unconsciously clenched on the tender skin at Charlie's waist as he saw what was happening, but she hardly felt it. Both of them stood frozen with horror, staring out at the scene unfolding below them.

Chapter Thirteen

In ghastly slow motion, they watched an immense wave appear beyond the reef, build and build in mighty splendor, then roll untouched over the protective barrier straight toward Carol and the wriggling puppy she grabbed for in the waist-high water but lost and grabbed for again—

Ben gave an inarticulate shout and began to run as hard as he could. Too far, he estimated, running faster. He was too far away, and the wave was building and building.

Carol had the puppy. She glanced over her shoulder, struggled through the shallows and gained the sand. With one more terrified glance behind her, clutching the dog awkwardly to her chest, she ran desperately for the sandbag barrier while behind her the wave seemed to gain momentum as it rolled inward.

A tall figure in sodden khaki was also beyond the barrier now, running like a disjointed scarecrow toward Carol.

Ben slowed, grabbed Charlie and wrapped her in his arms, restraining her flight. It was too late. They were too far away to help. All they could do was stand and watch the scene unfolding below them.

Carol staggered and went down on one knee. Tom reached her, yanked her to her feet, grabbed one hand and half dragged her along on the narrowing gap between them and the sandbag barrier.

Charlie knew she was screaming insanely as she watched the figures reach the ocean side of the sandbags, watched in impotent horror as the wave towered over the suddenly tiny figures. Then everything was a maelstrom of bursting water, flying bodies and confusion as Carol came flying over the sandbags, obviously shoved hard by Tom an instant before the wave broke over them.

The roiling froth obliterated the scene for an endless time.

When it settled, Carol lay in a motionless, crumpled heap, crushed against the inside edge of the sandbagged wall that had kept her from being swept away. Even as figures raced toward her, the puppy she still held wriggled and rolled weakly over in the sand.

Carol struggled to her knees. One of Kimo's policemen, first to reach the scene, pulled her roughly to her feet, scooped up the puppy and half carried Carol in a loping, clumsy race farther and still farther up toward the buildings as another wave, nearly as large as the first, grew and rolled inexorably inward, to crash and break over the barrier.

Charlie and Ben reached them, and Charlie's arms locked like a vise around Carol, while Ben pried the sopping wet, shivering dog out of Carol's grip. Both Carol and Charlie were weeping brokenly.

Ben's eyes met those of the policeman in a silent question, and almost imperceptibly, the young, bedraggled man shook his head. There was no sign of Tom Tanaka-Martin.

The ocean had taken him, and all anyone could do was wait for the tides to give his body back.

THE TIDES HAD SWELLED to their fullest and ebbed again before Kimo gently broke the news to a grieving Lani and the others that Tom's body had been found. The storm was ended, and nature perversely did her best to pretend it had never been. By afternoon, the sun shone hotly down on Reveille Reef, the birds were singing, and a deep sense of peace prevailed. The capricious ocean washed gently in and out, the line of debris and sand two hundred yards below marking the previous night's terrifyingly high watermark.

Lani had spent the first few hours after the accident comforting Carol. Incoherent with guilt, blaming herself for Tom's death, the tall woman had been on the verge of hysteria until Lani gathered her within a gigantic embrace of her huge arms and rocked her like a child until she quieted.

The men who'd given so generously of their time and effort during the long night were fed and had gone home to rest hours before a haggard and shaken Kimo brought the news that Tom's body had washed up with the late-afternoon tide on a deserted stretch of beach miles away.

Only the Reef's "family" gathered in Lani's trailer—Pogey, Ben, Charlie, Kimo, Eliza and the still sporadically weeping Carol, her face swollen and sore from tears, wrapped protectively in Kimo's arms.

Lani mopped absently at her own face now and then with a huge red bandana, but her voice was steady when she spoke. "You must listen, and understand, all of you. Tom died the way he would have chosen, as a soldier, in battle. With pride, with honor. He wouldn't want to return even if he could, because his life here was difficult." Lani sank heavily into her wide wooden rocking chair, and began to rock gently back and forth in time with her words. "When I first heard of the problems, the mischief making at the Reef, I suspected it had to be Tom Tanaka-Martin causing the trouble. I grew up with him, you see. He was my childhood friend long ago, before the war came and everything changed."

Lani's eyes took on an introspective, half-dreaming look.

"Tom's mother was Japanese, like my own mother. But my father was a wonderful, gentle Hawaiian man, and Tom's father was a strict, stern American, a military man stationed here." Lani shook her great head sadly. "He was a hard man, Colonel Martin. Tom's gentle mother quietly but persistently taught her son the customs of her race, while her husband insisted all the while that Tom was an American and must act like any other American boy. So Tom was always divided, torn between his loyalty and love for each of them, between the two sides of his heritage."

It was cramped in the trailer, and the door stood open to trap the breeze, because the afternoon had grown unusually hot. Sitting wherever there was space, most of the tired group had slept only an hour or two, and some, like Charlie and Ben, not at all.

Charlie had helped ladle soup, butter bread for sandwiches and make fresh coffee. Once, she'd slipped away and showered hurriedly, washing away the stiff and itching salt from her body and her hair.

There had been no chance for even a few private words with Ben in the tragic aftermath of Tom's drowning. People came and went, reports of the accident had to be made, and as usual, Ben quietly took charge.

But now he was here, with an arm around her shoulders, on Lani's couch. In a dreamlike trance, Charlie listened to Lani's voice, aware of the enveloping safety of Ben's embrace and of her own fatigue.

Her tiredness added to the aching sorrow she felt for the heroic old man. Lani went on with her story.

"Tom enlisted to please his father, and then the war came. Suddenly, Japanese boys were no longer allowed in combat units. Tom was considered Japanese. He was finally posted as general handyman here at Reveille Reef Club. His father was mortified, and Tom knew it. But here at the Reef Tom was happy. He was needed, relied upon and liked. He had a sense of self-worth."

Lani rocked, and sighed deeply. "Then came Pearl Harbor. Tom's father was killed by Japanese bombers, and Tom suffered a mental breakdown. In some fashion, he felt his father's death was his fault. He spent miserable years in mental hospitals on the mainland. Finally, two years ago, his old mother brought him back here to his home, and the priests at the Shinto mission took responsibility for his care. For the first time I think he was happy again, so close to the Reef where he'd felt he belonged. He puttered around harmlessly until the renovations began." Lani shook her head in sad recognition of her friend's dilemma.

"Tom didn't understand; he knew only that his beloved Reef was changing, that it would never be the same again, and it frightened him. He wasn't an evil man, and I tried and tried to reason with him, but often he was far away in his mind. I admit that when Ben needed someone to work here, part of the reason I agreed to come was Tom. I was afraid something terrible would happen because of his delusion.'' Tears rolled down her cheeks, and she didn't seem to notice. "Many, many times I went to the mission, and sometimes he seemed to know what he was doing. Then he was ashamed, and he would promise me it wouldn't happen again. But always he would forget." She looked around beseechingly at them. Many cheeks were as wet as her own as she cleared her throat.

"He couldn't put the parts of himself together, you see. He couldn't find a balance between past and present and future." Lani's tears fell freely, following the etched lines of her face, but her deep, rich voice never faltered as her words became a chant, an echo of an ancient funeral prayer. "Don't call him back. Don't be too sad for him. Let him go and play. Let him be accepted where he is laid to rest. Let him go in peace; let him go in silence. Let him, at last, be free to welcome each new morning."

"BEN, WHAT IS THIS Fungus Factory, anyway?" Charlie demanded. She'd fallen asleep on Lani's sofa with Ben's arm comfortingly secure around her shoulders, thinking of Tom, sad and tired but content to be in Ben's arms.

Then she'd awakened, still nearly sick with fatigue, to hear Pogey saying quietly, "The Fungus Factory's on the phone, Ben. There's some emergency down there with the automatic heating because of the storm and the power failure."

And Ben began to slide his arm carefully free and tuck his sweater more securely around her. He was about to sneak away when she sat up petulantly and demanded an answer.

"I heard somebody mention it before. Ben, I want to know. What is it? Where are you going?"

She'd felt a sharp concern for the total physical depletion evident in the harshly drawn lines of his face, but she had to ask, she had to know.

He studied her, tousled and heavy eyed, chin set stubbornly, and he glanced around at Lani and Pogey and Eliza, all watching the scene with unabashed interest.

"Walk over to my cabin with me, Charlie, and I'll try and explain."

He tried. He did his best, starting with the idea, the research, the experimenting. He described the technical details carefully, the wonderful simplicity of the mushroom-pineapple scheme, the plans he'd finalized for a similar factory, only with sugar by-products and beef cattle, to begin in the spring when the Fungus Factory was over its birth pains. And even through the fog of exhaustion his enthusiasm had been evident to Charlie, his almost fanatical dedication to something he loved.

She sat on his bed while he showered, changed clothes and poured out to her his ambitions for the Fungus Factory. He sounded like someone in love.

That was it. Ben had found something to love. A lump grew and grew in her throat as he went on and on, telling her things about his business she didn't begin to understand. The words were foreign—sporophytes, mediums, morel, residue.

She did understand the cost projections, the almost unbelievable financial success the factory was realizing already, only weeks after its opening. Apparently Ben was going to be financially successful on a scale far beyond Charlie's modest yardstick of success.

He stopped talking after a while, watching her expectantly. She cleared her throat and in a brittle voice said, "Well, this whole thing, it's wonderful. You must feel really proud of yourself, Ben."

She smiled at him with phony brightness.

Then, in a barrage of words she couldn't hope to contain, she wailed, "Why didn't you share it with me? How could you plan all this, accomplish all this, and never say one word about it to me? Did you think I wouldn't understand, that I wasn't educated enough to understand?''

"Charlie, it wasn't like that. Damn it all to hell, I knew this would happen," he cursed distractedly, coming to sit beside her and putting an arm around her stiff shoulders. She shook him off roughly and got to her feet to pace back and forth across the soft gray rug, agitated and hurt.

"All those nights together and you never said a word." She was trembling. As he moved to put an arm around her, he said contritely, "Don't, please, Charlie. I can explain; I want to show you the factory. I have to get back over there right away; it's urgent. Why don't you come with me? We can talk on the way."

"Can't," she snapped in that stubborn, closed way that was guaranteed to infuriate him. "I have work to do in the morning. You can understand that now, can't you? So leave me alone."

And she got up and hurried back to her cabin, ignoring his imperious, exasperated calls of "Charlie? Charlie!"

She locked herself in, stripped off her clothes, climbed into the shower and plugged her ears so she wouldn't hear if he banged on her door. He wouldn't waste much time trying, she thought bitterly. Ben was now a busy man.

Well, she'd mouthed off often enough about his aimless life-style, his lack of direction and ambition, his dreamy approach to his life. Now he'd changed and become just what she'd thought he should be all along.

She used a word Sister Mary Francis would wash Charlie's mouth out for using, but it didn't help. Tears mixed with the shower spray.

He'd changed completely. He'd succeeded at what he'd chosen to accomplish. He was financially successful, apart from his inherited wealth. He had purpose and direction to his life. Weren't those good things, wonderful things in a man you loved?

She slumped under the deluge from the shower head and wished she'd drown. What had ever made her think such changes would be an improvement in Ben? She liked the old

Ben much better, she decided mutinously. The fact was, this new Ben scared her to death.

What hurt most was that he'd been planning this scheme all along, letting her lecture him prissily about his wasted life. She remembered the scene at the restaurant and shuddered.

What a fool he must have thought her. What a fool she thought herself. He'd already been an innovative factory owner, and she'd treated him like a child in need of scolding.

The water poured over her head, and she reminded herself that at least she should feel grateful that she hadn't had a chance to implement the mad scheme she'd concocted for proposing to him. Viciously, she rubbed herself with soap, lathered shampoo into her hair and rinsed it out.

What had she been thinking of, to believe Ben needed her as she needed him?

The truth was, Ben had proved he didn't need her at all. If he couldn't talk with her about this factory of his, what did they share?

And he was so professional all of a sudden, as if this business side of him had been lurking there all along, waiting to emerge at the right moment. Reluctant admiration for Ben stirred despite her efforts to subdue it.

Ben was—what was the word? *Entrepreneur.* He was a genius of sorts, she guessed. And what would a genius need with a carpenter?

She gave up, too tired to think anymore, too tired even to cry. She dried off and then peeked out the window.

Sure enough, the yellow Jeep was gone. The reef was deserted in the silver spill of the moon.

PERHAPS IT WAS the absence of the haunting bugle in the early dawn that awakened Charlie the next morning.

Her first thought was for Ben, and she shut her eyes tight against the pain. She'd lost him.

Tom was gone, too, before she had a chance to know him, to tell him how much his morning serenades had meant to her.

The deep exhaustion and aching muscles, which were the aftermath of filling sandbags, had faded to just a twinge here and there, she realized, stretching her legs and swinging them cautiously out from between the warm sheets. She propped her feet on the wooden sideboard of the bed and drew her knees to her chin, wrapping her nightshirt and then her arms around her bare legs.

Ben was lost to her. She had to accept that and find a way to get on with her life, impossible as it now seemed.

Well, there was always work. She'd bury herself in work. "Get real, Charlie; up and at 'em; time's wasting," she admonished herself with an attempt at the old spirit, but it didn't seem to do much good.

Well, the best thing to do now was to finish this job as fast as possible and go back to Bellingham, where she belonged.

She thought of Papa and Rosalie. She thought of finding an apartment of her own. Where she used to belong.

Funny how much Hawaii had begun to feel like home. She pulled on her old, tattered cutoffs and a shrunken T-shirt, tied her disreputable Adidases on her feet and ventured outside.

The eastern sky was starting to show traces of pink. The sun would rise soon. Her shoulders slumped in total dejection, Charlie slowly took in the storm-battered buildings of the Reef.

The main lodge had suffered most of the storm damage. Charlie shook her head in disgust as she strolled toward it. Those deck supports would have to be replaced, and there was an ugly waterline on the wooden siding. Glancing up, she saw a gaping hole where shingles had been torn away by the wind. There would be considerable water damage to the attic, probably seeping down through the bedroom ceilings.

All that work, torn apart in a capricious moment. She moved to the shed and found the extension ladder, dragging it over to the side of the lodge. Might as well assess the damage right now. They'd have to order the shingles and get at it today.

Carefully, she settled it against the wall and scampered up. The ladder was tall enough to allow access to the topmost part of the roof. Bent in half like an agile monkey, she headed for the peak and perched there, high above, surveying the reef.

The green ocean was rolling in as always from the horizon, breaking on the rocky line of the reef across the lagoon. Ben had told her one day there was nothing between these waves rolling in, no land mass between Oahu and the Fiji Islands, Shanghai, Tokyo. He'd told her stories of exotic places and made them come alive for her. He'd taught her to dream.

He'd believed in her in a way she hadn't dared believe in herself, arguing that if she wanted to, she could go back to school to become an architect.

Charlie wrapped her arms around her breasts, afraid to confront the preposterous idea seriously but knowing the time had come to do so.

The money was now available, if she were careful. And Cossini Construction seemed to have dissolved itself, unless she wanted to go about the painful task of hiring new carpenters, chasing new jobs, hurrying through the days with no thought beyond tomorrow's tasks.

"Slow down, Charlie," Ben had told her so often. "Take time to listen to your dreams. What's so great about hard work, anyway?"

An agony of longing for Ben sent a shudder through her. If only she hadn't been so stubborn, so critical, so bad-tempered. If she had it to do over, she'd treasure the lazy hours he tricked her into spending with him. She'd be more ladylike; she'd curb her temper and her tongue. Not that it would change anything. But he'd remember her differently.

She adjusted her bottom on the hard roof and flung herself wholly into fantasy.

She'd never be critical of him again. She'd get a manicure once in a while. She'd remember to use the lotions and gloves he'd bought her so often. Would she try surfing?

She glanced down at the waves beyond the reef and shuddered. That was going too far, even for fantasy, but certainly she'd accept his ideas and not argue all the time.

Unless it was about building, of course. Ben didn't know beans about building. Or motors, either. He was impossible even about practical matters like gas and oil.

But she loved him. In spite of it? Because of it? She loved him.

Her shoulders slumped with sadness and longing.

Morning was breaking out over the water. Sunrise was glowing orange against the indigo shades of Reveille Reef, and the purple ocean stretched beyond sight to meet a smoky sky.

Reveille. To awaken. A dormant part of herself had awakened here at Reveille Reef, and with it an awareness of what she was and what she could be: the product of her heritage—hardworking, tough, Italian American—but she could be female without being like her mother, she could love without rules and conditions and limits, and could relax without the world falling apart.

Relinquish the old, keep the good parts and embrace the new. Wasn't that what Lani was always going on about? Wasn't that the real lesson of Tom Tanaka-Martin's tragic life? Too bad she'd learned it too late.

Watching the sunrise, Charlie lost herself in wistful dreaming.

THE JEEP HAD RUN out of gas half a mile from the Reef, and nothing was open this early in the morning, so Ben walked. Rocks and sand kept getting in his leather sandals, and his ankle still ached when he put this kind of pressure on it, but he was determined.

The last emergency at the factory had subsided an hour before, and Ben was on his way right now to ask Charlie to marry him, before the phone started ringing, or another hurricane came, or some other damn thing happened. Life had become a three-ring circus, and he enjoyed it—hell, he loved it—but there was a limit.

Look what had happened last night. If he'd had time to break the door down into Charlie's cabin, put a half nelson on her and make her listen, this whole mess would be solved by now.

He needed Charlie, he thought petulantly. Lani had said that everyone had a soul mate, and Charlie was his other half. He'd spent every spare, stray moment during the busy night preparing a lengthy marriage proposal, just as Gennaro had suggested. It was concise, businesslike, rather like a résumé for a job. It covered every single possible eventuality in a marriage contract between them, with every concession in Charlie's favor. And he'd forgotten and left the damn thing on the packing crate he used as a desk at the factory.

He turned into the Reef's driveway. Everything was silent except for the birds. His eyes flickered over the buildings, and then he saw Charlie, perched on the roof, silhouetted against the dawn.

He might have known she'd make this as difficult for him as possible.

Sighing with resignation but resolute with purpose, he started gingerly up the ladder.

It was the transfer from ladder to roof that did it. He glanced down. His leather sandal slid on the still-damp shingles, and the ladder jerked to one side.

Charlie had heard the ladder, and when his head appeared, she came down the incline like a frantic crab, grabbed his arms and pulled for all she was worth. His lithe strength saved them both. He found a foothold on the roof's edge a bare instant before the ladder toppled, crashing grandly to the earth far below.

His maneuver landed him half on top of Charlie. His weight pinned her beneath him, and her breath came in shallow gasps. He looked down into her delicate, lovely face. Her nose was peeling a bit from sunburn.

"Charlie, I'm sorry I didn't tell you about the factory. I wanted to surprise you."

"Ben Gilmour, you damned half-wit," she panted up at him furiously, "You're up on a slippery roof with leather sandals."

His thick blond eyebrows quirked above the grass-green eyes, and he stared down at her with that teasing, innocent grin.

He tried to gain purchase with his foot, but it slipped twice more before he could move enough to let her breathe normally.

"You see, Charlie," he went on conversationally, "the whole thing took me by surprise. I wanted it to be a success before I showed you."

"I must have told you a million times not to climb roofs in those stupid shoes," she raged, fear fueling her temper as she imagined what might have happened. "You could have fallen down and broken your fool neck." The awful thought made her weak.

She clung to him as they moved cautiously up the incline, his feet slipping and sliding at crazy angles, scaring her nearly to death all over again.

"I wanted to impress you. After all, what did I have to offer you? You're innocent and tough and vulnerable and independent. You know exactly where you're going. You know what you want out of life."

More than anything right now, she wanted to reach a safe spot for both of them on this blessed roof.

"Would you kindly stop yapping and be careful?" she begged desperately as he slid a few feet down and then once again caught hold and levered himself up beside her. At last, he was safely straddling the peak, and she slung her own bare leg over as well, weak with relief. She took a deep breath and really let him have it.

"Of all the idiotic, stupid things to do, this takes the prize. You could have killed yourself. What were you thinking of, climbing up here when you know very well—"

He reached over, took her face between his palms and said slowly and forcefully, "Shut up and listen to me. I love you, Charlie."

She stopped between one word and the next, lips a little open in that way she had that made him long to kiss her. He would in a minute.

"I love you. I want to live with you and raise children, whatever kind you want. I'm going to marry you, and I won't take no for an answer, if I have to keep you up here till we both starve. I need you Charlie."

Here we go, Ben thought with resignation. *Here come all the objections, the arguments, the stubborn denials Gennaro had said to expect.*

He slid his palms down her cheeks and rested his hands on her narrow shoulders. He noticed the faded message on her black T-shirt, and under any other circumstances he would have laughed. It read simply, Because I'm the boss; that's why.

He felt a tremor run through her like a shiver shaking her slender, beloved body beneath his hands. The sun was up, and it made golden highlights in her wild curls and reflected a sort of radiance in her deep blue eyes.

"You need me?" she said at last with a little gulp. She remembered Ben telling her that the only real reason for doing anything was need, that he'd never needed anything enough to pursue it.

Yet here he was, pursuing her up a ladder to a rooftop, with the wrong darned shoes on, as usual. A genius who needed to be told what shoes to wear. A man who loved and needed her as much as she loved and needed him.

She didn't wait for him to reaffirm it.

In a shy whisper she said simply, "I need you, too, Ben. I love you. I want so much to be your wife."

Careless of his precarious perch, he wrapped his arms around her in an exultant embrace, feeling her heart hammer in cadence with his own. Their kiss was a long, unhurried promise of delightful tomorrows.

Above them were the swaying palms, the white birds calling over the sun-swept lagoon, and all around them was the paradise that was their Hawaii. They could hear what might have been the whispering of voices along the shore, light and laughing and telling of eternal love, mixing with the far-off, haunting tones of a bugle playing reveille.

But they knew it was only the sigh and crash of the eternal sea.

Harlequin American Romance

COMING NEXT MONTH

#177 BEWITCHING HOUR by Anne Stuart

Despite Sybil's position as secretary of the Society of Water Witches, her psychic skills were notoriously mediocre. When Nicholas Fitzsimmons entered her bookstore, her suspicions were confirmed: Nick was a skeptic who scoffed at premonitions and everything else that mattered to her. But, despite their great differences, there was an attraction that could not be denied.

#178 THIS DAY FORWARD by Elizabeth Morris

Business was brisk at Weddings Unlimited, and it was expanding in ways that Andrea Kirkland had never dreamed of. But none of this on-the-job experience helped her relationship with Matt Donaldson, who stubbornly insisted that he was not entitled to love. That is, until the citizens of Laurel Valley stepped in and said their piece about happy-ever-after.

#179 SILENT NIGHT by Beverly Sommers

Nancy didn't have a spare minute. She taught English to some of Manhattan's toughest kids. After school her time belonged to Joe. But keeping busy wasn't enough. For her own sake, and for Joe's, she had to find answers to the nightmarish enigma of her old life—before she was free to live her new one.

#180 INTIMATE STRANGERS by Saranne Dawson

Patrick had returned from the dead. Megan was terrified of seeing him again. They'd been newlyweds twelve long years ago when he'd been sent overseas. So much time had passed—and they had changed. Could Megan find anything in him that she'd loved and cherished a lifetime ago?

Janet Dailey
Americana

Don't miss a single title from this great collection. The first eight titles
have already been published. Complete and mail this coupon today to
order books you may have missed.

Harlequin Reader Service

<u>In U.S.A.</u>
901 Fuhrmann Blvd.
P.O. Box 1397
Buffalo, N.Y. 14140

<u>In Canada</u>
P.O. Box 2800
Postal Station A
5170 Yonge Street
Willowdale, Ont. M2N 6J3

Please send me the following titles from the Janet Dailey Americana
Collection. I am enclosing a check or money order for $2.75 for each
book ordered, plus 75¢ for postage and handling.

_____	ALABAMA	Dangerous Masquerade
_____	ALASKA	Northern Magic
_____	ARIZONA	Sonora Sundown
_____	ARKANSAS	Valley of the Vapours
_____	CALIFORNIA	Fire and Ice
_____	COLORADO	After the Storm
_____	CONNECTICUT	Difficult Decision
_____	DELAWARE	The Matchmakers

Number of titles checked @ $2.75 each = $_____

N.Y. RESIDENTS ADD
   APPROPRIATE SALES TAX $_____

Postage and Handling $____.75____

                              TOTAL $_____

I enclose _____

(Please send check or money order. We cannot be responsible for cash
sent through the mail.)

PLEASE PRINT

NAME _____

ADDRESS _____

CITY _____

STATE/PROV. _____

BLJD-A-1

ATTRACTIVE, SPACE SAVING BOOK RACK

Display your most prized novels on this handsome and sturdy book rack. The hand-rubbed walnut finish will blend into your library decor with quiet elegance, providing a practical organizer for your favorite hard-or soft-covered books.

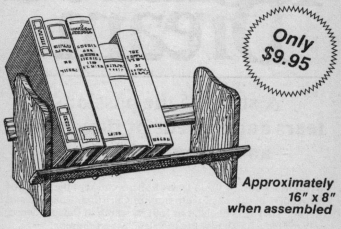

Only $9.95

Approximately 16" x 8" when assembled

Assembles in seconds!

To order, rush your name, address and zip code, along with a check or money order for $10.70 ($9.95 plus 75¢ postage and handling) (New York residents add appropriate sales tax), payable to *Harlequin Reader Service* to:

In the U.S.

Harlequin Reader Service
Book Rack Offer
901 Fuhrmann Blvd.
P.O. Box 1325
Buffalo, NY 14269-1325

Offer not available in Canada.

BKR-1